FINDING FIONA

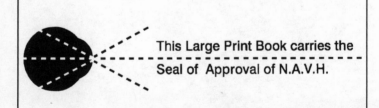

This Large Print Book carries the
Seal of Approval of N.A.V.H.

MAINE SHORE CHRONICLES

FINDING FIONA

MARY FREMONT SCHOENECKER

THORNDIKE PRESS
A part of Gale, Cengage Learning

GALE
CENGAGE Learning·

Detroit • New York • San Francisco • New Haven, Conn • Waterville, Maine • London

GALE
CENGAGE Learning

LIBRARY OF CONGRESS CATALOGING-IN-PUBLICATION DATA

Schoenecker, Mary Fremont.
  Finding Fiona / by Mary Fremont Schoenecker.
    p. cm. — (Thorndike press large print clean reads) (Maine
  shore chronicles)
  Includes bibliographical references.
  ISBN-13: 978-1-4104-3231-5
  ISBN-10: 1-4104-3231-9
  1. Missing persons—Fiction. 2. Time travel—Fiction. 3. Large
  type books. I. Title.
  PS3619.C4493F56 2010
  813'.6—dc22   2010030144

Published in 2010 by arrangement with Tekno Books.

Printed in the United States of America
1 2 3 4 5 6 7 14 13 12 11 10

This book is dedicated to my granddaughter, Alyssa Marie Simms.

Muse extraordinaire and dedicated critique partner, she walked each step of the way with me, grounding me in twenty-first century dialogue. *Merci du coeur,* Alyssa.

ACKNOWLEDGMENTS

My special thanks for help and expert advice from reference librarian Sally Leahey, McArthur Library, and Janice Beal, UNE Library, Biddeford Maine. To librarians of the Sarasota County and Charlotte County Florida Library Systems: Roxane Bennett, Roland Marcotte, Janis Russell, Michele Strickland, Cris Walton, and Tamar Wolfe, my gratitude and appreciation for their continuous support, assistance with research, and opportunities for book talks and signings. Special thanks also to Helen Wikoff, Friends of the Library Chairperson at Elsie Quirk Library. Libraries are this writer's best friends.

A special acknowledgment goes to my editors, Alice Duncan and Martha Reinhardt. While I am responsible for the story, it would not shine without their help.

Thank you to Hodding Cotter for the quote paraphrased in Chapter One: "There are only two lasting bequests we can hope to give our children. One of these is roots, the other wings."

They are not dead who live in the lives
they leave behind.
In those whom they have blessed they
live again.
— Maya Angelou

Prologue

Cotton Mill Loom Room, 1905
Pain blazed in her head. Shards of sound reverberated. The vibration of machinery thrummed in her ear and rattled her cheek pressed against wooden floorboards. A loud whistle sounded and the motion stopped.

Footsteps.

A corner of the hood covering her head was lifted.

"Holy Mary. It's a girl an' she's bleedin'."

It's a woman's voice. Maybe Clare . . .

She tried to open her eyes but the pain was fierce. Thoughts scattered.

It's me, Maddy . . . help . . .

More footsteps.

"She just fell through the door like the devil himself was pushin' her. She's bad hurt, Mr. MacDill."

"Calm down now, Molly. Go get water and rags from the washroom. Hetty and I will see to this." The foreman peered at the body lying face down, a puddle of water pooling on the floor around it. His brows drew together in concern.

"Let's get this wet coat off him, Hetty."

"It's a *she*, I tell ya," Molly called back.

Mr. MacDill raised the limp figure in his arms just enough to allow Hetty to unfasten the hooks of the yellow coat. Hetty pulled the sleeves away one at a time while the big Scot balanced the body against his bent knee.

MacDill's eyes widened when the coat fell away. "Good Lord! It *is* a lassie." He stared at long tendrils of wet hair plastered to a pale, china-doll face. He gingerly cradled the girl's bleeding head in one beefy hand.

Hetty knelt, clutching the strange yellow coat to her heart, gazing at the girl clad in men's trousers.

"For God's sake, put the coat down, Hetty, and sit. I'm goin' to move her so's she's lying wi' her head cradled in your lap."

More footsteps. Something clattered on the floor.

The foreman stood, shifting from one foot to the other, staring at his bloodied hand and shirtsleeve. "Molly, you clean her up a bit. See if you can staunch the bleedin' while Hetty holds her. I'm goin' for the mill agent."

12

Molly nodded, kneeling at Hetty's side.

Hetty's rough, warm hands held the girl's cold ones.

"Mère de Dieu. Elle tremble beaucoup. Calme-toi. Le secours arrive," Hetty murmured.

"Sufferin' Jaysus, Hetty. You'd be shakin' too if ya blew in outta nowhere with a cracked head. Yer tellin' her to lie still, an' she prob'ly don't know a word yer saying. She don't look like any of the Frenchies I ever seen in this shop."

"Je la connais."

"What? What d'ya mean, you know her? I learned enough of yer French in the eight years I been workin' here, but for the love of God, woman, speak English. How can you know this creature in men's clothes?"

Hetty shook her head vigorously, frowning at Molly. *"Elle n'est pas une creature.* She . . . how you say . . . eh, she *la professeur."*

"A teacher!" Molly threw the bloody cloth into the basin. She held a clean dry rag to the wound and brushed back the matted hair from the girl's face. "Are ye daft, Hetty? If this waif is a teacher, then I'm Mother Superior."

CHAPTER ONE

Biddeford Pool, 2005

"Sweet won't cut it, Maddy. You say this guy is hot — not like double-yawn Claude. You need to go brassy and sassy, maybe even a little sexy."

Maddy stopped rocking in the big wooden chair. "Hold it. I never said Claude was boring. He's intelligent, good looking and . . . and —"

"Dull."

Maddy snickered. "Oh, Clare. You know I don't love the guy, and I'd never agree to anything permanent with him, but my Dad thinks Claude would make an ideal son-in-law."

"I can see why your father would think so. Money. Big law firm. Plus his uncle's the priest who taught us theology at Saint David. Your path to the altar is already paved in your Dad's eyes, so tell me, girlfriend, what are you gonna do about it?"

"I've been trying to back away from Claude ever since I met Patrick. Wait till you see him. He's gorgeous. Tall, rugged, sleek-muscled. He has coal-black, wavy hair and dimples to die for."

"Geez, Maddy, when am I gonna meet him?"

"Good question. I just got introduced myself. When Rosie introduced him as 'Paddy,' he cut me a look with the most incredible blue eyes, raised an eyebrow and gave me a cocky grin. 'The name's Patrick, Miss Fontaine,' he corrected. Never said another word; just whisked Rosie out the door."

"I'm not following. Where *did* you meet him, and who's Rosie?"

"His sister, Rosemary Donovan, is one of my students. She has a solo in the eighth-grade play I'm directing. Her brother, Patrick, always picks her up after rehearsal, and that's how I happened to meet him."

"Well, *Miss Fontaine,* you have access to records at Saint David. Find out about the family. Seems pretty simple to me."

"I've already checked Rosemary's file. The Donovans are new to Saint David's. I think they transferred from public school. There are five kids and the mother's a widow. Patrick's the oldest. I think a little older than us. Next a sister, Fiona, then Rose-mary and twins, Meagan and Moira."

"Sounds like an Irish litany. Where do they live?"

"Down near the river where the old mill houses used to be."

"That's not far from *Tante* Margaret's."

Clare stifled a yawn and glanced at her watch. She was draped over a wicker settee on the front porch of Maddy's house, still wearing the wild print green shirt and white pants of her ER uniform. "Speaking of *Tante,* I'm due in town at her house right about now."

Shielding her eyes from the dropping sun, Maddy gazed at gilded breakers crashing the sea wall down Fletcher Neck. "Almost sunset, CeCe."

"Ayuh." Clare ran her fingers through her short, spiky hair, and stretched. "And I'd love to stay and watch the sunset, babe, but . . ."

A car drove up the pebbled driveway at the side of the house. "Perfect timing, 'cause here comes your loverly stepmother."

A green Volvo stopped by the wide front porch and an attractive redhead leaned out of the car window.

"I thought I'd find you two out here. Saw your car in the back, Clare. Would you mind

17

helping Madelaine in with my groceries? Put things away for me, will you, Maddy dear? I have to dash back to pick up your father at the country club. Oh, and Clare, be sure to give my regards to your Aunt Margaret."

"I'll do that, Mrs. Fontaine," Clare called out, turning to roll her big eyes at Maddy.

Maddy reached up to squeeze Clare's shoulder as they walked down the steps to the rear of the car. She looked at the very different shadows they cast on the drive. *Clare, tall, solid and square sure dwarfs my shadow. Thick and thin,* she thought. *We've come through a lot together.*

The trunk lid popped open. Maddy held her long hair away from her face as she raised the lid to lean inside. Clare grabbed two bags of groceries into her sturdy arms. Maddy lifted the remaining small carton and knocked on the trunk after she slammed it shut. Kathleen sped away in the green Volvo as the girls carried the groceries up the steps and into the house.

"Maddy, Maddy," Clare said, "I'll never understand why you don't come live with me in the apartment. It would be easier on both of us to share the rent, plus you'd be out from under Ms. Congeniality's thumb."

"It isn't her that keeps me here. Well, in a way it is, but it's really my father. Every time I talk about getting my own place, he has a dozen reasons why I should stay."

Maddy set the carton on the kitchen table, and counted off on her fingers. "The house seems big since my brother moved to New York. I can save money living here. It's not that far to drive to school. On and on, he goes. I think he feels I've grown away from him since college. Now that I'm back . . . well . . ." She raised upturned palms in a shrug.

"Your Dad oughta hear that quote about roots. 'The only lasting thing we can give our children is roots and wings.' *Tante* is the only mother I've ever known, and she spouted that little gem to me right after graduation. She even helped me find my apartment."

Maddy pursed her lips. "I know. Your Aunt Margaret is a piece of work, but I think the real reason Papa wants me here is so I can do some bonding with his new wife. Get to know her and —"

"Bond with Kathleen?" Clare cast her eyes heavenward. "I've already said more than I should about Ms. Congeniality. I'm outta here, babe. But, hey, if you still want to talk about this Patrick guy, come over to my

19

place tomorrow. I've got Sunday off, and Nurse Clare is in for some serious schmoozin'." Clare did a little happy dance around Maddy. "See ya." She waved her fingers over her shoulder before the screen door banged shut.

Maddy closed her eyes and a picture formed in her mind.

The kindergarten room at Saint David's. Looking up at the black habit and starched wimple of Sister Felicity looming over us . . . Clare, a chubby little girl with big gray eyes peeking around the girth of her Aunt Margaret, dancing around her and grabbing hold of my hand. It was an instant reckoning that never let go.

Maddy pushed the grocery carton to the side and slumped into a chair at the pine trestle table. Her face had the porcelain beauty and doe-shaped green eyes of her mother. She tossed her hair back from her shoulders and stared, chin in hand, at the wainscoting skirting the walls of the kitchen. *It was Mom's idea to keep the bead board in place and refinish it. She was big on restoration. Keep things the way they were.*

Well, things aren't the way they were anymore.

She pushed back her chair and left the kitchen. She paused at a big, oak sideboard in the dining room. Centered above it, two crystal hurricane lamps flanked a gilt-framed watercolor painting. Her fingers gently traced over the initials at the lower corner, J F 92. *Julie Fontaine.*

It was like touching a piece of the past. *Mom painted the roses the summer we moved into Francois's Fancy. The summer I was eight.*

A sprawling, weathered, clapboard Victorian, Francois's Fancy's tall windows faced the ocean. A porch spanned the entire front of the house, wrapping around it to the pebbled drive that opened on Mile Stretch Road at the back. Beyond the front porch, a lawn extended down to rocks and a sandy beach. It was not unlike other cottages that lined Maine's shore at Biddeford Pool.

Maddy looked across the oak dining table. A stretch of rose-sparkled sand glistened in the setting sun framed by the west window. She tapped her hand on the table, walked out into the hall and grabbed a jacket off the hall tree.

A cold wind blew in from the sea, heralding the fall season that sent summer residents away from Maine's rocky coast. Maddy didn't want to think about leaving Biddeford Pool. The huge tidal lagoon was *home.* She sat again in the porch rocker, watching the tide rising before the sunlight faded.

Two children and a man jogged on the beach. The children's heads bobbed above the rocks as they jumped in and out of waves streaming to shore. The man playfully circled the children, picking up the small girl and running ahead with her to the shrieks of the older boy. Their high-pitched laughter carried on the wind.

In her mind's eye it was she, her brother, Paul, and Papa running on the beach. She pulled the hood over her head, bounded down the steps and crossed the lawn. Picking her way among the rocks, she found a flat one at the edge of the sand. She sat and slipped off her sneakers, pushing her feet into the soft sand.

The dropping sun glinted off waves lapping the shore. She'd miss the soothing sound of breaking waves if she moved out of Dad's house.

Maddy watched until the man and children were tiny stick figures far down the beach. She pushed her feet apart in an arc, spreading the sea moss and sand until her toe dug up an oyster shell. The shell's opalescent lining caught the last sliver of light.

Her fingers pressed against the front of

her jacket where a gold shell locket hung between her breasts. Her mom had painted a miniature scene inside for Maddy's sixteenth-birthday gift.

A horn blared twice, then three times. Maddy twisted around to face the house. Twilight had gone but there was no mistaking a car idling in the drive with its headlights on. She pushed into her sneakers and wiped at the sand on the seat of her jeans. Making her way carefully over the rocks, she moved toward a person running down the dark lawn.

"Maddy!" Clare nearly tumbled them both to the ground in a breathless hug. Clare's eyes darkened as she looked into Maddy's puzzled face. "You weren't in the house, so my best guess was you'd hear the horn if you were on the beach."

Maddy pulled away, shocked to see tears in Clare's eyes. "What is it? What are you doing back here?"

"Kathleen rang the house over and over. When you didn't answer she called *Tante* Margaret's just as I got there. It's your dad, Maddy. He's at the Medical Center with Doc Halliday — they think it's his heart."

CHAPTER TWO

Visions of her father being carried into the hospital flashed in and out of Maddy's head as Clare drove like a mad woman on Mile Stretch Road. "What did the hospital say? Or Dr. Halliday?"

"I work there, babe, but I wasn't there when they brought him in, and I can only tell you what Kathleen told me. The medics had already taken your dad to the hospital when Kathleen arrived at the club."

"But didn't she say what happened?"

"Yes. She said he collapsed on the eighteenth green at the golf course. Doc Halliday was in the foursome, and he took charge until the ambulance arrived. He's in good hands, Maddy."

Thunder rumbled and rain started to blow in gusts across the road. Maddy edged forward on the seat, gripping the sides. Clare slowed down on Pool Road, to swing right onto Alfred Street. When the Medical

Center came into view, she couldn't miss the audible groan from Maddy's lips.

They hurried through the emergency room doors. "I'm going to stay right beside you," Clare said.

Neither was prepared for Kathleen when they walked through the double doors into the triage station. Smeared mascara and red eyes would have given her away, but it was her forlorn, lost-soul look that gripped Maddy's heart. She hesitated until Clare pulled her forward to the doctor who stood beside her stepmother.

Kathleen caught Maddy's hand, pressing it to her face. "Maddy, dear, this is the cardiologist, Dr. Mercier. Doctor, this is Jack's daughter, Madelaine."

The doctor looked from Kathleen to Maddy. "Your father has had a stroke, Madelaine. He has not regained consciousness, but from what Dr. Halliday told us, we're moving ahead with TPA drug treatment given intravenously. At this point we're still testing."

"Testing?" Maddy looked from the doctor to Clare, her face pale, her eyes questioning.

"We've done a Carotid Ultrasound and a CTA. I was just telling Mrs. Fontaine that the nurse is getting your father ready for an

25

MRA. That's an angiography that lets us evaluate any damage to the arteries —"

"Can I see him?"

The doctor looked at his watch. He flapped a hand, indicating the curtained bed space along one wall. "Well, just for a minute."

Clare steered Maddy forward through the curtain. An attending nurse smiled at Clare with a puzzled look.

"Doctor gave her a minute with him," Clare said. "This is Professor Fontaine's daughter, Maddy."

The nurse nodded and moved outside the curtain.

Maddy stood staring at the bed for a long moment. Jacques Fontaine was hooked to a respirator and a tube was anchored to his strong wide mouth. The only sound was the EKG monitor that blipped as squiggly lines moved across a screen.

Clare gently guided her close to the edge of the bed. Maddy grasped the metal rail of the bed, startled by the whoosh of a blood pressure cuff on her father's arm. She stared at the graying hair at his temple. "Do you suppose he can hear me if I talk to him?"

"Some say yes, they can. I would try."

Maddy swallowed hard. "I love you, Big Jacques." She shivered and put a hand to her mouth to squelch a sob. Clare's arm was around her, tugging her away from the bed just as the nurse walked back into the curtained space and pulled the curtains open. "Ladies, I'll have to ask you to step out now."

Maddy followed Clare as though she were sleepwalking. "I hardly ever call him Big Jacques anymore." Her lips trembled. "Not since Mom put a stop to Big Jacques–Little Jacques when Paul was big enough to go to school —" Maddy stopped suddenly, a frisson of fear in her eyes. She grasped Clare's arm. "Paul! I have to call him."

"Maybe Kathleen has already done that."

"No, she wouldn't know how to reach Paul. Do you have your cell phone with you?"

"Right here, Mad," Clare said as she patted her shoulder bag. "But let's go out and check with Kathleen first."

Maddy gave her a desperate look. "You don't understand, and I can't get into it right now, but *I* must be the one to call Paul."

Clare led Maddy to find Kathleen at a small waiting room near the entrance to the emergency room. She stepped back, clearly trying to distance herself.

"Do you mind being by yourself here for

a while, Kathleen?" Maddy asked. "I'm going down the hall with Clare to try and call my brother."

Kathleen's eyes widened, darting from Clare to Maddy. "I'll be fine, dear. I hope you can reach Paul. You know I would have —"

"It's okay," Maddy reassured her, "we'll be back as soon as we can."

Clare pushed through the second door after the waiting area. "Good, there's no one here just now. It won't be a problem, anyway. We're not supposed to use cell phones, but I have mine set on vibrate, so sit here at the table. I'll get us some coffee."

Maddy punched in the numbers on the cell phone. It rang until Paul's voice mail kicked in asking the caller to leave a message.

"Paul, this is Maddy. There's been an emergency and I need you to contact me right away. I'm at the medical center, so please call this number: 694-2236." Maddy put the phone in her jeans pocket.

Clare set two coffee cups on the table. "No answer?"

"Just his voice mail. I don't know why he's not answering."

"Well, it's six o'clock. Maybe he's still at work, or out to eat."

"Oh, God. I didn't even think of the time. Paul will be devastated if he thinks the message is about Dad, especially after the rift between . . ." Maddy put her face in her hands and shook her head as though to clear her mind.

"Tell me, babe. Maybe I can help. There's very little I don't know about Paul and you and Papa Jacques."

"It was all such a terrible scene. Dad just couldn't let it go. When Paul got the job offer from New York, my father more or less booted him out of the house."

"But why? What happened?"

"Paul asked to do a portrait of Kathleen at the end of the summer and Dad and she agreed to it. I was a little surprised because Papa rarely encouraged Paul's art."

"I don't think your dad was ever comfortable with Paul as *artiste*."

"No, he wasn't, and my mother could never understand why he didn't respect her talent showing up in Paul. Mom always encouraged him, and was thrilled when he chose art history as a major in college. She would have been real happy about the job offer."

"I agree, but it's like your brother's been kind of drifting this year, don'tcha think? Not doing much except painting and partying is what I've heard. Maybe your dad was just happy to see him go."

"Well, that isn't how it went down. Before the job offer came, Dad walked into the studio one day to check the portrait's progress. Kathleen had been posing in a gauzy long white dress, but when Dad took the drape off the easel, he discovered Paul was . . . he was sketching Kathleen nude, with a long swan back, curvy buns and big boobs."

"Whoa!" Clare choked on her coffee. "Excuse *moi,* but that's awesome."

"You can imagine my father's reaction. It wasn't 'awesome.' He was furious. I've never seen him so unreasonable. He wouldn't accept any of Paul's explanations. The job offer at the art museum came right after that, and it couldn't have been better timed. Dad said he hoped this job would help Paul mature. Told him: 'Contact your sister when you get settled. I don't want to hear from you until you've settled down.' "

Clare's cell phone vibrated, and Maddy grabbed it from her pocket.

"Paul. Thank God you called right back. There's no other way to tell you, but straight out. Dad's had a stroke and he's in pretty bad shape."

Clare stirred her coffee and closed her

eyes at the long pause.

"No, he's probably going into intensive care next . . . no, not conscious yet. They're doing tests. I'm going to stay right here at the hospital with Kathleen, but I need you. Can you get a plane out tonight?"

Clare nudged her. "I'll meet his plane," she whispered.

"Clare can meet you at the airport. Just call and let us know when you get a flight, okay?" Maddy's voice began to tremble.

"Yes, I'll try." She snapped the phone shut and handed it back to Clare.

"What did he say?"

"He'll come. He just said 'hang tough, babe.' "

Clare held out her arms and Maddy crumpled into them.

Fortified with *Tante* Margaret's sugar cake and a huge cup of coffee, Clare met the red-eye at Portland airport. She tried to concentrate on I-95 traffic in a driving rain while Paul peppered her with questions on the way into town.

"Don't gloss anything over, and spare me the medical jargon. Is he talking? Moving? What are his chances?"

"Well, it's pretty dicey. They moved him up to ICU for monitoring right after you

31

called with the flight number last night. I left Maddy and Kathleen pretty late."

"God, Clare. I don't know how I'm going to handle this. My conscience is on overload." Paul ran his fingers through his thick, raven hair. "Kathleen," he moaned. "Jesus, Mary and Joseph."

Clare shot him a quick glance. "My Aunt Margaret's been calling on them, too, wearing out her rosary since late yesterday. She always says, 'God will steady your heart when the floor shifts beneath your feet.' You'll be okay. Just remember that your sister needs a strong shoulder right now."

"Is she still seeing Claude Duval?"

"Ayuh. But not as much. She just met some new guy who really turned her on, and —" Clare's cell phone blared with the theme song from *Sex and the City*. Paul jerked forward, spreading his palms on the dashboard. "God, Clare, you couldn't miss with that one. Where's your phone?"

She was rummaging in her bag with one hand; found the phone and clicked it open. The rain pelted the windshield so hard, Clare had to scrunch forward, trying to see the road. Handing the phone to Paul, she swerved out of the passing lane. "Go ahead, I've got my hands full."

"Paul Fontaine here." A long pause, and

Clare's hands tightened on the wheel. "Hold on, Maddy. CeCe, are we near the exit yet?"

"We just passed the 208 one-mile sign. Ten minutes, tell her. Maybe fifteen in this blasted rain."

Paul looked at his watch and listened for what seemed like forever. Removing a crumpled handkerchief from his pants pocket, he wiped his forehead with his left hand. "I know, sis. That's probably it. We'll be there as soon as we can. Love ya." He clicked the phone shut.

"Probably it? What's it? What's happening?"

"Maddy's on the edge of falling apart. Doc Halliday is with them. He insisted Kathleen and Maddy take a break and try to eat some breakfast with him. Maddy barely made it down to the cafeteria. She's dizzy and faint, and now Doc is sending her home."

"I wouldn't wonder. It's been a shock."

"That's what Halliday said."

"No change in your dad?"

"Yeah, Doc says he's out of danger now and he'll stay with Kathleen until we get there." Paul slapped a hand to his forehead. "Oh damn. Kathleen!"

CHAPTER THREE

The sounds of the EKG monitor jarred the thoughts that raced through Paul's mind. He stared at the shadow of beard on Jacques's olive skin, at his bushy dark eyebrows arched over closed eyes.

Those eyes could rivet me in place with one fierce look. Wake up, Pa. We're not done here. The portrait . . . it was a beginning, just a beginning. Blip, blip, blip. He looked up at the monitor, then down at his hands. *Mom . . . taught me beginnings* — Paul's eyes blurred with tears.

He shook his head, wiped his eyes with a handkerchief and walked away from the bed just as Kathleen came in. She looked fragile and more vulnerable than he had ever seen her.

"Clare just called from the house and left a message at the nurse's station. Your sister is fine and finally getting some sleep. You probably should do the same, Paul, but if you wouldn't mind, can we talk for a bit, first? There are some things I must tell you." Her sad green eyes mirrored the sincerity of her plea.

They walked toward a bank of windows at the end of the hall. Early morning sunlight streamed through the glass, firing Kathleen's red hair with glints of gold. "Your father and I had a long talk after you left for New York. He's a very proud man, Paul, but I think he finally became reconciled to the fact that there was nothing wicked about your intentions . . . about the painting, I mean."

"Wicked? God almighty, Kathleen!"

"Wait, I'm not saying this right. At first your father was suspicious. Not of you and me, of course. But of your intent. He couldn't get past the nudity, Paul."

Paul's face reddened, his mouth clamped in a straight line. "He never listened to my explanation, either. Artists don't think in terms of nudity. I was blocking in face and figure. If he had waited —"

"I know, and I think he was beginning to understand but . . . then you were gone, and the painting was gone too." Kathleen heaved a sigh and turned to the window. "What happened to the painting, Paul?"

An elevator door behind them suddenly

opened and a young man walked directly toward them. He gave Kathleen a hug, "Mrs. Fontaine, I'm so sorry," then he extended his hand to Paul. "I just got the news from my uncle. They didn't give me much information downstairs, except that visitation is restricted, so I thought I'd come up to see if I could be with Madelaine. Is she with your father, Paul?"

"No." Paul took in the pin-striped gray suit, dark red tie and white shirt. Claude Duval fit the Yuppy image from his short, neat haircut to his polished, tasseled loafers. Claude had eased into full partnership in his father's law firm right after law school. Paul knew him in college. He didn't particularly like him, even before Maddy.

Strain was visible on Paul's finely chiseled features; a muscle twitched in his cheek. "My sister's not here. She . . . Doc Halliday gave her a sedative and she's home resting."

Kathleen grasped Claude's arm. "I can't take you into ICU, dear, but I can tell you what the doctor said. Come with me to the visitors' room. It's just down the hall. Paul? Coming?"

"No, I'll take *my ten minutes* in a while," he said, with an unmistakable edge to his voice. "I'm going down to get something to eat. Later, Kathleen." Paul pushed the elevator button.

He dialed Clare's cell phone number from a booth in the lobby. "Hey, CeCe, how's Maddy doing? Still asleep? No. No change here yet. Kathleen's holding forth with Claude. Ayuh, Mr. Brooks Brothers himself. He came looking for Maddy. I know, I know, but he's not the pick of the tree in my book.

"Look, Clare, I know you have today off. Is there a chance you'll be coming back here later? Aunt Margaret? Great! Could she swing by here and pick me up? Thanks, pal. Auntie Mame is the best. Just tell her to watch at the entrance for the guy wearing wrinkled clothes and a day-old beard."

Paul's guilt about leaving Kathleen faded fast when he got back to the ICU waiting room. Kathleen's head rested on Claude Duval's shoulder. She appeared to be asleep. When he saw the uncomfortable look on Claude's face, Paul wiped his hand over his mouth to cover a grin and signaled toward the ICU with his thumb. He tapped his watch and Claude nodded stiffly as Paul walked away.

Hands clenched on the metal bar of the bed, Paul stared at his father. Nothing seemed changed. A pretty blond nurse came round the curtain. He stepped back as she checked all the tubes and made notations on Jacques's chart.

Paul spoke softly to her. "Clare Chamberlain is coming in at noon to be with my father. She works in ER, but it's her day off, and I guess Doc Halliday arranged this private duty for her. Do you know Clare?"

"CeCe? Ayuh, as a matter of fact I do. She's a hoot. We were in training together. Know your sister, too. Maddy's a sweetheart."

Paul looked at his watch. "Well, I'm due to catch a ride home. If you see Mrs. Fontaine in here, would you do me a favor and tell her Clare's on her way?"

"Sure will."

His conscience nagged again when he thought about leaving, but when he got back to the waiting room, he could see that Claude had managed to shift Kathleen's head to a pillow on the sofa. He was standing beside her, brushing red hairs from the shoulder of his coat as Paul approached.

"I feel guilty leaving your stepmother, but I'm due at a meeting at the office," Claude said. "Glad you're back, Paul."

"I'm not back. And she's just *Kathleen* to me." Starting toward the door, he lowered his voice to a near whisper. "Forget the stepmother crap. They've been married less than a year, for God's sake."

Claude shifted uneasily, opened his mouth to speak, then closed it.

Paul glanced over his shoulder at Kathleen's prone body. "I need to crash for a while myself. I've got a ride back to the house, and CeCe's on her way in to take over."

Tante Margaret Chamberlain was a force to be reckoned with. Broad as she was tall, which was short by most standards, Margaret had a soft heart, a gentle touch, and the wisdom of the ancients.

Black hair, confined in a knot at the back of her head, shone as brightly as her warm, brown eyes. High cheekbones in a broad face were a throwback to her grandmother. Her grandmother was half Abenaki Indian. Having seven brothers, Margaret Lebrun Chamberlain was the only daughter of widowed French-Canadian logger Thomas Lebrun. Her father emigrated from Quebec with his mother and his eight children when Margaret was sixteen.

Margaret leaned across the passenger seat and pushed open the car door. "*Mon Dieu,* Jacques Paul, you're a sight for sore eyes."

"Is that a good or bad sight, Auntie Mame?"

She laughed and leaned over as Paul kissed her cheek. "You know, you are the only person who calls me that, but I don't mind a bit, eh. It's a good sight you are, Paul. Your little sister needs you."

"Yes, and I need her. Soon as I get a shower and a change of clothes, Maddy and I will drive back in to be with Dad. Kathleen's there in body only. She finally fell asleep in the visitors' lounge."

"You should take a nap yourself, *mon cher.* Not to worry. Clare will go to your papa as soon as we arrive at Francois's Fancy. My Jean Chamberlain, God rest his soul, would be so proud of our Clare."

"She's a brick, Auntie Mame."

"Are you hungry, Paul? I am going to take over your kitchen today. I will nourish your body, *mais oui,* and the Good Lord will nourish your soul. He promised."

The tempting smell of fresh-baked bread and spicy meat pie filled the kitchen. "Mmmm, this is so good." Paul scraped the last bite from his plate and beamed a smile at Margaret. "I haven't had tourtiere since 'Little Christmas.' "

"My pork pies are not reserved only for Noel, Paul. Your papa loves them anytime. I'm going to make gratin de raves too, and freeze it into small portions for when he comes home." She cocked an eye at Maddy. "You are not eating much, *ma petite.* Would you like a piece of my maple sugar cake?"

"No, thanks, Aunt Margaret. My stomach is still a little off. Maybe later, when we come home tonight. I'm anxious to get back to Dad. It seems like I slept away most of the day, Paul."

"Ah, but you needed that, and so did I. I'm good to go, whenever you say."

Margaret stood back, hands on hips, and smiled at the two of them. Paul rose and gave Margaret a big hug. He grabbed his sweater from a chair and settled Maddy's cardigan over her shoulders. She swept her long hair free from the yellow sweater and straightened her twill skirt.

"You are both good to go. *Très bon, mes amis,*" she said. She put an arm around each of their shoulders. "Think positive, Madelaine and Jacques Paul. Your papa will come home. I'll keep praying while I cook."

CHAPTER FOUR

Clare waited at the hospital lobby elevator. "There's been no time to tell you the good news. *Tante* called me to say you were on your way, so I came down to meet you. The clot-dissolving medication did its job. Dr. Mercier is encouraged with the MRA results, and he's moved your dad into a private room."

"Is he awake?" Maddy asked.

"Yes, but a little slow to respond. The test results showed no serious brain tissue damage, so that's the good part."

Paul gave Clare a kiss on the cheek. "Your *tante*'s prayers must be mighty powerful."

"Amen to that. Look where they got me," she said, her hands doing a flourishing sweep of her uniform. "I wouldn't have made it without her."

"Can you take us to his room now?" Maddy asked.

"To be frank, I'd like five minutes alone

with you guys first. Kathleen can be . . .
well, let's just say, I need a short break."
Clare grabbed both of their arms and led
them toward the cafeteria. "I also need a
drink." Her brown eyes danced mischie-
vously up at Paul. "Coke, that is. Fortifica-
tion, if you know what I mean."

"I hear ya," Paul laughed. Maddy turned
toward her brother, smiling and shaking her
head at the two of them as the three walked
into the cafeteria, arm in arm.

Maddy's shoulder brushed the arm of a
man walking toward them. He tried to
dodge, but the coffee he was carrying spilled
on his hand. "Damn," he muttered, setting
his cup on the nearest table.

Maddy broke away and came back to him
immediately. A flush warmed her cheeks as
she looked up at the perfect line of his jaw,
the flash of incredible blue eyes. "Patrick
Donovan?" she said in a shocked voice.
"What are you doing here?"

His brow furrowed and a glint of annoy-
ance flashed in his eyes. "You might say I'm
spilling my coffee, Miss Fontaine," he said,
as he wiped his hands with a handkerchief.

"I'm sorry. That was my fault. I wasn't
watching where we were going."

He took in the concerned look on Maddy's face, glanced at her companions and

shrugged his shoulders. "No, I'm the one should be sorry. That was a smart-ass answer. I'm here because of my sister, Rosie. She's in X-ray. It's taking forever, and I'm getting a little edgy."

"Rosemary? What happened to her?"

"She slipped on wet leaves coming out of church this morning, fell, and broke her arm. At least they think it's broken. That's why she is in X-ray."

Clare and Paul came to Maddy's side. When she introduced them to Patrick, she caught CeCe's puzzled look. "Patrick's sister Rosemary is one of the cast in the school play at Saint David. He's waiting for her to come from X-ray."

Recognition of whom Maddy was talking about registered when Clare heard Rosemary's name. "Did you come through Emergency with your sister?" she asked.

"Yes. It's only been about two hours, now," he said sarcastically, giving Clare's uniform the once over.

"Well, triage takes time, especially on a Sunday, if it's busy. I work there so I make no apologies. We do our best."

"And her best can't be topped," Paul said. "Clare came in on her day off to help with our Dad."

Patrick looked at Maddy. "Your father?"

She nodded, sudden tears welling in her eyes. "He's had a stroke." She reached up with one hand to the corners of her eyes with thumb and forefinger. Patrick impulsively took her other hand in his.

She looked down when she felt his callused palm and the warmth of strong fingers. A jagged scar ran around the joint of his thumb, wrapped his wrist, disappearing into his shirtsleeve. Maddy shivered when she met his gaze. There was a strange, soft look in his eyes. Tears tracked her cheeks and she opened her mouth, but no words came.

Clare saw Maddy begin to tremble. She impulsively took her arm. "Uh, I'm sure you'll excuse us, Patrick. I think Maddy needs to get upstairs to see her dad. I am the guilty one for keeping her down here in the first place. Coming, Paul?"

Paul's eyebrows arched. He shot Clare a quizzical look, then reached out to shake Patrick's hand. "Good luck with your sister."

Patrick watched them go. *And yours, too,* he thought, puzzled by the aching feeling he had in his gut when he looked into Madelaine Fontaine's tearful face.

"I don't know what came over me down

there. Maybe it was his unexpected kindness. I felt lightheaded for a moment. Weak as a kitten," Maddy said.

"Well, if he's as compassionate as he seemed to be, you'll see him again, for sure," Clare said, raising her eyebrows.

"Geez, will somebody clue me in here?" Paul asked.

"Patrick is someone I met through one of my students —"

"And she wants to get to know him better," Clare said, giving Paul a nudge and a meaningful look.

Paul nodded his head. "Oh, okay. Now I'm remembering our conversation coming in from the airport. So this is the guy you've just met, huh? I have to say, little sister, this guy makes Claude Duval look like a beached fish."

Maddy couldn't help herself. She laughed and popped Paul's arm with a fist. "I think you two are conspiring against Claude."

"Wouldn't be a bad idea," Clare said.

They were standing in the hall outside Jacques's room, having arrived just as Kathleen and Doc Halliday were getting ready to leave. They waited until the elevator door closed.

"I'm really beginning to wonder about *Mrs.* Fontaine," Paul said. "As soon as we got here, she was quick to take Doc Halliday's offer to drive her home. She gave me her keys and asked me to drive her Volvo home. That's the second time today she's latched on to a man."

"Well, in all fairness, she really wasn't in any condition to drive herself," Clare said. "She's only had catnaps for the last forty-eight hours. Her clothes are a mess and her thinking is not much better. I'm not her biggest fan, as you well know, but I am glad she left. I think it's time I leave you guys, too. Shifts will change in about five minutes."

"We can't thank you enough, CeCe," Paul said as they walked back with her to the elevator and said their goodbyes.

"Call me, no matter what or when," Clare said as the elevator doors closed.

"She's as blunt as she is tenacious, Mad, but a better friend you couldn't ask for. We're lucky, I guess," Paul said as they entered the hospital room.

They watched as their father's fingers clutched the bed sheet, but his eyes were closed.

"Should we . . . can he hear us?" Paul asked the student nurse who was filling a water carafe on the bed stand.

"The nurse assigned to Mr. Fontaine's

room will be in shortly, and she'll be able to answer your questions."

Maddy closed her fingers gently around her father's hand. "We're here, Papa." She could feel Jacques's fingers wiggle under hers. Her lips tipped up in a smile.

A motherly looking gray-haired nurse breezed through the door. Her snow-white, crisp, calf-length dress was in sharp contrast to the uniforms of the rest of the staff. A pin on her ample bosom read *Miss McCormack RN*. Paul and Maddy stepped back.

She checked Jacques's pulse and his head moved slightly on the pillow. "Waking up a bit, are ya? Praise be to God. 'Tis a good sign." A low moan escaped Jacques's lips. She smoothed his brow with long, practiced fingers.

"Behind that fine, broad forehead, you're thinking of something to tell us, aye?" She spoke as though Jacques were listening, and then cast a look at Maddy and Paul. "Your father, I'm guessing?"

Before they could answer, the door opened and Dr. Mercier walked in. "Good afternoon, Miss McCormack. You're right where they said you would be. I need a little consult after you finish with Mr. Fontaine." The doctor moved quickly to Jacques's side. "Well now, Madelaine," he said. "We have

48

some good news, eh?" He bent over Jacques, lifted his eyelids, checking his pupils.

"Yes, thanks to you, Doctor." Maddy touched Paul's arm. "This is my brother, Paul Fontaine. Dr. Mercier is Dad's cardiologist."

The doctor shook Paul's hand and gestured for them to walk with him to the window at the far side of the room. He lowered his voice. "Recovery can sometimes be a frustrating process. After TPA treatment, most patients come out of it awake and talking normally. A few have a little difficulty understanding at first. It may be trying to you and the people closest to you."

Paul and Maddy looked at one another. Their expression was not lost on Dr. Mercier.

"For now, we must be thankful the clot-busting medication worked. Tests showed little brain damage. He will be monitored closely. We have a strong staff here, a whole team who will work with him in the rehabilitation process if he needs it, but you can play a part in all of this." He smiled at Paul and squeezed Maddy's shoulder. "I'm sure you will. I'll see him again in the morning."

The doctor turned and nodded to the nurse as he headed toward the door. "He's in capable hands. Top of the evening, Miss

McCormack."

Paul shot Maddy a puzzled look. He ran his fingers across his forehead, a gesture that would become habitual in the hours to come. "Well, babe, I'm afraid I'm not going to be much good at this," he said in a low voice.

Miss McCormack was suddenly at Paul's side. She put a strong hand on his shoulder. "Aye, but you will be, lad. Never underestimate yourself. I've been nursin' thirty years and midwife ten before that. I've yet to see a father's son falter when the goin's rough. You will find strength, *Macushla.* God willin'." She gave his shoulder a solid thump. "You do your part, and I'll be back shortly to do mine."

To Maddy, it looked as though Paul was ready to bolt out the door behind the nurse.

Paul shook his head. "First *Tante* Margaret and now Nurse McCormack. Damned if the French and Irish aren't in cahoots with the Lord!"

"Oh, Paul. She is right. You may have the soul of an artist, but you have strong Fontaine blood in your veins. Grandpa Frank took risks and ended up with Francois's Fancy. Papa's not about to let you go," she whispered. "Just say a few words to him."

They stood on either side of the bed. Paul

swallowed hard and gripped the bed rail, looking at his father's closed eyes.

"I'm here, Pa. Sometimes I think I never left." His eyebrows knit as he drew in his breath and let it out slowly. "The stories you used to tell, the old Indian legends. They play back in my mind a lot. I want to hear them again, Pa." Paul looked at Maddy, hunched his shoulders and sighed. She smiled and nodded her approval.

"Paul," came a faint response.

Both heads turned at their father's voice. His brooding eyes were open, staring at them. His voice sounded hoarse and the words came out slowly. "I remember . . . the storytelling time."

"Me too, Papa," Maddy said, reaching for his hand, relief in her voice. "You told such wonderful stories."

"I had a good teacher. Your Grandpa Fontaine told stories in good old French tradition."

There was a long pause and Paul's feet shifted nervously. He ran his fingers across his forehead. "Speaking of French tradition, Clare and *Tante* Margaret have been helping since you . . . you, uh, came into the hospital. *Tante* made your favorite toutiere, Pa," Paul said.

The hint of a smile on Jacques's face was

soon replaced by a frown. His eyes roamed from Maddy to Paul. "Where is Kathleen?" he asked.

Paul hung his head.

Maddy squeezed her father's hand. "Kathleen's home, getting some rest. Not to worry, Dad. She will be back before long."

Miss McCormack opened the door and Paul heaved a sigh of relief.

CHAPTER FIVE

They left the hospital around six. It was prearranged for Paul to drive Kathleen's car, so Maddy drove herself to Biddeford Pool. They were like ships passing in the night, Kathleen leaving to go back to the hospital just after the two cars arrived at Francois's Fancy. Later that evening, Maddy and Paul sat alone in front of the fireplace.

"I'm glad you made a fire, Paul. I think it's the first we've had this fall."

"Not cold enough, or Pa just doesn't take the time? Which is it?"

"Both, I guess. It's been the warmest fall I can remember, but then, as soon as Dad comes home every day, Kathleen has him following some new whim or a little routine she's devised. There never seems time for the old conventional stuff."

"I could see that happening before *le* painting."

"Did Kathleen mention the portrait to you?"

"Oh, yes. I danced around the truth a bit, but she didn't seem to know the steps. Then we were interrupted by Claude, *the man,*" he said, rolling his eyes.

"Claude called me when you were gathering wood for the fire. Wanted to come over, but I begged off."

"Thank God. You know how I feel about him. Kathleen will be back in a couple of hours — now that's a different kettle of fish, as Grampa used to say. There's something about that woman that gets under my skin, and it's not those beautiful curves I was painting. The thing is, half the time I can't tell if she is sly or spacey."

"I can't read her easily, myself. That's one of the things that makes life uncomfortable here."

"Why don't you move in with Clare? She says she wants you to."

"I was close to making that decision when the whole thing blew up with Dad."

"Luckily, my choice to get out was made for me, but I should really only take a couple more days before I head back to New York. The museum director was great about my leaving, but Pa is the big question mark. Did Clare give you any more skinny

54

on him?"

"I had a long conversation with her, and we talked mainly about Papa and Miss Mc-Cormack. Clare said that McCormack is old school, but has a long-standing record as the most valued nurse in the hospital. The doctors love her, especially Dr. Mercier, who is young, and definitely not old school in attitude."

"No wonder he wanted a consult with her. But what about Pa?"

"Well, it's like the doctor said. It can be a slow road for some, but Clare thinks Dad will be back in no time. You seemed to reach him today when you spoke about the past. Maybe there won't be any more mention of the painting."

"That would be a *cause célèbre*. As soon as I know he's in the clear for any complications, I'm out of here."

Maddy couldn't sleep. The scenes at the hospital were running before her eyes, nonstop. Her mind kept churning up images, first of Jacques, then of Patrick Donovan. She punched her pillow and pulled the down comforter up around her ears. She squeezed her eyes shut, but new images persisted. Her mother, then her grandfather, Frank. They seemed to be beckoning her away from Francois's Fancy. She got up, wrapped herself into an old flannel robe, and tiptoed down the stairs. She walked through the hall to a room she seldom entered.

It had been, at various times, a sunroom, a studio, and now it was Jacques's study. His desk and bookshelves dominated the room. She walked unsteadily to the lamp on Jacques's desk, turned it on. Her brow furrowed. Every shelf was crammed with books in haphazard fashion. His desk was piled with folders and papers. Her mother's framed artwork, hanging on the wall in a symmetrical design, provided a stark contrast to the bedlam on the bookshelves.

Maddy had never seen her father's bookcase or his desk in such disarray. Jacques kept his history collection here for use when he needed to research something for his classes, but he did most of his prep work in his office at the university.

Mom kept those books in classified order. One was never out of place.

Her eyes scanned the far wall. Corner cabinets filled with painting supplies flanked a window seat. An afghan covered the worn and faded cushion of the broad seat under tall east windows. She turned the lamp off. A shaft of moonlight spilled down, like a spotlight, on her mother's painting stool. Maddy visualized her mother perched on the stool, limned in light and softness. She rubbed her eyes, pulled her robe close around her neck, and inched past the stool to the window seat.

Kneeling on the cushion she could barely see the curve of shoreline at the far corner of the moonlit yard. But there was no mistaking the faint sound of breakers hitting the sea wall, or the wind whistling past the window. She curled up under the afghan on the broad seat, easing a pillow under her head. Maddy stared at the painting stool, sighed deeply and closed her eyes. She yearned for the room to be the way it was.

The smell of coffee woke her, and she padded on bare feet to the kitchen to find Paul scrambling eggs and lathering *Tante*'s toasted bread with strawberry jam.

"I knocked on your bedroom door. When you didn't answer, I guessed you were still asleep."

"I wasn't there. I slept in the studio."

Paul gave her an earnest look. "That bad, huh?"

Maddy nodded, taking a seat at the table. "Too many memories here, Paul."

"Ayuh. Couldn't agree more." He poured coffee and pointed to his eggs. "Want some?"

"No, I'll just have one of the toasts."

"Same old, same old."

"Yes, but things are going to change. I've made a decision. After we see Dad this morning, I'm going to talk to Clare about moving in with her."

"Now that's a kick-ass decision, Mad. Perfect timing. We can take care of a move before I leave. Dad isn't here to give you an argument, and when he does get home, Kathleen will be too busy with him to give you grief. Herself must have been out of here bright and early this morning. Her car is gone."

"Do you think she'd miss my help here?"

"Kathleen? Hell, no."

"Slow down, Paul. You must have picked up on some of that New York City driving. We're on Main Street. Remember? Downtown Biddeford, and this is *my* car. I said you could drive us to lunch, but you're flying like Clare was when we told her about my decision to move in."

"I've never seen CeCe so excited. She was bouncing around that ER like Miss McCormack. I think you're gonna be fine in

CeCe's apartment. She is not going to let you have one sorry minute that you left Francois's Fancy."

"I know she'll be a great roomie. It's not her I'm worrying about. It's Dad."

"But the doctor said he's starting him in rehab today. What could be better news than that?"

"I mean, Dad and me. I couldn't tell him I'm moving out. I haven't even told Kathleen yet."

"Later, babe. Let me help you with that later, okay? Big brothers have to be good for something. Now tell me why we had to drive down to Main Street to eat lunch at the Café."

Maddy put on a confident smirk as they pulled into a parking space across from the Café. "When I called Saint David's this morning to tell them I would be back to my class on Wednesday, I inquired about Rosemary Donovan. She is my eighth-grade student, remember."

"And she is Patrick Donovan's sister."

"Yes," Maddy said with a grin. "And it just happens that Patrick's mother is a part-time cook at the Café." An enormous smile broke over her face.

"I got the picture. Okay. Showtime, babe."

Inside the Café, Maddy marched up to a

waitress tallying checks at the counter. The waitress smiled at Maddy. "Be right with ya," she said.

"Thanks, but before we sit, could you please tell me if Mrs. Donovan is in the kitchen?"

"Nope, not today. She only works three days. Tomorrow, Thursday and Saturday mornin's. If it's Eileen Donovan yer looking for, her son's one of our regulars. He's in the back booth and I'm just about to bring him his check."

The waitress moved through the small café, Maddy and Paul close behind her. She stopped at a booth, placing a check on the table. "There you go, luv," she said.

Patrick Donovan looked up, holding a coffee cup to his lips. He abruptly put the cup down. Genuine surprise registered on his face. His eyes fixed on Maddy with a steady blue-eyed gaze. His mouth twitched.

"It seems we're destined to meet over a coffee cup, Miss Fontaine." Patrick stood and shot a hand to Paul. "Paul, isn't it?"

"Yes," Paul replied, shaking hands and cocking his head toward his sister, "and *Maddy,*" he emphasized.

Maddy looked up at Patrick. His stature made her feel very small, but she gave him a confident grin. "I prefer Madelaine," she said.

Patrick laughed. "You remember our first meeting, too, I see. Well, then, Madelaine it is. Would you like to sit down? I've just finished, but I'll have a topper on my coffee."

Paul nudged Maddy into the booth, sliding in after her. "We only have time for a quick sandwich. Have to get back to the Medical Center," Paul said.

"How is your father?" Patrick asked.

"He's holding his own, now, thank God. He's starting therapy today," Paul said.

"How about Rosemary?" Maddy asked. "She's been on my mind."

"Her arm's in a cast, but she's back in school today. I'm sure you wouldn't know her arm is broken because, obviously, you're not at Saint David's if you're here on Main Street."

Patrick finished his coffee and cleared his throat. "Actually, I don't think I've ever seen you in the Café." He smiled. "I'd definitely remember it if I had." His smile had a taunting quality to it.

Maddy felt her cheeks warm. Two can play this game.

"What about you, Patrick? Do you work downtown?" She watched a muscle twitch in his jaw. Suddenly, the waitress was back, pouring coffee in Patrick's cup. "You folks like to order?" she asked.

Paul ordered cheeseburgers for both of them. Patrick silently sipped his coffee, watching Maddy over the brim of his cup. He checked his watch.

"On a time clock, Patrick?" Maddy asked.

She noticed a flashing glint of steel gray in his dark blue eyes. "No. My time's my own. I have a woodworking shop in the Biddeford Complex," he said.

"The old mill buildings?" Paul asked.

"Yep." Patrick kept a steady gaze on Maddy while he stood and picked up his check. "Got to get back. I'm working on an order for the carriage trade. Top-drawer stuff." He grinned, inclining his head in a mock bow. "Madelaine."

"Stop by sometime," he said, clapping Paul on the shoulder. He was gone before Maddy could think to answer.

Back at the Medical Center, Paul and Maddy visited Jacques in the hour before Clare's ER shift ended. They had prearranged to meet her back at Francois's Fancy after her shift.

Convinced that Jacques was making good progress, Paul told his father he was book-ing a flight back to New York the next day. "I may come back up for Thanksgiving, but in the meantime, with all these ladies looking after you, you'll be back at the university in no time, Pa."

"Clare should be here in the next ten minutes. Between her car and yours, we should be able to get all your stuff loaded and over to her place in one trip, don't you think?"

Maddy swallowed a bite of sharp cheese. "Maybe, if I leave my stereo equipment here. But I've got tons of books, a DVD player, my laptop, and all my clothes. I guess I could leave my summer stuff here. I noticed a lot of your gear is still in your closet."

"Ayuh. Got to have a port in the storm. I'll probably come up to celebrate the holidays. Speaking of celebrations," Paul said, holding up his glass of wine, "let's toast your new digs."

"I hear a car, and it's three-thirty on the button. It has to be CeCe. Let's wait for the toast. Don't forget that I want help with Dad's study when we finish upstairs. My mind won't rest until I know those books are back the way Mom always kept them."

Clare came into the kitchen carrying two

large cartons. "Whoa! No fair, guys. You're one up on me with the wine and cheese. I was going to break some goodies out as soon as we got everything over to Elm Street." She dropped the boxes at Paul's feet. "I'm sure Maddy's stuff will fill these."

Clare flopped into one of the pressed-back chairs at the kitchen table, stretched out her legs and reached for the cheese and crackers.

"Right on time, CeCe, and you even came equipped. Where have you been all my life?" Paul asked, handing her a glass of wine while he kissed her cheek.

"Bullcrap, Paul," she said, laughing. "You're such a tease. Seriously, now, I want to hear all about your lunch at the Café."

Maddy looked at Paul, her mouth twitching. "Surprise, surprise. Rosemary's mother wasn't at the Café, but Patrick was."

"And?"

Paul raised his eyebrows. "If you think I'm a tease, you should have heard the banter between the two of them," Paul said. "I caught desire and innuendo in the repartee, if you can imagine that combination."

Clare raised her wine glass. "To Patrick. Now tell me what he said, Maddy, before we pack one thing."

"Patrick Donovan is a man of few words.

He seemed cordial at first, but a little caustic at the same time. His sister is back in school with a broken arm. He did tell us he has a woodworking shop in the Old Mill Complex," Maddy said.

"His eyes were glued on Maddy the whole ten minutes we were with him, and before he left, he did say to stop in sometime," Paul added.

Clare took another sip of wine, stood and grabbed an empty carton. "I'd say go with the flow, Mad. But first things first. Let's go upstairs and get your clothes packed. I put a rod across the backseat of my car so we can hang some stuff and pack the rest flat."

"I'll put all the heavy gear — books and music stuff — in your car," Paul said, "and then I'll start on Pa's shelves. I know you want that done before we meet Kathleen at the club."

"Meet Kathleen?" Clare said, stopping in her tracks.

"Paul is going to help me break the news about my move over dinner at the club. We're supposed to meet Kathleen there at seven. You can come too, CeCe. Paul's flying back to New York late tomorrow, so we're trying to let Kathleen in on the move tonight. That way she can smooth the path for me telling him tomorrow. Tomorrow will

65

be my last day to spend with Papa at the hospital, and I don't want him to be stressed."

Clare shook her head. "I don't think so. I'd rather dinner be just the three of you. I would be more comfortable going to Papa Jacques's room tomorrow when you're ready to tell him about the move. I can manage that a hell of a lot better than dinner with Kathleen."

Everything was packed in the two cars by five o'clock. Clare left Maddy and Paul in Jacques's study with a promise of snacks and more wine when they arrived at her apartment.

Paul pushed the last book into place on the shelf as Maddy leafed through a book from a pile that had been on Jacques's desk. "I've never seen this book before," she said. "*Stories and Legends of Old Biddeford.* I bet there's some neat stuff in here that I could use with my class. I think I'll borrow it and mention it to Dad tomorrow." Maddy looked around the room. "Everything else looks great, Paul. Anything we've missed that you can think of?"

Paul's gaze fell on the painting stool. "Nothing but the portrait."

"The portrait? What do you mean?"

"I mean that Kathleen's portrait is unfin-

ished business which I'm going to personally take care of later. Much later."

CHAPTER SIX

A bell sounded as Maddy opened the door of the shop. She looked around, bewildered, at the small anteroom. *This must lead to cavernous factory space beyond,* she thought. Stools stood on either side of a drafting table to her left. An exquisite small table stood on a low wooden platform to her right. Its curly maple grain glowed with a satin-smooth finish. Business cards filled the table's single open drawer.

Maddy ran her fingers over the tabletop and lifted a card from the drawer. Imprinted on the card was a detailed sketch of the table. Beside the sketch —

Custom Designs
Patrick Donovan — Cabinetmaker

"Can I help you, Madelaine?"

The sound of her name on his lips startled her, producing fluttery feelings in her chest.

"I was hoping your invitation to stop by

was a sincere one, Patrick Donovan," she said, holding up his business card. "Did you actually design this table . . . and this card?"

"Yes. And yes. My invitation? I rarely say things I don't mean. The table was my first creation. The sketch of it gives a little panache to my card, *n'est-ce pas?*"

Maddy laughed to hear French words come from his mouth. "Patrick, you are . . . talented and clever. I mean no offense when I laugh, but you surprise me."

"What? The French, or the talent?"

"The French, of course."

"To be honest, those are the few French words that I know."

"Well, you obviously know your trade, which probably doesn't depend on a knowledge of the French language." She gestured to the open doorway ahead and flashed a smile. "Care to give me a tour of what lies beyond? I'm amazed by the renovation of these old factory buildings, and more than a little curious."

Patrick glanced at his watch. "Whoa, four-thirty, already. Actually, I should have closed shop half an hour ago. But then, if I had closed, I would have missed you."

The teasing note in his voice disappeared as he came close. He took her arm. "Come, I'll give you a quick tour, but only if you promise to tell me why you *really* came here today."

Maddy felt heat creep up her neck. She gave no reply as Patrick guided her through the open door. They stepped into a large partitioned space. High windows lined the west brick wall that was obviously an original outside factory wall. Lumber stood in neat stacks on long racks beneath the windows. The opposite wall held a lighted workbench and woodworking machinery. A worn, old sofa stood beside an antique Hoosier cabinet at the far end of the room.

"The back room," Patrick said, sweeping his hand in an arc from left to right.

Maddy's nose twitched at the smell of fresh-cut wood, oil and shellac. She let her eyes roam around the room. "May I ask how you got started in all this?"

"My grandfather. He had a small wood shop before I was born. It was a sideline for his job at the mill." Patrick pointed to racks behind the workbench. "Mostly hand tools."

"These are his tools?"

"Some of them. I still pamper those that were his, keep them in shape. I use them mostly for finishing. Fine knives, chisels and planes, files and such." He talked as he walked, pointing things out. "My grandfather did most things by hand. If he knew a chestnut tree was cut down, he'd help bring the logs to the sawmill. He'd buy a plank or two and let it air dry. Eventually, he'd match the wood up with an idea, or a wish that someone had."

"Is that how you operate? I saw your drafting table, and you obviously sketch first, and then . . ." Maddy inclined her head to the woodworking machines.

Patrick nodded and pointed to part of a drawer secured in a vise on the bench. "That's part of my current project."

He stopped to lean against the bench next to a band saw, resting his hand atop the saw. "There's a balance between machinery and finishing. Cabinetmaking takes concentrated thinking — move wrong and you can lose a finger or a hand." He held up his left hand. "My thumb was almost severed. Luckily, some doc knew how to reattach it. Luckier still, it was my left hand." He pointed to the band saw. "My grandfather had just bought it. I was twelve."

Maddy's eyes widened as she reached to touch the jagged scar. "And you continued to learn this trade since then?" She stared into his eyes, an incredulous look on her face.

He caught her hand, wrapping his fingers around it. "You might say so. Most of it,

71

anyway, came from my grandfather. He was something of a *seanchai* in his own right."

"A *seanchai*?"

"An Irish storyteller or poet. Aye, and he kept me entranced with tales about wood, he did." Patrick laughed at his own attempt to speak with a brogue.

"My grandfather worked at the mill most of his adult life. The woodworking was on the side, but I learned most of what I know from him." He raised his eyebrows at her, sending an impish grin. "Some of his Irish expressions, too. *Sweet Jaysus* I heard often enough when his feelings were rising." He wiggled his eyebrows. "They kind of stuck with me."

Patrick straightened and pulled her forward with him. Holding tightly to one hand, he moved deftly around sawhorses that occupied the middle of the floor.

She looked up at his angled jaw, couldn't take her eyes from the deep dimples and sensuous mouth.

"Enough about my family. Come sit for a minute, Madelaine, and tell me about you." They scuffed through wood shavings toward the back of the room. "If you don't mind the sawdust on the sofa, I'll make you a cup of tea."

A cup of tea? This man was an enigma.

Maddy focused on a hot water carafe on the Hoosier cabinet. Cups, spoons, a tea caddy and sugar bowl all lined up neatly on its porcelain shelf.

She sank into the worn cushions, fastening her eyes on the piece of furniture that was taking shape near the sawhorses.

"Tea is Irish breakfast," he said, handing her a cup. "My mum got me hooked on it for an afternoon pick-me-up."

"Suits me fine," she managed, staring at the honey-colored cherry wood of a cabinet in progress. "Is that the 'carriage trade' piece you mentioned at the Café? The wood is so beautiful."

"Yes." He fastened steady blue eyes on her as he balanced his cup and sat beside her on the sofa. "My grandfather taught me about the richness of wood. There's an intimate relationship between wood and tools, you know. 'Your fingers and eyes are tools.' " Patrick looked at his hands, sipped his tea. "Skilled fingers, a sensitive eye, and the wood."

His mouth quirked slightly as he looked into her eyes. "But I'm waiting to hear about you, Madelaine. You came to my shop because . . . ?"

Maddy gulped her tea, gasping as the steaming liquid burned her tongue. She let her breath out slowly, and put her cup down on the dark, oiled floor. "I told you I was curious about this old mill project."

"Just one particular building?" His smile had a taunting quality.

Maddy's mouth quirked in a grin. "I'm . . . uh, I'm always looking for ideas to use in my Social Studies class. This would be a good starting place for a local history project. One that shows how these old buildings can hold promise for the future." She slanted a look up at him as she drank her tea. He was listening thoughtfully.

"A family business is becoming a rarity these days. I think your sister Rosie would be proud if I chose your shop for a field trip and study. Maybe your sister Fiona would like to help."

He was suddenly quiet. Instead of interest, she saw that his eyes took on a dangerous glint and his jaw tightened. Patrick shook his head. "I don't think so," he said.

"But, why not? It might even be good for your business, and —"

Her voice faded when Patrick suddenly picked up her cup and carried their teacups to the cabinet. He returned to the sofa, faced her, scowling. "This is not a family business, and my answer has to be no, Madelaine." There was finality and an unmistakable edge to his words.

Bewildered and a little hurt, Maddy stood, narrowing her eyes. "I seem to have misunderstood when you spoke about your grandfather. The idea of a school project just sort of developed in my mind as we talked." She swallowed the lump rising in her throat. "But it was not my original reason for coming here."

She looked down, then her eyes snapped up and met his for an instant. "I thought we . . ." She turned away without finishing and stood. Spine straight as a broom handle, her feet fairly flew through the back room, heading for the front of the shop.

Patrick was speechless for a minute, then he moved quickly after her, catching up as she reached the front door. "Madelaine. Wait." He spun her around, held her by the waist, feeling her slender body shudder. Bending low he brushed his lips very gently across hers and pressed his cheek to hers. His breath was hot and sweet against her face.

His voice was husky. "My decision about your project has nothing to do with you, personally. I'm glad you came here today. I wanted you to."

Their troubled eyes met. As the implication of his words penetrated, a thrill went

75

curling deep down inside her. She felt her breath catch.

"Patrick . . ." Her hand rose to his cheek, lingered for a second. It took all of her strength to push away. Not to throw her arms around his neck and kiss him back. "I have to go. It's been a very long day." She opened the door and set its bell to jangling.

Get a grip, she told herself as she walked toward her car. *This is impossible. He turns my spine to jelly . . . one minute tenderly teasing, the next he's cold and abrupt. Something is wrong. Something is definitely wrong.*

It wasn't in Patrick's character to speculate why he did what he did, yet with her, he knew he wanted to be never less than gentle.

I should have told her I loved her green eyes.

I should have told her that I ached to gather her in my arms.

I should have explained my abrupt decision.

I should have told her about Fiona.

"I can't believe the last forty-eight hours, Clare. My dad didn't seem the least upset when we told him I'd moved in with you. Of course, Paul had laid it out pretty straight to Kathleen the night before at dinner. Fortunately, she had Papa all primed.

76

Paul said Kathleen could be cunning when she wanted to be, and she was probably glad to have Papa all to herself."

"I thought you would tell me all about that after school today, but you weren't here," Clare said, plumping up the pillows before she stretched out on the sofa. "I had big-time emergencies all day yesterday, and I couldn't get up to the third floor. Didn't even have lunch. I'm pooped."

"I know. Paul said you only had time for a peck on the cheek when he came down to the ER to say goodbye. When I got home from taking him to the airport, it was after seven, and you had left to take *Tante* Margaret to her social club. We've got tons of catching up, CeCe."

"Well, out with it. Start with where you were after school today."

"First I called Dad's room at the hospital. He was in therapy and Kathleen said everything was going smoothly. Then I volunteered to drive Rosemary Donovan home. We had a nice long talk. When I told her I met her brother Patrick at the Café, she seemed less reluctant than usual to talk about her family. Poor Mrs. Donovan has had a lot of heartaches. I learned that she lost a son, Daniel, two years ago, and then her husband last October. Rosie said that

Patrick kind of took over as man of the family."

"I didn't know there was a brother."

"Me either. Daniel was second eldest. Rosie's usually sweet and shy, but she did tell me that she was Danny's favorite. He had leukemia, and I could see that talking about him made her sad, so I changed the subject; talked about Patrick's woodworking shop —"

"I knew it! You went there, didn't you?" Clare sat straight up and playfully tossed a pillow at Maddy. "I thought this was leading to a big announcement from my *wily* roomie."

"I don't know about wily. I came away from Factory Square very confused."

"Well, start at the beginning. What was his shop like?"

"That part was amazing. The restoration of those old mill buildings is fantastic. There's a small front room where he has his drafting table and a beautiful example of his work, an absolutely elegant little table. His cards were in the table drawer." Maddy reached in her pocket and tossed the business card to Clare.

"Hmm. Very impressive," Clare said, studying the card. "Way to go, Patrick."

"The back room, where he does his work,

was even more impressive. It's a big carved-out space at one end of the first mill building. The outside wall is the original brick. The partitioned opposite wall has all his tools and machinery. He even has a Hoosier cabinet and an old sofa in the back."

"Don't tell me. I can see it coming. You made love on the sofa."

"Clare! Are you out of your mind?"

Clare laughed. "Well, what was he like? What did he say?"

"At first he was teasingly nice. He gave me a tour and talked about how he got started in the business. He reminisced about his grandfather, who taught him most of what he knows. Patrick seems very sensitive, almost sensual at times. Then he made us a cup of tea."

"A cup of tea? That's sensual?"

"Well, he was. I mean, he was intriguing and sensual when he talked about his work. That is until I got the bright idea of asking if he would allow his shop to be part of a history project for my class."

"What's wrong with that? He doesn't like kids?"

"No. I think it's because I mentioned his family getting involved. Oh, I don't know what set him off, but something did. He totally refused my idea. Shut me off."

Maddy snapped her fingers. "Just like that. He's the most mystifying person I've ever met."

"That's a bummer. I thought the guy would be compassionate. You know, like he was at the hospital."

"At the end, he was. When I tried to leave he kissed me. It was a tender, sweet kiss. He told me he really wanted me to come to his shop. I was flabbergasted."

"And?"

"I left."

"Maddy! *Tu es fou.* Crazy, crazy." Clare grabbed Maddy's left hand. "Time to ditch Claude. No ring, no intent, no Claude. I wouldn't care if he had a six-figure income and was every mother's dream. I'd blow him off."

That was typical Clarespeak. Clare Chamberlain was outspoken, sometimes crude. She knew more street talk than sailors, but she was often right on the mark.

CHAPTER SEVEN

The next morning, Maddy woke from a dream. She woke to a gentle whisper, a voice deep within. It was something her mother used to say. *Follow your heart. Keep a sweet spirit, a gentle heart.*

Mom?

It was a breathtaking dream. Patrick was kissing her, gently at first, then with a ferocious need. This time Maddy didn't pull away from the thrum his kiss set off in her chest. She wrapped her arms around him and kissed him back with a need that matched his.

She wanted to linger longer in the dream, but she could hear the shower running in the bathroom. Clare had to be at work before Maddy, so they'd agreed on a routine. Maddy would get breakfast and clean up. Clare would cook dinner on nights they would both be home.

A plan was hatching in her mind as she

put out the breakfast things. She would keep Rosemary after play rehearsal on the pretext she needed coaching. Maddy was determined to find out more about Patrick, and Rosie was a good place to start.

Maddy ended play rehearsal after the third scene. "Okay, listen up, guys. This is a one-act play, but each scene is important. I'm going to work with individuals on stage directions for the last scene. Rosemary and John, will you both stay, please? I want to work on John's entrance before Rosie's solo. The rest of you may leave, and remember, no rehearsal until next week."

Maddy stood in the wings. "Take it from the top, John. Stride in from stage right with strong, forceful steps, then pace like you are really thinking. That's it. Good. Keep glancing at Rosie on the loveseat, and let me hear your lines.

"Almost perfect, guys. Rosemary, I want you to remember not to upstage John when you leave the loveseat. He must be the focus of the audience until your solo. You can go now, John, but you still need to practice your lines at home. Don't forget, no rehearsal tomorrow."

As soon as the boy left the auditorium, Maddy walked out on the set and sat on the loveseat. "I do want to hear your solo, Rosemary, but sit here with me for a minute first. Something is bothering me that I'd like to talk about with you."

Rosemary looked glumly at her cast. "Is it about my arm?"

"No, no. Your cast doesn't interfere at all with the role you play."

"If it's about my lines, I promise I'll spend more time on them this weekend. My mum, she'll help —"

"It's not your lines, Rosie, but it is about your family. I hoped you could help me understand something about your brother Patrick."

With eyes downcast, Rosemary chewed on her lip and heaved a sigh. "I'll try, Miss Fontaine, but Paddy and me, we butt heads a lot. He's real strict about what he thinks I should and shouldn't do."

"I hear you, but just listen for a minute and tell me what you think. I visited Patrick yesterday and asked him if he would consider his shop being part of a school project to study the restoration of the old factory buildings. I suggested his wood shop could be a core example of a successful family business. I mentioned that I thought you would be proud to be involved, and that your sister Fiona might want to help."

Maddy heard Rosemary's quick intake of breath and saw a flush creeping up the girl's neck.

She looked wide-eyed at Maddy. "That can't be, Miss Fontaine."

"That's what your brother said. Can you tell me why, Rosie?"

The girl's face was a mix of sadness and embarrassment. " 'Cause Fiona's gone."

The auditorium door suddenly opened and Patrick strode down the aisle toward them.

He took in the near empty stage and called up to them. "Practicing late, Miss Fontaine, or is it just Rosie not knowing her lines?"

"Stop there, Patrick, if you would." Maddy called to him as he reached the middle aisle. "I was giving Rosemary some extra coaching, but I really want to hear her solo. Could you wait just a bit longer and hear her sing? Your sister needs to get used to an audience. She has a sweet voice, but she needs to project more. Have a seat and let's see if you can hear the lyrics from there. I'm going to listen from the back of the auditorium."

With her back to Patrick, Maddy whispered. "Just relax, Rosie, and forget about our conversation for now. Sing as though

84

you are trying to reach me in the back."

Maddy exited the stage by the left stairs and walked quickly to the back. "From center stage, Rosemary. Let me hear it in the last row."

Rosemary's voice had perfect pitch, a lilting sweet soprano. She didn't look at her brother, but seemed to concentrate on reaching Maddy at the back, just as she was told. At the end of the song, Maddy smiled to see Patrick putting his hands together enthusiastically. Applause echoed through the empty auditorium.

Maddy walked directly down the aisle to stand beside Patrick. "I could hear every word of the lyrics," she called up to Rosie. "That was lovely, and I'm glad your brother agrees." To Patrick, she whispered. "Your sister needs that affirmation. Thanks for waiting." Maddy started toward the stage, but he caught her arm.

"We need to talk, Madelaine . . . to finish our, uh, conversation from yesterday. Can I pick you up later tonight?"

Taken off guard, there was a barely discernible quaver in her voice. "I . . . um . . . guess it would depend on the time. I've hardly gotten settled in the apartment and —"

"You've moved? I thought your family was

85

one of the year-rounders out at the Pool."

Maddy shot a quizzical look his way. "Well, we are. I mean, my father is, but I'm not any longer. I've moved in with my friend Clare."

"Okay. So where is that, and what time could I come by?"

Maddy could see Rosemary approaching, and there was no time to think. "Eight o'clock will be okay, and it's the apartment building before you get to Pearl Street. I don't know the number, but you can't miss the yellow siding," she whispered. She managed a smile before turning her attention to Rosemary. "Your solo will make a grand finale, Rosie. Aren't you glad your brother thinks so, too?"

Patrick cleared his throat and nodded. "Ye sang clear and sweet, me darlin' Rosie. That's what Grandpa would've said." His dimples deepened as he smiled and ruffled her hair. "But I'm saying I'd better be getting you home before Mum gets worried."

Rosemary blushed, looking shyly at Maddy.

Patrick helped his sister into her jacket and started up the aisle, Rosemary in tow. "Thank you Miss Fontaine," Rosie called over her shoulder. "See you tomorrow."

Maddy watched them leave. Impulsive,

unpredictable and irresistible. *No wonder I have this gnawing apprehension about being alone with him.*

Maddy hurried out of the kitchen, headed toward her room. "That was really good lasagna, Clare."

"Thanks. Gonna change for your big date?"

"I don't consider it a date, but I don't want to be in these school clothes any longer."

Maddy showered and dressed. She tucked a moss-rose turtleneck shirt into navy corduroys, threading a new silver belt through the loops. She fastened her shell locket around her neck and took up the blow dryer to give her hair one last turn with a round brush.

"I haven't seen you fuss like this in a long time, babe." Clare stood in the bedroom doorway. "Does this mean that Claude is history?"

"I haven't told him that, but I'm doing it real soon."

"No regrets?"

"I'm a little sad about it, but only for Dad's sake. That's how I met Claude, remember? Kathleen invited him to their wedding reception and she kind of pushed him after that. He's the longest relationship I've ever had. Dating, I mean."

Maddy sighed and smoothed her hands down her jeans. "But we've never . . . Claude never made me feel like this." She waved both hands in front of her like she was shaking. The doorbell rang.

Clare left to answer the door while Maddy ducked back into her bedroom. She stood staring into her closet, finally choosing a burgundy leather jacket. Walking into the living room she shrugged her arms into it and stopped short of the counter. Her mouth dropped open.

Patrick was leaning over the narrow bar that curved around to separate the kitchen from the living room.

Clare held a forkful of lasagna to his mouth. "He said it smelled good in here, so I was offering him a taste of the leftovers."

Maddy was surprised to feel a pang of jealousy as she watched Clare acting so spontaneously natural with Patrick.

"Mmm, it's as good as it smells, Clare." He turned to smile at Maddy. "And you are looking mighty fine, Madelaine."

"She's a mighty fine person. Only been living here two days and already gives this place a touch of class."

Maddy rolled her eyes at Clare and moved

to open the door. "Later, CeCe," she said.

"Bye, guys. Have fun," Clare called, sending a foxy grin their way.

"What was that nickname you called her?" Patrick asked as they walked outside the apartment complex.

"CeCe? Two C's. I spell it with an e when I write it, so that's the way I say it. It's just short for Clare Chamberlain."

"Sounds French to me. She is French, same as you, right?"

"That's right. Clare's parents were killed in a car crash, and she was raised by her Aunt Margaret. We've known each other since we were kids. We grew up tight. Actually, she's my best friend."

"At first, I thought she might be a wood-pile cousin of yours. You two are obviously pretty tight, but she has a very different personality than you. She seems like the type you can count on for a little sass."

Patrick stopped beside a silver GMC truck, a wide grin on his face as he opened the passenger door. "CeCe is probably the kind of person who wouldn't mind riding in my . . . uh, truck. Would you care for a ride, *mademoiselle?*"

Surprised, but charmed, Maddy said, *"Oui, monsieur."* She climbed in with a little boost from Patrick. The inside of the cab was more surprising than the outside. It was uncluttered, neat, and clean as a whistle. "Where are we going?"

"To a quiet little spot across the river. A new place that just opened on Water Street, if that's okay with you."

They were across the bridge and into Saco in minutes. "Sounds great. How did you find out about this place?"

"Actually, I do business on both sides of the river. The carriage trade piece you saw in my shop was requisitioned by a mill manager who lives here in Saco. He recommended T.J.'s Wine Bar to me. I kind of liked the name. T.J. were my grandfather's initials. Myself, I hang out sometimes at Mulligan's, but I think you'll like the wine bar."

Maddy did like it. It had soft lights and cushy booths. Framed French scenes and California winery posters covered the walls of a long narrow room. Opposite the booths, rows of wine racks flanked a small bar; more stock than she'd seen in posh cafés in Portland.

"I'm impressed," she said as she took a seat.

There were a few couples seated in booths. Soft jazz oldies muffled the conversations around them. Sarah Vaughan was singing

"The Nearness of You."

Maddy remembered hearing that song on one of her mother's favorite albums. She felt cosseted. She sat quietly, listening and wondering if it was the place, the music, or Patrick that produced the feeling.

"Well, I hope you know what you'd like. I know nothing about wine," Patrick said. He ordered a bottle of beer and Maddy agreed with the waiter's suggestion of Gossamer Creek Chardonnay.

Reaching across the table, Patrick clinked his glass against hers. "Let's drink to new beginnings," he said, fixing his gaze on her mouth. *"Slainte."*

"Is that an Irish toast?"

"Yes." He raised his glass. "It means good health." A muscle rippled in his cheek and he set the glass down after taking a big gulp of the beer. "I've got to get something off my chest, Madelaine. I owe you an apology."

"Oh? I hope it's not for the kiss." She grinned at him.

"It's not for the kiss. Never for the kiss." He smiled nervously, then ran his fingers through his hair.

"I gave you a flat refusal when you asked if my business could be part of a school project."

91

"That, I remember." *I remember the kiss more.*

"I should have explained why I refused. It's complicated, but my shop is *not* a family business, even though it's sort of tied in to the Donovans." He looked away momentarily. "It exists because of my grandfather. When he died, he left a good sum of money in a trust for me until I reached age twenty-one. The contingency stated that the funds had to be used to start a woodworking shop. Gramp's will had the effects of a bombshell in my household. My father resented it big-time. Never did get over it. That's when he began drinking."

"Isn't your father deceased?"

"He is, but he was alive six years ago when Gramp passed on. I was sixteen at the time, still in high school."

"Sounds like your grandfather had a lot of faith in you."

"Yeah, a hell of a lot more than my father ever did. My grandfather wrangled himself into the good graces of a mill manager years before I was born. The manager was a Boston man like my grandfather, but a man of wealth and power. They both came over from the old country. The old guy had pulled himself up by his bootstraps, and moved up fast. He took a liking to Gramp.

Did him lots of favors, and my grandfather returned his trust by building things for him. When the manager died, he left a tidy sum to Thomas J. Donovan, his faithful friend."

Patrick closed his eyes for a second. "And that, Madelaine, is where my seed money for the business came from." Patrick sat back and seemed to relax. He raised two fingers and nodded to the waiter passing their booth.

After their drinks were replenished, Maddy ran a finger round and round the rim of her wine glass. "Thank you, Patrick, for explaining, but I have to say that your explanation sounds more like your cabinet-maker's shop really is a family business. Rosie told me that you've assumed head of the family since your father and brother died."

Patrick shot her a surprised look. "She told you about Danny?"

"Yes, just a little."

"And my da?"

"Just that he died suddenly last year."

Patrick took big gulps of his beer, swiped his lips with the back of his hand. He fixed his gaze on Maddy's shell necklace. "And did she tell you about Fiona?"

"When I asked about your sister, Rosemary said that she was gone."

Gone. The word made it sound like she was dead.

Patrick groaned. It was a jarring sound in the midst of soft music and soft voices. He drew a deep breath and stared into space. "It's not a pretty story." His eyes darkened to indigo. He cracked a knuckle with his hands pressed together. The arrogant tilt to his chin didn't match the expression of reluctance on his face.

"It's been a year and there are still no clues to where my sister Fiona is, or the bastard that took her away from us."

"Took her away?" Maddy reached a hand to cover his scarred wrist. "Patrick, I can see that you are upset. I don't understand all this, but it's okay if you don't want to tell me any more."

"You really *don't* understand. Fiona's disappearance tore my family apart. My father died that same month, and my mother hasn't been the same since."

Maddy's face registered shock. Patrick suddenly grasped her hands in his.

"God knows why I've told you any of this, Madelaine. I wanted tonight to be good . . . for both of us."

CHAPTER EIGHT

A crowd of college kids came into T.J.'s Wine Bar. Noisy conversations erupted, destroying the cozy ambience. Patrick released Maddy's hands. He shot the students a jaded look, finished his beer and stood suddenly to signal the waiter. It seemed to Maddy that he couldn't leave fast enough.

Back in the truck, Patrick grasped the wheel at three and nine, concentrating on getting over the bridge. It was a short drive back to Elm Street, but thick fog had rolled in, leaving a mist over everything, making it difficult to see more than a block ahead.

Maddy tried to quell her angst. The music from the wine bar filtered through her mind . . . "The Nearness of You." She glanced at Patrick, staring ahead, focusing on the fog-shrouded streets. The tension in the truck was almost tangible.

He parked at the curb in front of the

apartments and turned to face her. Placing a hand on her shoulder, he broke the silence.

"I'll understand if you don't want to see me after tonight — if you want to end this . . ." His words drifted off, but his eyes conveyed a different message.

She flattened her hands on his chest, her gaze raking his face.

"End this?" She shook her head. "What happened to your sister is sad and terrifying, but it doesn't change anything about tonight. I liked being with you, Patrick. I understand now why you are so protective of Rosemary."

He took her hands in his and held them tight. "It's best you know the whole story about Fiona, and it's better you hear it from me. I don't want Rosemary reliving it in any conversations with you. Can I tell you what happened?"

She nodded her head. "Of course."

Patrick took in a deep breath. "This goes back to June of last year. Fiona met a guy at the *La Kermesse Festival,* end of June. My mum chewed her out for being out half the night. I don't usually go to the Franco festival, so I didn't see him. *No one in the family has ever seen him.* Fiona described him to Rosie. Tall, handsome, the usual crap. Hell, I don't think Rosemary was even tuned in to boys then. She is such an innocent."

"Did Fiona tell Rosemary his name?"

"Fiona never told anyone his name, called him her prince. She sneaked off to meet him on the sly all the rest of the summer and always gave Mum some shady excuse about why the guy didn't come to the house. By the end of September, my father demanded to meet him, and that's when the shit hit the fan."

She watched his blue eyes go soft and sheepish when he looked at her.

"Sorry, Madelaine." He ran his fingers through his hair. "Fiona may have thought this guy was her Prince Charming, but believe me, this was no fairy tale. He was a sneaky SOB." Patrick looked off into the hazy light from a street lamp, the muscle in his cheek twitching, his finely chiseled features silhouetted in the misty light. "Fiona was pregnant. She left my mum a note saying she wasn't going back to school. Said she was going away and we were not to look for her until she contacted us. She never did."

Maddy put her arms around his neck, laid her head on his chest. "Oh, Patrick. I'm so sorry."

"My family always covered up about Fiona to others, but that didn't take the hurt away. That day in my shop when you mentioned her, I couldn't bring myself to tell you about it. You were something soft and sweet that came to me, Madelaine." He gently lifted her chin with a finger, brushed her hair away from her face and stroked her cheek with the back of his fingers. "I didn't want you to know about her."

She pressed a finger on his lips and shook her head. He grasped her hand, kissed her fingertips and then her lips, slowly, gently . . . thoroughly. She felt the tingling down to her toes.

Clare was watching TV when Maddy let herself into the apartment.

"Only nine forty-five? That was a short talk — date — whatever," she said, watching as Maddy pulled off her jacket and sat beside her on the sofa. Clare clicked off the remote. "You look a little flustered, girlfriend. Are you okay?"

Maddy needed no encouragement to tell her what happened. She began with Patrick's mention of CeCe's personality and the truck. Clare hooted. By the time Maddy finished telling her about Fiona, Clare was no longer laughing.

"That is bizarre. I don't understand how someone could just disappear and leave no trace. Didn't they search for her?"

"I asked that very question. Patrick said they went to the police and declared her missing. They questioned her girlfriends, inquired at the café where she had a summer job, checked the bus station, the train station, the airport. Nothing.

"After all that, Mr. Donovan wouldn't allow any more searching. 'Fiona's almost eighteen,' he said, 'she made her bed. Now let her sleep in it.' I guess their father was a bitter, prideful man."

"My *tante* wouldn't have stopped there. She would have searched and searched, come hell or high water. *Tante* knows most of the big shots who work *La Kermesse,* and I'll bet she would have found a clue. Somebody at that French festival might have seen them."

"Well, it was a whole year ago, and it's still hard for Patrick to talk about it. I can see that he endures the hurt it caused his family. He took it into his heart, you know? I just don't think he wants things stirred up any more."

"Then why did he bring it up at all?"

"For one thing, he's protective of Rosemary and his two younger sisters. I think he was responsible for them transferring to Saint David this year. And secondly," Maddy said, looking into Clare's eyes with a half smile, "I guess he wanted to be up-front with me because he didn't want the scandal to spoil things . . . for us."

"Aha. There's an *'us.'* I'm beginning to like this guy more and more. I don't want to spoil things for you either, babe, but there are three phone calls you need to know about. Claude called you twice. I forgot to tell you about the first call that came yesterday on my cell phone; then he called here tonight."

"And the third call?"

"From Kathleen. Your father's coming home from the hospital tomorrow. She thought you'd like to stop at the house after school to kind of welcome him home."

She couldn't tell if it was longing or dread that made her turn toward the small harbor. Maddy's breath caught on a sigh when the ocean stretched to the horizon beyond the fishing docks.

It was dusk, but she could clearly see sailboats, fishing boats and small craft bobbing in their moorings at high tide. Vermillion and gold banners painted the sky. She let the car idle in front of the docks, rolled down the window to let the sound of the surf fill her head, the salt air twitch her nose and the colors of the sunset soothe her soul.

Several minutes passed before she slowly turned the car back up Mile Stretch Road to Francois's Fancy.

"Hello the house. Anybody home?" Maddy entered from the back door, almost colliding with her stepmother in the kitchen doorway.

"Kathleen. How's he doing?"

Kathleen took Maddy's arm, leading her up the hall toward the wide entry to the living room. "He's doing just fine, but he'll be staying downstairs for a few days."

"I hear you, and it's just till I get my sea legs," Jacques called out from the living room. Jacques sat in one of the wing chairs flanking the fireplace, legs propped up on an ottoman. "I can really manage the stairs, but Doc wants me to take it slowly."

Maddy put on her best smile. "Hi, Papa." She bent to kiss his cheek. "I'm so glad you're home. You're looking really good. Any other rules besides no stairs?"

"Oh, yes," he said, reaching for her hand. "No driving for a week, avoid stress, and most important, a low fat diet. Ugh."

"I'm not surprised about that. CeCe thought that would happen. Clogged arteries are the devils, she said, and *Tante* Margaret's cooking has to go on hold." Maddy sat by his feet on the ottoman. "Anything I can get for you?"

"No, thanks, babe, but the sun's well over the yardarm and I think I'll have my scotch now."

"Is scotch allowed?" Maddy asked.

He nodded his head, crooking a finger at Kathleen. "One a day. Everything in moderation. Right, my dear?" He pointed to a beginning pot belly. "And while you're at it, Kathleen, maybe Maddy would like a glass of wine."

"Yes, darling," she said, pouring scotch into a glass from a decanter on the table. "I'll get some wine from the kitchen. Be right back, Madelaine."

"Well, now, Kathleen tells me you and Paul tidied up my study while I was in the hospital. I know it was bad, but I just kept putting things off after classes started, and things kind of got away from me."

"I hoped you wouldn't mind our doing that," Maddy said, patting his knee. "I just couldn't stand the mess."

Jacques smiled pensively at her. "You're more like your mother every day, Madelaine, and just as beautiful as she was." He closed his eyes for a second. They were misted when he opened them and reached for her hand. "Now then, how about you? Are you happy with your first month at Saint David? How's it going at the apartment?"

"The apartment's fine and everything's great at school. I've met someone new, Papa. The older brother of one of my students." She glanced at Jacques to see his reaction. "His sister has the lead in a play I'm directing for my eighth-grade class, and incidentally, I borrowed a book of legends from your library —"

The sound of a male voice at the back door stopped her in mid-sentence.

"Are you expecting anyone, Papa?"

"Claude called earlier looking for you, and Kathleen told him you were going to be here late this afternoon. Maybe it's him."

Jacques didn't miss the frown on her face as Claude strode into the living room seconds later, Kathleen on his heels. Claude went directly to Jacques's chair, extending his hand.

"Glad to see you're home, Dr. Fontaine, and looking well, too. I'm not surprised, given there are two lovely ladies here to take care of you." He bent to kiss Maddy's cheek.

Jacques sipped his scotch, watching Maddy's face.

Kathleen put a tray down on the coffee table, and cleared her throat. "You two must not be communicating about Elm Street, hmm?" she said, raising an eyebrow to Maddy. She poured wine and handed them each a glass.

Maddy stood by her father's chair, knowing full well what Kathleen meant. She exchanged glances with Kathleen and sipped her wine.

"It's not that *I* haven't tried," Claude said. "Maddy has no cell phone, and with no answer here until today, I tried Clare's cell phone and then her apartment. She acted like I was a telemarketer."

There was a heavy pause. "She was probably leaving it up to me to tell you, Claude," Maddy said, looking from her father to Claude. "I've moved into town. Into CeCe's apartment."

Confusion registered on Claude's face and for once he was at a loss for words. There was another uneasy silence.

Jacques tried to ease the awkward moment. "But Maddy knows where home is, right, babe?" he said. "The door's always open."

"Of course, Papa." She finished her wine, and sat once more at Jacques's feet. "In fact, I need the counsel of Le Professeur this weekend, if you can spare me some time. I have a local history project coming up with my class."

"How about tomorrow afternoon? Kathleen has bridge at the club —"

"I don't have to go to bridge, darling," Kathleen said.

"But I insist you take some time for yourself. I'm really not an invalid, and it will do me good to have Maddy here testing my memory about a subject that's dear to both of us."

Maddy was grateful that the awkward situation was ending on a good note as far as her father was concerned. She set her glass on the coffee table and leaned in to the wing chair to kiss Jacques's forehead. "If I'm coming back tomorrow, Papa, then I don't want to tire you any more today. I'm sure Kathleen has supper to get ready, and CeCe's expecting me back at the apartment."

That wasn't exactly true, and Maddy sucked in her breath as she moved to Claude's side. "Are you ready to leave, Claude? You can follow me into town if you like."

Claude hid his frustration well. He offered his good wishes for Jacques's recovery as he said his goodbyes, then he followed Maddy out the back door. As he opened the door of Maddy's Honda for her, he spat out three words: "I'll follow you."

This wasn't working the way she'd planned. Claude was more persistent than patient. He was considerate when at his best, but dogged and intimidating at his worst.

Claude hopped out of his Beamer on Elm Street and raced to Maddy's car. It happened so fast, she started when he jerked open the door.

"You didn't seem very welcoming when I arrived at your father's. I don't know if I'm welcome here, either, Maddy. Your move into town and the distance you've put between us lately . . . it isn't just your father's illness, is it?"

Maddy gathered her books and purse and got out of the car, her mind racing a mile a minute. "No, it isn't, but you are welcome to come in and hear me out."

She spoke rapidly as she led the way into the apartment. "I was less than honest back at Papa's. Clare's not expecting me. She has a dinner date, but we do need to talk."

Be calm, be honest, and pray he will understand. Better to be hurt with the truth than . . .

She put her books down on the kitchen

bar. A covered casserole sat on the counter; a tented note with her name scrawled on it was propped against it. Probably something Clare fixed, she thought. Maddy gestured for Claude to sit in the living room.

She hung her blazer in the hall closet and came to sit beside him on the sofa. "I've been waiting for the right time, but I guess there isn't a right time and you deserve honesty, Claude." She looked at her hands. "I think we should end this relationship."

Claude pushed his back against the cushions, an incredulous look on his face. "Relationship! I can't believe you're saying this. It's more than a relationship. I'm ready to take it to the next level. I've been seeing you all summer and I thought I'd proven my commitment."

He snapped up straight, gripped her by the shoulders and pulled her close. "I . . . I want more than this for us. I thought you knew that." Crushing his lips against hers, he tried desperately to deepen the kiss.

Maddy pressed her hands against his chest, pushing him away. His fingers dug into her arms, and she turned her face to his shoulder.

He kissed her neck and pushed his tongue into her ear. She shuddered and hunched her shoulders.

"Is this what's missing, Maddy? Is this what you've wanted all along?"

Guys she dated at college had pushed like this to move relationships to an intimate level, but she had always denied them for her own good reasons. No sex until she found true love. That had been her conscious choice.

She jerked back, shaking her head. "No. I . . ." She looked into his eyes. "No, I don't want . . . I'm sorry, Claude. I don't love you." She pushed herself into the farthest corner of the sofa.

He went silent for a moment, eyes blazing.

"Is there someone else?"

She closed her eyes and drew in a breath. "Yes," escaped her lips on a sigh.

The apartment door burst open.

"Hallo, hallo. I'm back."

Both heads snapped around to the door. Margaret Chamberlain stood in the entry clutching two bags of groceries. "Oh, *excusez-moi,* Madelaine. I didn't know you were having company. Didn't you see my note?"

Maddy rose quickly and crossed the room, glancing at the note propped against the casserole. "I'm sorry, *Tante* Margaret. I thought the note was from Clare and . . ."

She shot a frustrated look at Claude. "We've only been here a few minutes."

Claude came directly to Margaret. "Let me help you, Mrs. Chamberlain," he said, taking the bags of groceries into the kitchen.

"When my Clare told me she was going out tonight, I brought the casserole for you, Maddy. I wanted to make a salad to go with it, but your refrigerator . . . it's pretty empty, eh?" Margaret pursed her lips with mock scorn as she waved a finger at Maddy. An instant later her frown turned to laughter and she drew Maddy into her arms for a hug.

"Only teasing, *ma chérie.* I know you've had no time for shopping." She picked up the note, dangling it in front of Maddy. "This told you I would be right back with some fixings, and there is plenty now for you and your guest," she said, turning to grin at Claude.

CHAPTER NINE

Claude was not smiling. "Thank you, Mrs. Chamberlain, but I'm unable to stay." He shot an accusing look at Maddy. "Unforeseeable circumstances," he said in his clipped, lawyerly tone. "Maybe some other time." He nodded to Margaret as he walked out of the kitchen. Claude inclined his head toward Maddy in a stiff and formal way, sending her an icy look. He was out the door without another word.

Grabbing Maddy's hands in hers, Margaret's brow furrowed. "Aw, Madelaine, it is my fault, eh? I interrupted something?"

"No, no. It's good you came when you did, *Tante*. Actually, you helped," she said with a half smile and a resigned shrug. "I'm not going to be seeing Claude Duval anymore."

"*Sacre bleu!* I arrived in the middle of a breakup?"

"Mercifully, at the *end, Tante*."

"Aye yi yi. Come sit at the table, Madelaine. My Clare has been hinting to me about this business with Claude, but I didn't expect to be witness to the ending! Let me fix you a cup of tea with your supper. You'll feel better, and me, too."

Maddy's face suddenly exploded in tears and laughter.

"What? What did I say?"

"Tea. A cup of tea! Oh, *Tante,* let me tell you about a cup of tea," was all she could manage between convulsive gulps of laughter.

By the time Margaret finished tossing a green salad and serving her scallop casserole, Maddy had told her all about Patrick Donovan, his cabinetry shop, his family and his sister Fiona's disappearance.

"Maria sainte, mère de Dieu," Tante said, closing her eyes and shaking her head. "How sad for his mama."

"And for Patrick. He takes responsibility for his family now. Although he does very well at his shop, his mother works a few days a week cooking at the Café. I think, in the beginning, she did it to help out the Café owners. They were friends who employed Fiona in the summertime and sympathized when she disappeared. Now it's probably just something to occupy Mrs. Donovan's mind. Her heart is broken."

"No one has found his sister?"

"They stopped looking. Mr. Donovan put an end to it."

Margaret slowly shook her head. "More's the pity. What you tell me reminds me of things that happened in my own family. My *grand-mère,* Henrietta, you know she was part Indian, eh?"

"Yes, Papa told me that long ago."

"In Quebec, her uncle was a shaman of the Saint Francis tribe."

"Is that like a spiritual man?"

"Yes. Shamans were in touch with good and bad spirits, and they were healers. Before she came to the States with us, the French called my *grand-mère Guérisseur.* Healer. *Ma grand-mère* had powers, but only good spirits. She had knowledge of things before they took place."

"You mean like a seer?"

"*Oui.* She could stop bleeding and heal the sick, too, but the *curé* in Quebec forbid it, so she stopped." Margaret paused, giving Maddy a doleful look. Taking Maddy's hand in hers, she spoke softly. "Someone in my family died, needlessly, *ma chérie.* Bled to death."

Maddy's eyes widened. "Oh, no! That must have been terrible for your grandmother. It's unbelievable that the Catholic Church could have such strong influence on the French people."

"Believe it, Madelaine. Faith, language and customs. To the people who came to Biddeford from Quebec, *la survivance* was everything. I, too, am an example. When I was young, I prayed to the Holy Spirit to let me be a nurse. He gave me Clare instead, and see what happened? She became the nurse. God works in wondrous ways."

"I think you are a nurse at heart, *Tante*. You are always comforting those who are troubled, or suffering. You were there for Papa Jacques when my mother died."

"*Oui,* I would have loved to do more . . . for her, your mama Julie. But —" She closed her eyes and threw up her hands with a shrug.

"Clare says you used to have visions. You could talk to those on the other side. Can you still do that?"

"I don't know. The sisters discouraged such things, so I stopped trying. Just like *ma grand-mère* stopped healing, and just like Mr. Donovan stopped looking for his daughter."

"Patrick's father stopped for the wrong reasons. He was a heavy drinker and a prideful man. He left his daughter's fate up to her, all because of scandal and disgrace. The man was drunk when he died of a heart attack just three weeks after Fiona's disappearance."

"More's the pity for your poor Patrick."

Madelaine tried to pour more tea into *Tante*'s cup, but Margaret shook her head.

"*Merci.* I have been here too long tonight. I don't want my Clare to come home and find me still here. God forbid that she thinks I meddle."

Maddy gave Margaret a hug. "Impossible for you to meddle today, *Tante.* I'll tell Clare that you actually saved the day for me."

Clare came into Maddy's room, dragging one foot after the other. "Ohmigod. Maddy, Maddy, I thought this friggin' night would never end." She kicked off her shoes and flopped down on the end of Maddy's bed. "Look at me." Clare lifted her legs straight up in the air and back down on the bed with a thud. Her blouse was ringed with sweat, one sleeve ripped at the seam. Maddy could see long runs in her panty hose.

"What happened?"

"Dr. Harold Stone was what happened. Big mistake to go out with an intern who is, quote, 'polite and mannerly' on duty. We got through dinner okay, but as soon as we got into the car to ride out to the Pool for a nightcap, Dr. Stone became Horny Harry."

Maddy put down the book she was reading; tried to smother a giggle at the same time that tears were glistening in her eyes. "Oh, CeCe, this is the second time tonight I cried when I laughed." She rubbed her fingers over her eyes, trying to compose herself. "I thought you told me Harold was the best intern on surgery rotation."

"He is. He'll make a damned good surgeon. His hands are like lightning, striking all over the place, fast and devastating."

Maddy eyed the torn stockings. "He didn't —"

"No, but he sure as hell tried! My *tante* didn't raise a pushover, babe. That's one thing I've totally agreed with you about since high school. We get to choose when, and with whom, the big event takes place. Somebody we really, really love, and it certainly ain't Horny Harry."

Clare sat up and shifted closer to where Maddy sat cross-legged at the head of the bed. "Now tell me what you mean by laughing and crying a second time tonight."

Maddy laced her fingers together in her lap. "You would have been proud of me, CeCe. Claude came out to the Pool while I was there, and when I left Papa's house I invited Claude to follow me here. I thought, 'Now or never. I'm going to try to be honest and break it off with him.' I guess it worked."

"What do you mean, you guess?"

"When I told him I wanted to end our relationship, he tried to force the issue. Things got a little heavy, so I told him right out that I didn't love him. That did it. That and your Aunt Margaret. She came through the door the very moment I said there was someone else. Claude couldn't get out of here fast enough."

Clare shook her head slowly. "Go figure. My *tante* to the rescue. I bet she cooked for you, too."

Maddy laughed. "How did you guess? She also stocked the fridge. I told her all about Patrick over supper. Then she made tea — like Patrick did. Remember? That was when I laughed through my tears."

"I remember," Clare said, finally flashing a grin. "So what else? Did you tell her about Patrick?"

"Yeah, I did. I told your *tante* all about Patrick's family over supper, and the mention of Fiona somehow led to a conversation about *Tante* Margaret's grandmother."

"Ohmigod. Henriette, the *guérisseur?*"

"Yes. We talked about the early French

who came to Maine, and the Native American Indians who lived here first. Like in this book." Maddy held up the book. Clare yawned as she gave the book a casual glance.

"She probably knows a lot about that stuff. How long ago did she leave?"

"About eight, I guess. She said she didn't want you to think she meddles."

"Ha! When pigs fly. *Tante* doesn't meddle. She *immerses* herself into stuff and before you know it, the world has changed. Hey, I'm glad she was here, really, but I'm super glad to see the end of Claude Duval."

"So was Paul. Right after *Tante* left, Paul called and I told him all about it. We talked a long time. He told me about some history between Kathleen and Claude. Stuff I never knew, like when Kathleen's first husband, John Murphy, was killed in an accident. Claude was a shoo-in for Murphy's place in the Duval-Murphy law firm. That's how Claude and his father ended up as guests at Papa's wedding reception. They were *Kathleen's* friends. You know the rest of the story."

"Yeah, I know. Pursuit was the game, and Claude Duval was the game master. From the minute he laid eyes on pretty Miss Madelaine — *Cherchez la femme.*"

"Urgh," Maddy groaned. "I have to get

him out of my head. After Paul's call, I had to focus on something else, so I started reading this book I borrowed from my dad's library. There are some really fascinating Indian legends here."

Maddy started flipping the pages until she came to a picture of Indian canoes on the shore at Fortune's Rock. She pointed to the illustration. "I'm going over to the Pool tomorrow to get Papa's advice about how to use this in my project at school."

Clare yawned again as she looked at the page. She stood and stretched, knocking twice on Maddy's wooden headboard.

"You need sweet dreams tonight, babe. I need to take a shower and scrub myself clean of Horny Harry. Tomorrow, while I'm slaving in the ER, you can wade back in time with Papa Jacques." Clare tweaked Maddy's bare toes as she headed out of the bedroom. "Get some sleep, Miss Fontaine. You're a free woman."

"From what you've told me about Patrick Donovan, I can understand why you've taken a fancy to him. He sounds responsible, hard working, and talented, but I'm not sure you were wise to sever all ties with Claude."

"There was no sense in continuing, Papa.

I would be living a lie. Claude is serious. I'm not."

"He's from a very good family, Madelaine."

"And you think Patrick's not?" she said a little testily. "He's Irish working class. Is that it?"

"You know better than that. I simply meant that you'd want for nothing with Claude Duval. I haven't anything against the working class. My father worked with his hands in the ship-building trade. He worked hard to give me an education. His only fault was gambling. You know —"

"We wouldn't have this house if grandfather hadn't won it in a poker game." Maddy bit her lip and sighed after finishing the sentence for him. "Oh, Papa, I mean no disrespect to Grandpa Frank. I was so young, and I really remember very little about his winning this house. The man he gambled with must have been pretty desperate, huh, to put up this house as a stake in a poker game? Who would do such a thing?"

"Not a desperate man. A foolish and wealthy man. Remember, it was the end of season, and summer people were going back to their homes in Boston. He was probably tired of the open-up, fix-up and close-up routines that these big, old summer places required. I think this house dates back to the turn of the century, or close to it. Your mother and I helped Grandpa do a lot of work to make it a year-round home."

"I know, and Mama named it Francois's Fancy just before Grandpa died." She reached for Jacques's hand. "We had the kind of happiness here that I couldn't expect to have with Claude Duval. I don't love him, Papa, so please, can we not talk about it anymore?"

She looked up, trying to gauge her father's reaction. He passed a hand over his face as though he wished to erase his distress. He nodded slowly and smiled.

"All right, my dear, I promise."

Jacques reached for the book in Maddy's lap. "So this is how you want to begin your social studies project? With the Indian legends?"

"Yes. I thought I'd give research assignments on the Abenaki Indians; incorporate some of the legends from this book with the students' findings. Next, I'll move into the Colonial period in Biddeford, and finally, the mill industry that brought all the French here from Canada."

"I'd approach it with a little different sequence if I were you, Maddy. Spark some interest first by letting them *hear* the legends, then follow up with individual research on the Indians. You could integrate the project when you come to the Colonial period. Have them write stories or letters. The colonists were great letter writers. Your students could interview some of the descendents of early families. Write skits or plays about Winter Harbor. There's a wealth of history to digest and illustrate."

"I knew you'd be the perfect muse I needed, Papa. Those are wonderful suggestions. Would you start us off by coming to my class to read some of the legends to the kids?"

"No, no, babe. There's a far better choice than me for that task. If you start with legends, Margaret Chamberlain would be a natural. She's a legend herself."

"Let me get this straight. You intend to ask *Tante* to come to your class to read legends and talk about her Abenaki ancestors. You want me to see if Miss McCormack at the hospital would be willing to be interviewed about midwifery. You want me to cook a fabulous dinner for Patrick. I assume that's to soften him up about using his shop for a field trip, yes?"

"Well, those are some of my plans, but they may not happen in that order. I'm just trying to line up my ducks so I can get started next week."

"*Tante* will probably agree. McCormack can be persuaded later. Cooking I can do, but Patrick — he's all yours, babe. Not that I wouldn't want to sidle up to his bodacious body and do a little coaxing, but hey, you saw him first."

"CeCe, you're as much a tease as my brother. Seriously, though, is next Tuesday too soon to plan a dinner? I'd like to invite both Patrick and *Tante* Margaret."

"Maddy, that could be a lethal combination."

Maddy chuckled. "Well, you said she immerses herself in situations and great things happen. I figured a little of Aunt Margaret's magic can't hurt."

Clare rolled her eyes. "Be wary what you wish for, Miss Madelaine. You never know, girlfriend. My *tante* might end up talking to someone on the other side."

CHAPTER TEN

"That was a delicious fricassee, Clare," Margaret said. "Don't you think so, Patrick?"

Patrick Donovan looked at the broad-faced woman. Her brown button eyes twinkled to match her smile. It was an unexpected question, and he felt embarrassed that he hadn't offered a compliment to Clare sooner. He'd been musing over his dinner invitation as Maddy cleared the table.

"Yes. It was really good chicken." Raising his eyebrows and smiling at Clare, he handed his plate to Maddy. "Clean plate," he said.

"There are lots of ways to fix *poulet*. You taught me well, *Tante*," Clare said. "I've pretty well perfected the dish since you gave me the recipe, but I throw in a few things on my own when I make fricassee. You don't have to fish for compliments for me, though.

Patrick knows I can cook. He sampled my lasagna last week. Right, Patrick?"

"Sure did," he said, rising from his chair and chuckling. "I think it's time for me to pitch in with kitchen duty. Can't let Madelaine do it all alone."

"Oh, Maddy and I have a deal," Clare said. "I cook and she cleans up. But since you are offering to help, c'mon, *Tante*. You and I will go in and look over the legends." She stood and led Margaret away from the small dining area to the sofa in the living room.

Legends? Patrick walked to the corner of the kitchen where Maddy was loading the dishwasher. His eyes fastened on the curves of her body as she bent and reached. *I'd like to wrap her in my arms.* He stood behind her, placed his hands on her shoulders.

"Can I help?" he said softly behind her ear.

Tingling charges curled down her spine. She drew in a breath and turned to face him. "Thanks, but I'm about done in here for now."

His eyes glinted as he met her gaze. "Will we have time to talk later?"

She tipped her head at an angle, grinning at him. "I hope so." Maddy took his arm. "Let's go in and see what Margaret thinks about the legends."

Legends again. He frowned and stopped her. "Maddy, I don't know what you're talking about."

"Didn't Rosemary tell you about our class project?"

"No," he said in a questioning tone.

"I was sure she would tell you, else I would have mentioned about Margaret when I called to invite you to dinner. Clare's aunt is here because she's coming to Saint David's School tomorrow. She's going to launch my class social studies project by reading an Indian legend and talking about her French and Indian ancestors."

Patrick raised an eyebrow at her. "And I'm here because . . . ?"

"Because I want you to be."

Clare was laughing heartily as they came into the room. "Oh, *Tante,*" Clare said. "You crack me up. The kids are going to love it if you read it like that."

Maddy and Patrick sat on a loveseat opposite the sofa. Jacques's book lay open on the coffee table in front of them. Maddy picked it up, placing it across Patrick's knees. "Is this the one you were reading? The one about Kuloscap?" She pointed to the story about the Algonquin hero of the Abenaki tribe. "It's my favorite, you know."

"*Oui,* that's the one, Madelaine. You think the kids will like it too, eh?" Margaret asked.

"Definitely. A perfect choice to inspire them to read the rest of the legends on their own."

"*Tante* read it with great body language," Clare said.

"Always good to start with a little laughter, *mes amis.* Some American Indian tales can be pretty heavy. Later the children can read about Squando, the Sagamore of the Saco Indians. Is better *later,* to read the frightening stories."

Maddy pointed to the book's sketch of a whale for Patrick's attention. "This legend is about a whale that gives an Indian, named Kuloscap, a ride on his back. The whale asks the Indian for a pipe, some tobacco and a light after the ride. When the whale swims away a long plume of smoke is seen trailing after him. The legend says that whenever a whale was seen off shore blowing a stream of spray, Indians would say that brother whale is smoking Kuloscap's pipe."

Patrick's dimples deepened as he caught Margaret mimicking a spouting whale while Maddy talked. He said, "The kids should like the story. I doubt that Rosemary has ever heard anything like that."

"I want my class to be able to place events

in their correct historical framework. I want them to create a sense of identity with the past. These tales have been handed down, kind of like your grandfather's storytelling," Maddy said.

"Your grandfather was a storyteller, Patrick?" Margaret asked.

"Aye, he was a *seanchai*. That he was." He grinned at Margaret and winked at Maddy. "Came over from County Mayo to Boston when he was a lad, and the leprechauns followed him from the old sod." He laughed at his own attempt at a brogue.

Clare laughed with him. "Ah, now we have two actors in our midst, Mad."

"Actually, three. Patrick's sister Rosemary acts and sings in our class play." Maddy closed the book, placing it back on the coffee table.

"Sounds like a winning combo," Clare said.

Maddy pursed her lips, nodding her head. "Patrick could make it complete if the class could come to his shop on a field trip and see what clever entrepreneurs there are at the Old Mill Complex." She flashed him a quick look.

Patrick frowned. "So that's why I was invited to dinner? Casting out nets, huh, Miss Madelaine?"

Clare rose and grabbed Margaret's arm. "C'mon, *Tante,* I better get you home before the sidewalks roll up in Biddeford."

Maddy and Patrick walked Margaret and Clare to the door. "Shall I bring Henriette's wedding regalia to school tomorrow, Madelaine?" Margaret asked.

"That would be special, *Tante,* if you would. And thanks for coming tonight. I know you don't like to drive at night."

"And that's what I'm for," Clare said. "Nighttime rendezvous." She wiggled her eyebrows. " 'Night, Patrick."

Margaret gave Maddy a hug and surprised Patrick by planting a kiss on his cheek.

"I live not far from you, I think, Patrick. Maybe we meet again, eh? I'd like to hear some of your *grand-père*'s stories."

Patrick grinned at her with a shrug. "Maybe so, Mrs. Chamberlain."

"Call me Margaret, *s'il vous plaît,*" she said. *"Au revoir."*

When the door closed behind them, Patrick let out a whoosh of breath. "That's quite a pair. What did she mean by Henriette's wedding regalia? Who's Henriette?"

Maddy took Patrick's hand and moved toward the loveseat. "First, I *wasn't* casting nets when I invited you, and I *will* tell you about Henriette. She is Margaret's grandmother. That's where Margaret's Indian heritage comes from. Henriette was half Abenaki. She wore a beaded elk-skin tunic when she married Thomas Lebrun in Quebec in 1904. Margaret's grandmother had mystical powers, according to *Tante,* and so, incidentally does Margaret . . . in a way."

"What do you mean, in a way? Is she a psychic?"

"Yes. She can commune with . . . the other side, but —"

Patrick plopped down into the loveseat, pulling Maddy down with him. "Margaret, a psychic! Unbelievable," he said, slowly shaking his head. "My grandfather probably would have believed in that bunk, but I'm not sure I do."

"It's true. She's gifted in a special way, but she rarely uses her gift because the nuns frowned on such things."

Patrick quirked his mouth and nodded. "Sounds like the good sisters," he said with a tinge of sarcasm in his voice. "How did Margaret end up in Biddeford, anyway?"

"Her story's not much different than a lot of French families. They were back and forth to Canada in the early years, just trying to scrape a living out of mill wages. Henriette had been to the States with her husband, went back to Canada much later, a widow with a son. Her only child, Clement, married and had eight children in Quebec. Margaret was his last child. *Tante*'s mother died in childbirth. Eventually, Clement brought his children and his widowed mother, Henriette, back to Biddeford. I'm told the grandmother practically raised Margaret." Maddy grew suddenly quiet, staring at her hands.

Patrick folded his hand around one of hers, reached up to touch her mouth with his index finger. He gazed into her green eyes. "That was quite a history lesson in less than two minutes, Miss Fontaine. Rosemary says you are the best teacher she's ever had. Care to teach me some things?"

Maddy blushed, meeting his gaze. "I don't think I could teach you anything new, Patrick Donovan."

"Try me," he said pulling her into his arms. He cupped her face and touched his lips to hers.

His kiss felt like velvet and flame. There had been nothing like it from anything she could remember. She didn't want the kiss to end, but at the same time, something tugged at her, pulling her back. It was becoming more and more difficult to control her reaction to him. She buried her face in his neck.

"I don't know what's come over me. Something seems to propel me toward you, Patrick. I've wanted you to kiss me since that first time in your shop. Yet, when you're near, I get the feeling someone is watching me, telling me to slow down."

She heard his soft moan.

Gently, he squeezed her shoulders, raising her face to his eye level. "You've been haunting my thoughts, too." Too damned much. He looked into her eyes, then pressed his lips to her forehead. "We will take it slow, Madelaine."

She reached her arms around his neck and rubbed her face against his cheek. "Promise?"

"I promise," he said.

Maddy leaned back against the loveseat. "I didn't tell you the other reason you are here tonight, Patrick. You found something early in life that you wanted to do, right?"

"Yes. And something tells me I know where this is leading."

"I want the kids at Saint David's to know about your shop. Actually, to see, firsthand, the whole mill complex, so they can focus on the kinds of possibilities that are in the future for them."

Patrick's mouth twitched. He stood, put his hands around her waist and lifted her from the loveseat to stand beside him. "My sister is right. You care about the kids and that's why you are the star teacher at school, Miss Fontaine. Would you consider being my *étoile?*"

"*Étoile?* How did you know the French word for star?"

"I'm not telling. There are lots of things I'm not ready to tell . . . yet. But yes, you may bring your class to my shop — when I say so."

Maddy met Clare for coffee after *Tante*'s presentation at school and couldn't wait to tell her about it. "*Tante* Margaret was the highlight of the morning. The principal made a surprise visit to the classroom while she was performing, and heaped praise on both of us at the end of the period."

"How about the kids? Were they enthused?"

"God, yes. She brought Henriette's silver pendant with the jasper stone, and her bead and feather headband along with the wedding tunic. She taught them Abenaki words and, of course, her reading of the legend was the *coup de grace.*"

"I'm not surprised. *Tante* is a natural for something like that."

"That's what my father said when I first

talked to him about my class project."

"Papa Jacques should know." Clare suddenly put her hand over her mouth. "Oh, crap, I almost forgot. There was a message from your dad on the phone yesterday. We were so busy getting the dinner together last night that I didn't remember to tell you. You really should get a new cell phone, babe. I'm terrible about messages, and not everybody knows that you are living with me now."

"I know. I've been putting it off since my old phone got trashed. In the weeks before Papa's stroke I really didn't miss having one. Paul and Claude and you were about the only ones calling me, and you know the end of that story."

"Yeah, well, now that Patrick is on the scene, you better use your mitten money to buy a new cell phone."

"Okay, okay. Will do. Now, how about you paying for the coffee while I use your cell phone to call my dad?"

Clare rolled her eyes, handed the phone over and waited while Maddy went outside.

When Clare came to her, Maddy was huddled near the door with her back to the wind, talking on the phone. "I should be there in about twenty minutes, Kathleen. Okay. Not a problem."

"What's up?"

"Papa ran a little fever yesterday and he thought he was coming down with the flu. He was calling to ask me about my mom's old cold remedy, but I think he just wanted me to come over to see him. At any rate, Kathleen says he's feeling better today. I'm to stop and get lemon verbena and honey, so I better get going."

"I can't believe Kathleen is so friggin' helpless that you're still doing her errands."

"Whatever," Maddy said with a shrug, resignation in her voice. "I gotta go. This wind is really getting bad. Don't wait supper for me. I'll probably go out to the mall."

"Not to worry, I'm working the late shift tonight, so whatever's left over goes."

Maddy found Jacques bundled up on the window seat in his study, a book in his lap. She gave him a hug and brought a hand to his forehead. "No more fever? I brought the ingredients for Mom's best cure. I didn't see Kathleen anywhere downstairs. Shall I go fix it for you?"

"I think the fever is gone and Kathleen isn't here, so I'd appreciate it if you would fix the toddy. Claude called right after you did. He was asking if he could swing by here on his way to the club."

134

"Claude?" A shivery frisson of distrust ran down her spine, but she tried to keep her feelings disguised.

"Yes. He said he had some papers he needed to go over with Kathleen. I would imagine it's about her late husband's estate. I don't like to get into all that with Kathleen. Claude is very capable." He paused to meet Maddy's gaze. "At any rate, he didn't want to disturb me, so Kathleen went with him to the club. They'll take care of business and she'll be back shortly."

Sounds kind of fishy to me, but I guess the less said the better . . .

"Okay, Papa, Mama's remedy coming up." She tucked the afghan around his legs and hurried out of the room. "I'll be right back," she called over her shoulder.

Maddy returned from the kitchen in ten minutes carrying a tray. "Hot tea. Lemon verbena to quiet your heart, honey to smooth your throat, and a good shot of brandy to chase away the germs. This should fix you right up."

Jacques's eyes looked sad to Maddy as he took the cup. "I think of your mother, Madelaine, and of Paul. I miss Paul. I've never told him why I often dismissed his artistic ability. When he was younger, I think it was because I wanted him to be athletic

135

and masculine, and he was neither. That was wrong of me. After your mother died, well . . . whenever I saw a brush in Paul's hand, it brought Julie to mind. It's hard to explain, and —"

"It's okay, Papa. Not to worry. Drink your tea and I'll tell you about Aunt Margaret's visit to my class."

Jacques's smile brightened his eyes. "I'll bet she was wonderful."

"She was, and the kids ate it up. Even the principal praised her. I had a list of readings and writings the students could choose as a follow-up to the legends, and they were eager to sign up for them."

"Margaret is a very special person, Maddy. I'm pleased she was there for you. She's been here for all of us at one time or another."

"I just learned something surprising about her, Papa. Margaret has psychic powers. Did you know that?"

Jacques shifted uncomfortably and sipped his tea. "Yes, she's gifted, but she hasn't done anything like that in a long time."

"Do you believe in those powers? I mean, can *Tante* really commune with the dead?"

Jacques's eyes darkened and he stared at Julie's painting stool. He spoke softly. "I believe that it's possible, but Margaret doesn't discount the power of prayer," he quickly added. He looked toward the wall that held his wife's paintings. "Margaret has been with me many times in prayer. From her lips to God's ears," he said very softly.

Maddy swallowed the lump rising in her throat. She walked to the window seat, leaning over Jacques's shoulder. Leaves were swirling in the wind that whistled around the windows. The sky was already darkening. She shivered. "I think we're getting a storm."

"Didn't you hear the national weather warning this morning? After the number of Atlantic hurricanes last year, I make it a habit to tune in the weather watch every morning. They put out a warning early today of a fast-moving hurricane just off shore of the Carolinas. It'll probably move out to sea, but those storms are fickle. Would you want to stay the night?"

"Thanks, Papa, I'll take a rain check, no pun intended." She flashed a grin and leaned against her mother's painting stool. "I promised myself that I'd go out to the mall today and buy a new cell phone, and just in case we *are* getting a big storm, I better stock up on candles and maybe even a flashlight. I don't think Clare does much in the way of preparedness for stuff like that."

"It's good you have each other, Maddy. Clare is dependable in other ways, much like her Aunt Margaret." He smiled at the mention of Margaret's name, closed his eyes for a second, seemingly thinking.

"I'm really grateful that you were here to make your mother's toddy for me, but maybe, with this hurricane threat, you should run along and do your errands. Kathleen will be back any time now."

Jacques rose from the window seat and came to Maddy's side, carrying his teacup. "I'll walk you to the kitchen. Something tells me I should check my own cupboards for batteries and candles."

CHAPTER ELEVEN

The latest cut of the Dave Matthews Band blared from Clare's iPod dock on the kitchen bar.

"Clare!" Maddy shouted as she let herself into the apartment. "Would you come get these things?" She dropped soggy shopping bags down near the door. "I'm taking my shoes into the bathroom to dry. I don't want to drip all through the apartment. You wouldn't believe the wind and rain out there. The mall parking lot was flooded."

Clare looked up from the kitchen island. With rolling pin in hand, she danced around the kitchen bar toward Maddy. "Hey. Didn't hear you come in."

"Oh Lord, Clare. I know that iPod is the latest and greatest, but we're getting the tail end of a hurricane. Can you turn it down, or off?" Maddy cat-walked toward the bathroom, toting her shoes. "I want to turn on the weather."

"Chill out, Maddy. It can't be that bad. I'm in the middle of a chicken quiche here, trying to use up all the leftovers from the other night. Just rolled out my pie dough."

"Well, I hope you have power enough to bake the quiche, 'cause everyone is saying we're in for a major power outage. The wind and rain are wild out there and the river is cresting."

Maddy was back in the kitchen pulling things out of the bags. "I didn't know if you had candles or a flashlight and batteries, so I bought some. They'll come in handy if the power goes, and . . . *voilà!*" She held up her new cell phone. "So will this."

Clare looked up with a big smile. "Hallelujah! Now tell me about Papa Jacques. Is he feeling any better?"

"He's better. I tried to make it clear to him about my break with Claude. That caused a little friction. Then I made my mom's tonic for him and he got a little nostalgic. This stroke must have triggered some serious mortality thoughts. He talked about Mom and Paul for the first time in ages." Maddy leaned her elbows on the bar, chin in hand, watching Clare finish the quiche.

"All good, I hope."

"Yeah, but I didn't let him dwell on them.

Didn't stay long, either, because Claude was out to the club with Kathleen about some legal stuff and I didn't want to chance his coming back to the house. Besides, the storm was getting worse and I had shopping to do. I even bought one of those plastic raincoats. It covered everything but my feet."

"Smart move, babe." Clare put her quiche in the oven and followed Maddy into the living room.

Maddy sat in the rocker programming her new phone. She copied Clare's cell directory for *Tante* Margaret's number and the hospital.

"No problem with dad's or Paul's numbers, but I haven't memorized Patrick's shop number yet." She dug through her purse to find Patrick's business card. "Might just need it in this storm."

"Come to think of it," Clare said, "I did have a heads-up about the storm. Three accidents came into ER this morning, all weather related, just south of here. My friend Suzie called me about it after she went off duty. Told me to bear up for my shift. It's a zoo at the hospital. Just my luck to be on double shift tonight, but you know me, babe. I'm just takin' things as they come." Clare put the TV on.

A channel-six anchorman interrupted a report from Iraq with a local news flash: "A weakened hurricane, wobbling back and forth along the coast, barreled in at Cape Arundel, swamping low islands, knocking down telephone poles and power lines. Hundreds of thousands are without power from Martha's Vineyard north. Police and fire officials are cautioning shore residents who have not evacuated south of Portland to remain in their homes and follow emergency procedures. Major flooding is expected in the Saco-Biddeford area."

The TV screen was suddenly filled with lines before going black.

"Damn. Now I have to dig out my little radio *Tante* gave me. It's a good thing you bought batteries, Mad, 'cause I haven't used that thing in ages."

Clare rooted around in the cupboard above the refrigerator until she found her small portable radio. She set it on the bar, pushed the on button and tuned the dial to a local station. Amazingly, it came on with only a little static.

"Two families were driven from a duplex late this afternoon in downtown Biddeford when fire broke out on Bradbury Street. High winds hampered the efforts of fire companies as smoke poured from the back

142

of numbers ten and twelve. Mutual Aid had things under control within an hour, but three residents of number twelve were taken to the Medical Center suffering from smoke inhalation."

"Maddy. Did you hear that? Bradbury Street. That's pretty close to *Tante.* Didn't you say the Donovans live on Bradbury?"

Maddy's face paled. "Yes, but I don't know their house number."

Clare grabbed the phone book. "Maybe they're listed." She flipped the pages, her finger stopping on a line. "Ohmigod. Donovans are number twelve."

Still clutching the two cell phones, Maddy came to Clare's side and stared at the phone book. "Patrick was probably home when it happened. He told me he seldom works past dusk. Did they say *three* members of a family? Do you think I should check at his shop?"

"Let's take things one at a time. You sit and call his shop. Call your dad next, and I'll check *Tante.* She always listens to the radio news and she's bound to know about this." Clare looked at her watch and suddenly slapped a hand to her forehead. "Oh God, am I ever screwed up. I'm working double shift tonight. I'll just put the quiche in the fridge, and then I'm out of here.

Gotta run, babe. Stay cool until you hear from me."

Maddy clutched her seashell locket, pacing the floor in front of the entertainment center, willing the silent TV to come back on. She lit all the candles and listened to Clare's portable radio for a while, but that did nothing for her jangled nerves.

Everything was okay when she checked at the Pool, but no one answered at Patrick's shop. Clare called as soon as she got to the hospital. *Tante* knew about the fire, but had no details. The only Donovans admitted were the mother and twin girls. The hospital had gone on generator and Clare had no time to talk.

Maddy stopped at the recessed shelves flanking the television. Lifting a small, silver-framed photo from the shelf, she stared at her mother's face. She had constancy and courage in every crisis. If only —

She grabbed her cell phone on the first ring.

"*Tante* Margaret? I can hardly hear you. You're breaking up on me. Are you okay? No, Clare's working the night shift, remember?" A long pause followed while Maddy listened. She looked at the phone in her hand as though she was hearing things, then

144

put it back to her ear. "Patrick's mother? The mill? Say that again. I'm losing you — must be your phone line. *Tante?* Hello? Hello? Oh, God."

Maddy grabbed a note pad from the kitchen and scribbled a note to Clare.

Tante called — very agitated — said something about a vision!! Last words I caught were Patrick and old mill before her phone went dead. I'll be back. M

She propped the note next to Patrick's business card on the kitchen bar.

Maddy changed into jeans and one of Paul's old flannel shirts. She shoved her cell phone and flashlight into the deep pockets of her old wool jacket. No sense using that plastic raincoat; the wind would whip it to shreds. She pulled an oilcloth slicker and a pair of Wellingtons from the boat-gear box stashed under her bed.

Even the gear was scant protection for the sheets of rain that slanted across Elm Street. Rain blew inside her hood, pelting her eyes and soaking her hair minutes after she left the apartment. Getting from the apartment building to her car wasn't easy, but it was minor trouble compared to the nightmare facing her when she got the car started. The roadway was pitch black. She inched the Honda along Elm Street to the end of the block.

Her headlights illuminated a huge tree limb near the intersection of Pearl Street. A sign dangled from a bent pole. Pieces of picket fence were strewn like Legos along the curb. Maddy slowly maneuvered around them, passing three abandoned cars stalled in deep water. She gripped the wheel tightly, praying out loud. Her little Honda sputtered and died twenty feet ahead of the last stalled car.

Maddy looked through the windshield at the slanting rain. She could barely make out the gabled roof and chimneys of the old mill buildings looming ahead like great, gray ghosts in the sky.

She opened the car door and stepped into cold water that spilled over her boots. Panic set in. Wind, sounding like a car roaring through a tunnel, pushed at her as she struggled to move away from the car. She fastened her eyes on the mill buildings, but sheets of rain clouded her vision as she struggled to lift her booted feet along the flooded walkway. A huge gust of wind pushed at her back like a giant hand, and Maddy flew across the mill yard like a duck in a pond.

A loud crack sounded behind her. Before she could turn, an airborne piece of metal slammed into her head, pushing her against a solid door. Her breath whooshed out of her. Her fingers dug at rough wood as her knees went weak. Dim light began to spiral like a whirling top.

CHAPTER TWELVE

Pain blazed in her head. Shards of sound reverberated. The vibration of machinery thrummed in her ear and rattled her cheekbone pressed against wooden floorboards. A loud whistle sounded and the motion stopped.

Footsteps came close. Someone lifted a torn hood away from her head.

"Holy Mary. It's a girl an' she's bleedin'."

It was a high-pitched woman's voice. Maybe Clare.

Thoughts scattered. It's me, Maddy. Help . . .

More footsteps.

Maddy tried to open her eyes and lift her head, but the pain was too fierce.

"She just fell through the door like the devil himself was pushing her. She's bad hurt, Mr. MacDill."

"Calm down now, Molly. Go get water and rags from the washroom. Hetty and I will see to this." The foreman peered at the figure lying face down, a puddle of red-tinged water spreading on the floor. His brows were drawn together in concern.

"Let's get this wet cloak off him, Hetty."

Molly called back. "It's a *she,* I tell ya."

Ian MacDill raised the limp figure in his arms just enough so Hetty could unfasten the hooks of the yellow coat. She pulled the sleeves away one at a time while the big Scot balanced Maddy against his bent knee, holding her head in one beefy hand.

Hetty clutched the yellow slicker to her heart, staring at the strange coat.

"For God's sake, put that coat down, woman. Sit against the wall. I'm goin' to move her so's she's lying wi' her head cradled in your lap."

More footsteps clattered on the floor. Maddy moaned as she felt herself being dragged, then settled.

The foreman shifted from one foot to the other. He was a tall, thin man, well past his prime, wiry and nervous, a Scot with a quick eye but a soft heart, for a foreman. He stared at his bloodied shirtsleeve and hand. "Molly, you clean the blood away while Hetty holds her," he barked. "I'm goin' for the mill agent."

Molly nodded, set a basin down and knelt at Hetty's side.

Rough, warm hands held Maddy's hands tightly.

"Mère de Dieu. Elle tremble beaucoup. Calme-toi. Les secours arrivent."

"Sufferin' Jaysus, Hetty. You'd be shakin' if ya blew in out of nowhere with a cracked head. Don't be tellin' her to lie still. She probly don't know a word yer saying. She don't look like any of the Frenchies I ever seen in this shop."

"Je la connais."

"What? What d'ya mean, you know her? I learned enough of yer French in the eight years I been workin' here, but for the love of God, speak English. How can you know this creature in men's clothes?"

Hetty shook her head vigorously, frowning at Molly. *"Elle n'est pas une creature.* She is . . . how you say, eh, *professeur."*

"A teacher!" Molly threw the bloody cloth she had been using into a basin. She held a clean dry rag to the wound and brushed back the matted hair from Maddy's face. "Judas priest, Hetty. Are ye daft? If this waif is a teacher, then I'm Mother Superior."

Voices drifted and floated on the air between bursts of pain. The words made no sense. Maddy felt hands tying something around her head. She felt like she was falling again, enveloped in a tunnel of fog, spin-

150

ning away.

Molly's eyes widened as she loosed the buttons of Maddy's wool jacket. She fingered a gold seashell locket dangling in the folds of the injured woman's shirt.

"Will ya look at this bauble hangin' round her neck," she said.

The door shut with a bang as she spoke. Mr. MacDill was back.

"Well now, lassies," he said, coming toward them with a wary gait. "This is the way of it. I got to think about this situation like Mr. McArthur would. The boss is over to Saco at a meeting, so it's up to me, ya see."

Ian MacDill stood with his beefy hands on his hips, looking from one to the other of the women on the floor. He had been in America for a dozen years. After escorting several Scottish women weavers hired to work at the cotton mill, he soon worked his way up the ladder to foreman.

Ian tolerated the Irish and French scuffles in Biddeford. It seemed they were always in conflict, except for these two. He tried to understand their differences, but a more unlikely pair than Hetty and Molly he couldn't fathom. He knew only that they were good workers.

Molly Carrigan was one of the few young

Irish women left who hung on at the mill after the strikes. She started when she was twelve, and now she worked six drawing frames with the young French widow, Hetty Lebrun. *Got to have grit, that one, carryin' a wee one an' comin' back to work in the same mill her husband was killed in.*

"I'll just have to take things into my own hands," he said, peering closely at the still-unconscious girl.

"She seems to come and go," Molly said.

"Looks like she needs some of that hair cut away, and stitching up too, most likely." He scratched at his beard and passed a hand over his bald head.

"Mr. McArthur does a lot for the poor and less fortunate, so best I try to help this wee lass." He put a hand on Molly's shoulder. "With no one knowin' the least of what happened here, ye ken? I haven't displeased Mr. McArthur yet, and I shanna do it now."

Molly loosened the wool jacket and opened the damp shirt at Maddy's neck. Her hand hovered over Maddy's locket. She pushed it out of sight, pulling the wool jacket around Maddy's neck. "Aye, sir. She needs helping for sure, an' mum's the word."

Molly's gaze shifted from the foreman to Hetty. "We could take her to our room at the boarding house and let Hetty . . . er, uh, bring her round."

"And how is that? What are ye sayin', lass?"

"Hetty Lebrun is gifted, you know. Healin' and such. She helped me mither afore she passed on. I was alone and Hetty come to stay with me after her husband died. She's . . . real good with her hands, sir." Afraid to say more and hoping Hetty understood her, Molly cast her eyes first at Hetty and then down at the cloth she held on the injured girl's head.

Ian shook his head, looking around at the quiet machines. When the seven-thirty whistle blew, the workers had filed out, unconcerned about a body in a faint near the door. The foreman went to a bin near the back. He pulled out a length of rejected drill cloth and dragged it back to the girls.

" 'Tis made strong enough for sails, so I'm thinkin' this'll carry her."

"How's that, Mr. MacDill? Ya might be hurtin' her worse."

"Nay, I wouldna want to hurt the lassie. I don't think I could carry her out to my cart meself. I'm none so young as I used to be. This'll do for a litter." He spread the cloth out on the floor beside Maddy.

"Hold her head still, Molly, while I lift her

onto it." Ian MacDill carefully laid Maddy onto her side. "Now if you two will bring up the corners by her head, I'll take the bottom corners. Hold her head still with your other hand, Molly, and out she'll go on this litter to my horse and dray."

Back and forth, to and fro. A gentle motion that seemed to be saying, "Wake up, wake up." It felt like the hammock that hung from the porch at Francois's Fancy.

Suddenly the motion stopped. Maddy's cheekbone felt the hardness of wood again. Forcing her eyes open, she squinted at what looked like the sideboards of a wagon. She opened them wider. Elm trees formed a canopy over her head. A shudder went through her, matching the rustle of leaves left clinging to the trees. Stately elm trees that lined the street had died out more than fifty years ago. One of the facts she'd found in her research for her history project. The jolting boards of the wagon were another reminder that this was not 2005.

She had to push through shadowy barriers between levels of reality. There was no gale-force wind now blowing at her back. No rain pelted her face. No flooding from the hurricane. The storm had lost its menace, replaced by a terror she had no power against. The clip clop of horse's hooves and the rattle of boards beneath her beat a steady rhythm.

"Ach. She's not as light as I thought," Molly said, tugging the litter through the sitting room door into a cramped bedroom. "Ease her down on the narrow bed by the window, Mr. MacDill. It's not so lumpy."

"There, now. 'Twas a good thing we did, bringin' her here in the dark of night with no one the wiser," Molly said. "Our lips are sealed." She made a motion with her fingers zipping across her lips, nudging Hetty at the same time.

"Aye. I'll see what luck you've had wi' her once you come into the shop in the morning." Ian searched Hetty's face, a look between fear and suspicion knotting his brow. "Tell me now, lassie, are ye a true *ban-lichiche?*"

"Mr. MacDill, how are we supposed to know the Gaelic? What on earth is a *ban-lichiche?*" Molly asked.

"In the old country she's a female healer."

"Well, Hetty is that, all right. Faith, an' the good Lord'll be on her side, too. The Frenchies are fearsome pray-ers."

He took a last look at the girl on the bed and turned to leave. "All right then, if ye have any trouble, send a message up to Jefferson Street."

Molly saw him out, locking the door behind him. "Trouble, aye. Trouble is just beginning. I've no doubt of that," she muttered to herself. She called to Hetty. "I'm putting the kettle on."

By the time Molly came to the bedroom with a tray, Hetty had removed Maddy's boots and clothes and covered her with a light blanket. She sat silently beside her, clutching Maddy's shirt to her heart, watching her intently. Hetty put a finger to her lips and pointed at Maddy, whispering "*Elle se réveille* — she is waking!"

"Thanks be to God."

Maddy's eyes had fluttered when they first laid her on the bed, then squeezed shut like a turtle ducking into its shell. Visions came swift and hard, seemingly far away, then close by. Dangling power lines . . . cars stalled in a flooded street . . . a voice speaking with a Scottish lilt . . . words fading in and out. A soothing voice . . . French. Now a harsh voice . . . Nurse McCormack?

Maddy opened her eyes slowly and tried to focus on the dark skin of a hand holding one of hers. A sliver of moon was barely visible rising in a window beside the bed. She heard the sound of squeaking bedsprings when she tried to move her legs. Fear was spiraling up her spine. Panic was setting in again. Where am I?

"I've got clean rags and a pair of scissors. I aim to see if that gash is healin' without stitches, an' I'm needin' a little help here, Hetty."

Hetty sighed, let go of Maddy's hand and placed the shirt at the foot of the bed. Molly carefully removed the cloth from the gash on Maddy's head. Dark, dried blood caked in her hair high above her right ear, making it difficult to see where the wound began and ended. She brought the basin closer and bent to the task.

Maddy moaned. She could see the broad, high cheekbones of the face hovering close to the window. Worry was etched on the woman's forehead. Dark eyes held a steady gaze at Maddy. A hand closed over her trembling fingers.

"Shhh. *Calme-toi.*"

Maddy felt a tingling sensation of warmth, and her racing heart steadied. *Something passed between this woman and me.*

Maddy jerked violently at the sudden grating snick of scissors close to her ear. She batted one hand in the air. Scrunching her shoulders, she tried to raise herself and confront the person wielding the scissors.

"No," Maddy cried in a weak, gravelly voice. Bile rose in her throat, and throbbing quickened in her head. She sank back on her side.

"Awright, awright." Molly held a thin clump of wet, matted hair and let it fall to the floor. "I'll let the bloody mess be, then. It was tryin' to help yer, I was, Miss."

Hetty placed a quieting hand on Maddy's shoulder.

"Madelaine. *Elle est* Madelaine," Hetty said.

Maddy's eyes snapped open.

Molly's eyebrows lifted. "And how, pray tell, Henriette Lebrun, are ya knowin' her name?"

"Madelaine *est du future.*"

"The future! Holy Mother. We're dealin' with Mr. MacDill and the mill wigs here, an there's no explainin' her comin' from *the future.* It's not so sure I believe it meself."

CHAPTER THIRTEEN

Henriette Lebrun . . . Hetty?

Maddy hardly dared to breathe. *If I stay real still, my throbbing head might ease.*

"What she needs is a cup of my tea," Molly said.

"Please," Maddy whispered, "if I'm not dreaming, someone tell me where I am, and who you are."

"I'm Molly Carrigan. Yer in me boardin' house rooms on Lincoln Street, an' lucky to be here," Molly said. "Before the whistle blew, you crashed through the mill door like ya was three steps ahead of the devil. Unconscious, soakin' wet and bleedin'."

"You mean the old cotton mill?"

"The very same."

"But why were you there in such a terrible storm?" Maddy asked, trying to raise herself on one elbow.

"Storm?" Molly said with a puzzled look. "Why to work, o' course. Me and Hetty tend the spinning frames."

Molly rolled a lumpy pillow into a bolster and pushed it against Maddy's neck and shoulders.

"Turn to this side and lie back easy, Miss. Let the bolster take the pressure off your head." The bed springs squeaked as Molly helped Maddy turn her body.

She angled her head slightly to the right on the pillow and stretched her legs out in relief. For the first time she could have more than a side view of everything. At the foot of the narrow bed a tall, young woman stood straight as a sapling. Maddy blinked and stared. It was the same broad face that had hovered over her before. Dark eyes met her gaze and held.

"*Je m'appelle* Henriette," the woman said.

Maddy's mouth opened, then closed without a word.

"She's called Hetty," Molly added with a nod, "but she's really Madame Henriette Lebrun."

Maddy's stomach clenched. Any thought that she was merely dreaming was dispelled by hearing that name. She drew a deep breath. "How did you get here — I mean, where did you come from?"

Molly spoke without hesitation. "I came from Dublin after my da died. I came with my mum an' uncle. My uncle brought us from Boston to Biddeford for jobs in the mill. Started as a spooler when I was twelve, an' 'fore I was twenty my mum died." Molly gave a sharp nod to Hetty.

Hetty clutched an odd-shaped, hammered silver pendant hanging from a rawhide thong around her neck. She rubbed the jasper stone at its center and began to speak French, so softly that Maddy could only catch a word now and then.

"I don't understand," Maddy said.

"She's telling you that she came here as a new bride from Quebec. Her husband was killed in a mill accident and she went back to Canada with her child."

Maddy frowned. "Then how is it she's here with you, and where is her son?"

Molly looked suspiciously at Maddy. *How does she know it was a boy that Hetty had?* "She came back to Biddeford with some Frenchies to work in the mill, but since she helped out when me mither died, Hetty stays with me. Her boy . . . er, uh, well, in time she saved enough to put him in a boarding school."

"Do you know the boy's name?"

Maddy watched Hetty walk slowly away from the door and around to the side of the bed. A calendar, hanging on a nail by the

161

bedroom door, had been hidden until Hetty moved away from it. Maddy blinked and stared. *September 1905.* The page blurred and came back sharply into focus in the early morning light. She swallowed a lump that rose in her throat. Yesterday was Friday, September 29, 2005.

"*Il est* Clement, my son. Clement Lebrun."

Maddy covered her eyes with a trembling hand and forced herself to breathe deeply. *This cannot be happening. Tante* Margaret . . . I need your help here.

Molly leaned over the bed, gently prying Maddy's fingers away from her face. She looked into tear-filled eyes and felt Maddy's forehead.

"No fever, Hetty. See if she'll take the tea now. It's my brew of willow bark laced with just a bit of brandy. I'm needin' a cup meself." Molly retreated to the kitchen, muttering and shaking her head.

Maddy awoke to a whispering voice within herself. Dreaming of Papa Jacques seemed to summon his spirit. He was reading from the Bible in her dream. *Time . . . the fullness of time . . . past, present and future come together . . .*

The room was cold and dark. Dawn

streaked the patch of sky framed by a bedside window. Maddy blinked at slivers of light slanting across the bed. She shivered and burrowed under the light blanket. The plunge into reality was frightening. Her eyes searched the shadows of the room. Where were her clothes? She looked overhead at a bare bulb mounted in the center of a plaster ceiling. A clothes press stood in shadows against one wall and a wooden washstand barely fit between the beds. Other than the calendar by the door, the only adornment was a crucifix hanging on the wall behind the table.

Voices drifted in from beyond the bedroom door, too hushed for Maddy to hear.

Molly faced Hetty. "You bring the porridge in an' get her ready, and I'll be off to see Mr. MacDill," Molly said. "I'll not be wantin' to lose a day's wage, but we'll see what himself says. When you go to her, Hetty, for heaven's sake speak some English. Sure and ya understand *me* well enough, an' she needs to understand *you*."

"*Attends! Ses vêtements?*"

"Call them clothes, Hetty! Say clothes. They're dry there by the stove. Look in the clothes press for my old brown skirt. *Jupe brune.*" She gestured, sweeping her hands from her waist to the floor. "And give her my next-to-best shirtwaist. God forbid she look like a boy."

Hetty shrugged her shoulders with a puzzled look.

"My *jupe*," Molly said, impatiently. "It's big enough to fit over those trousers she wears. It'll help. Understand?" Molly rolled her eyes toward the bedroom, shaking her head. "Her wool jacket will do, but she won't be needin' that weird yellow coat, so roll it up in the market basket."

All of Molly's directions were accompanied by hand motions. "I'll plead yer case with MacDill, but you better be at the mill door at twelve sharp. *Douze heures,* Hetty," she called over her shoulder as she hurried out the door. "Noon."

Hetty carried a tray of porridge and strong tea into the bedroom. She was surprised to see Maddy half sitting up with the covers pulled up to her chin.

"*Votre tête* is better, no?" she asked as she put the tray on the table.

Words were coming back. *She's asking how my head is.* A line from an old song that Grandpa Fontaine used to sing popped into Maddy's mind. Grandpa would point to her mouth, and then to her head and sing, *"Eh la bouche, Eh la tête."*

Maddy gingerly patted the hair over and

around her ear. "No bandage," she said, managing a weak smile. "It's not hurting, so it must be trying to heal."

"Ah, *oui*. Healing salve. Poplar balm and marigold. Heals good, *comprenez-vous*, Madelaine?"

Maddy nodded her head, eyeing the breakfast tray.

Hetty pointed to the tray. "You eat now."

She left the room momentarily and returned with Maddy's clothes folded over her arm. She placed them at the foot of the empty bed and opened the clothes press.

Maddy stared at the bowl and smiled at the small lump of maple sugar in the porridge. *Some things never change,* she thought.

She wrapped herself in the bedcovers and swung her legs over the edge of the bed. Swirling the sugar through the porridge, her first spoonful was cautious. No queasiness followed, so Maddy ate slowly, sipping the hot tea and watching Hetty arrange things at the bottom of the bed.

Socks, a worn-thin, high-necked shirt-waist, her own flannel shirt and jeans were placed in a row next to her wool jacket. Hetty held up a faded long skirt and placed it over the jeans, holding them both together for Maddy to see. Then she placed them around her hips. *"Voici,"* she said, her dark eyes flashing. She covered Maddy's shirt with the high-necked shirtwaist, and lifted the last item, the wool jacket, up to her shoulders. Hetty felt the heavy pockets bump against her hip. Frowning, she patted the pockets and carried the jacket to Maddy.

Maddy knew exactly what was there. She pulled her flashlight out of the coat pocket, pointing it at the bulb in the ceiling. "A light . . . *lumiére.*" She pointed it at the wall calendar, and her hand trembled. Yesterday was September 29, 2005. She shifted it to a dark corner of the room. *"Lumiére* to find my way in the storm."

Hetty took the flashlight in her hands, examining it carefully, clicking it on and off.

Maddy shook her head as though to clear it. No sense showing her the cell phone. It had no use here.

Hetty raised her dark eyes to Maddy, pointing at the flashlight. "Future," she said softly.

"Yes, but here is not future." Her hand swept around the room. "Why am I here? I came to the old mill looking for Patrick." As soon as Patrick's name flickered across her mind, something tugged at Maddy from inside. Her voice quivered when she looked into Hetty's eyes.

"*Tante* Margaret said —" Maddy stopped talking suddenly at the wide-eyed look on Hetty's face.

Hetty straightened her shoulders, drew a deep breath and closed her eyes. When she opened them, she handed the flashlight back to Maddy and collected the tray. She patted the clothes laid out on the bed. "You dress now, Madelaine, *s'il vous plaît.*"

Maddy looked out the window at outhouses behind the row of buildings. *No way,* she thought. After using the chamber pot she found under the bed, she took pitcher and bowl from the bottom shelf of the wash-stand. The cold water felt good on her skin. She patted her face gently with the rough towel hanging from a rod on the side of the stand. Her bruised cheek was tender to the touch.

She tried straightening the tangles in her hair with her fingers, but the task was hope-less. Suddenly she felt Hetty's presence behind her. Maddy stepped into the long skirt she was meant to wear over her jeans. As she fastened the buttons on the shirt-waist, she turned to see Hetty waiting, a hairbrush and comb in her hand.

Maddy nodded to her. "Yes, I know my

hair's a mess, but I'm afraid of the cut," she said, pointing to the spot above her ear.

Hetty gently stroked the brush through Maddy's long chestnut hair, carefully avoiding the gash. She swirled the hair into a bun and fastened it at the nape of her neck with an ivory comb. Gathering Maddy's wool jacket over her arm, Hetty led her into the sitting room.

The room was simply furnished, but two objects on a table drew Maddy's attention. The silver pendant Hetty had worn yesterday and a feathered, beaded, bridal headpiece lay side by side on the tabletop. Her pulse rate leaped when she fingered Hetty's pendant. The same curious design of the jasper stone set in silver. She could feel a lump rising in her throat and a curious feeling in her chest. Her fingers closed around her own shell locket, still hanging round her neck.

Hetty urged her to sit at the table. Pointing a finger at Maddy's locket, Hetty spoke clearly. "Your *maman,* Julie, *oui?*" Then, picking up the pendant dangling from the rawhide thong, she cradled it in one hand, ran her finger over it lovingly, then pointed to the headdress. *"Ma maman d'Abenaki."*

CHAPTER FOURTEEN

September 30, 2005

Clare walked the floor, cell phone in hand. "What time did you call her last night? Tell me again, *Tante,* what exactly did you say to her?" Clare listened patiently for several minutes. Suddenly, her eyebrows lifted. She opened her mouth and promptly closed it, holding her forehead in one hand. "We've got a problem here, *Tante.* Maddy's bed has not been slept in. She's gone. I'll be over as soon as I've made a few calls."

Trying not to rouse suspicion, but wanting to see if Maddy might have gone to her father's, Clare called Jacques at Francois's Fancy.

"Just checkin', Papa Jacques. Did ya have any damage from the storm? A tree came down and . . . er, uh, what did you say? Maddy's young man?"

Clare choked on a cough, placed her hand over the phone and looked up at the ceiling

— Lord, don't tell me Jacques is still talking about Claude. "Uh, Jacques, this connection isn't too good and I gotta little emergency to take care of here. I'll have Maddy call you, okay? Bye."

She grabbed Patrick's business card from the counter and dialed the number. No answer. "That was wishful thinking," she said to herself. Patrick was in nowhereville last night.

Forgetting that it was Saturday, she dialed Saint David's School and listened to a recorded message. "Due to extensive flooding in the area, school will be closed until further notice." She ticked off on her fingers. Not at Papa Jacques's. Not at Patrick's. No school. Clare clapped a hand to her head.

There's got to be a clue in Tante's vision. Okay, Margaret Lebrun Chamberlain, you've got some explaining to do.

"Run that by me one more time, *Tante*," Clare said, her tone obviously tense. "You had a vision. Both Maddy's mom Julie and your grandmother Henriette were in it. And?"

"It all went so fast, *ma chérie*. Julie's presence was very strong at first. She was calling me to the mill. She was very agitated and frightened. *I* thought it was something to do with Patrick. You know, because his shop is at the mill complex."

"Yes, I know that, but what would Maddy's mom have to do with Patrick?"

"Nothing and everything. Now that I put it together in my mind, Julie was only concerned about Maddy being at the mill. When I telephoned to tell you about my vision, Maddy thought I was saying that she needed to go to the mill to find Patrick. I didn't have a chance to explain that Henriette was the dominant force in my vision."

"Wait. I don't get it. You're skipping a whole generation here — Maddy's mom and now your grandmother!"

"*Les mères.* It's the *mothers,* don't you see? The mother sense was aroused. Mothers have a powerful force, *chérie.* Julie was trying to help Maddy so she came to me in a vision. Then Henriette came. *Grand-mère* practically raised me when my own *maman* died."

"Yes, I know, *Tante,* but I still don't get it. What does Henriette have to do with Maddy?"

"Let me start over, Clare. I was praying to God for Mrs. Donovan after I heard the news about the fire. That's when the vision started. Of a sudden, I could feel Julie Fontaine's presence right beside me. It was

171

a sensation I used to feel when I prayed with Jacques after Maddy's mama died. This time, Julie was upset, but I couldn't tell why. My grandmama appeared. Henriette is a *seer, oui?* She knows why Julie is upset and she knows about Mrs. Donovan."

"How can you tell that? Did they speak to you?"

"*Mon Dieu,* no. I sensed it. I could see very clearly the old cotton mill, and Henriette was there, and . . . and then my lights in the house flashed off and on again — like a sign. I was frightened, eh, *ma chérie.* I went right to the phone to call you, but only Maddy was there."

"It's okay, *Tante.* You did the right thing. If I had been home and got your call, I would have thought you were talking about Patrick when you got to the part about the mill."

"But I hardly got the message to Madelaine when the phone went dead. Then the lights went off for good." Margaret took a shaky breath.

Clare wrapped her arms around her aunt, murmuring soothing sounds. "It will be all right, *Tante.* We're going to find Maddy. Not to worry."

Patrick stood beside his mother's hospital

bed. He didn't like looking at the oxygen tubes in her nose or the intravenous drip. He fastened his eyes on her hands.

"If only I'd brought Rosemary home when school let out, none of this would have happened, Ma."

"Paddy, love, you cannot blame yourself for this. We didn't know it then, nor do we know the cause, yet. The smoke seemed to be seepin' into our house from the McGinns' next door. I checked the kitchen and the upstairs. Nothin' was wrong up there, but the rooms were filling with smoke. I came back down and tried to get the girls out, but that's the last I remember."

He looked into her blue eyes, the mirror image of his own. A frown crossed his face.

"Aw, Mum, I might have got you out sooner and you wouldn't be lying here like this. I should never have driven Rosie out to Biddeford Pool." Patrick drew a deep breath and raked his hands through his hair. His frown deepened. He wouldn't complicate things by telling her about the accident. "I've got a soft spot, and Rosie always finds it."

"Ah, well, give it up to the Lord, son. We cannot live with regrets. I learned that lesson with Fiona . . ." Tears welled in her eyes as she reached for Patrick's hand. "Your good intentions had a detour, Paddy, but your heart was in the right place. Rosemary is a dreamer, but she's safe and sound now. She's with the twins, isn't she?"

"Yes. They're all okay. It's you I'm worried about."

CHAPTER FIFTEEN

September 30, 1905

Molly Carrigan burst out of the mill door just after the noon whistle blew. She ran to Hetty and Maddy standing in a patch of sunlight on the far side of the mill yard.

Maddy was gazing at unfamiliar sights and sounds on the street. Gabled roofs and chimneys jutting to the sky. Horses pulling wagons and buggies under a regal canopy of elm trees shading both sides of the street. *Elm trees were my first clue yesterday when I rode in the swaying cart. I've only seen trees like that in old pictures of Biddeford.*

"Aye, and it's glad I am you made it, Hetty." Molly's hand clasped Maddy's shoulder. "Are ya steady on yer feet, Miss?"

"Yes," Maddy replied hesitantly, casting an uncertain look at Hetty. "Hetty's been trying to help, but none of it made much sense." *Hetty spent hours talking to me in broken English about Tante Margaret and my mother, and even Patrick's mother.* "Truthfully, I'm kind of confused."

"Never ye mind, Miss Madelaine, I'm a might confused meself," Molly said as she patted Maddy's arm. "Hetty'll see ya safely to . . . uh, wherever it is yer goin'."

Molly placed her hand on her hip. "Hetty," she said, pointing her finger, a sharp edge to her voice. "Ya know I've little time to spare if I'm ta get me noon broth. You must listen up. MacDill gave me this to take her on the horse car." She thrust silver coins into Hetty's palm. "He can do no more today, but he promised ta see that you get yer six dollars and fifty cents weekly wage *if* yer in tomorrow, for sure. Me thinks he's bein' right generous because yer takin' care of —" Molly jerked her head in Maddy's direction. "— things."

Hetty murmured, "*Merci, merci* to Monsieur MacDill." She kissed Molly on both cheeks.

Molly squeezed Maddy's hands and cocked her head, flashing a broad grin. "I've no more time, but I wish ye well, Miss Madelaine. May the good Lord keep ya in his hands and never close his fists too tight." Abruptly, Molly turned and hurried back to the mill door.

"Come," Hetty said, urging Maddy away

from the mill yard. They started down the road, passing rows of tenement buildings, a bakery, and a cobbler's shop. Bunting and flags decorated the shops. A sign over the bakery read *50th Anniversary.* Maddy's head was turning from side to side to view both sides of the street. Nothing looked familiar. It wasn't until they came to an intersection of a dusty side street that Maddy suddenly felt a sense of belonging. A horse car stood under the sign for *Pool Street!*

The car's canopy roof reminded Maddy of pictures she'd seen of a trolley car. Along the roof a banner read *City Charter Golden Anniversary — 1855–1905.*

Rows of benches in the open car were empty, save one. The horses shook their manes and whickered when the conductor rang the bell. Hetty tugged Maddy forward, paid the fare and chose a seat, protectively placing Maddy on the inside aisle of the bench.

The only other passenger sat opposite her, a well-dressed, middle-aged man. He tipped his derby hat and nodded in their direction as he drew on a pipe clenched in his teeth. The scent of tobacco wafting their way brought a sharp image to Maddy's mind. Grandpa Fontaine was never without his pipe . . . right up to his last birthday.

She did some mental math and a startling thought followed. Grandpa Fontaine was only two years old in 1905! Francois's Fancy probably didn't exist then — or did it?

As the horses clopped along the dirt road they passed farms that Maddy had no memory of, but still they were on Pool Street. The gentleman broke the silence.

"Have you enjoyed the festivities for the city charter, ladies?"

Maddy glanced at Hetty who stared straight ahead.

"We . . . I . . . uh, the decorations in town were very nice." She nudged Hetty. "Hetty, why are we going away from town?"

"Your *maman* gives direction."

"My mother? But she's not —"

Hetty pursed her lips and squeezed Maddy's hand. When she opened her mouth, French words tumbled out so fast that Maddy could make no sense of them. She shook her head slowly and closed her eyes, wishing desperately that she wasn't on this horse car — wishing she had never left Clare's apartment.

A deep voice startled Maddy and her eyes flew open.

"She's trying to tell you how to seek some information that you need. Do you have a

178

friend who is missing?"

Maddy's head swiveled to the man seated opposite her. He spoke educated English with a slight accent that she didn't recognize. Warm brown eyes stared at her. She couldn't miss the questioning lift of his eyebrows.

"You speak French?" she asked.

"I speak three languages, miss. In my business it is vital that I do. I have clients abroad, you see."

"May I ask what you do, sir?"

"I build sailing ships," he replied. "As a matter of fact you will see my latest schooner in the bay presently. I hope to show her to its new owner today. That is, if he's still waiting for me." He looked at a gold pocket watch pulled from his vest. "My carriage broke a wheel earlier and this horse car was my only alternative, late though I shall be."

Maddy looked at Hetty sitting ramrod stiff on the bench. A market basket at her feet, she stared straight ahead at the road. If Hetty understood what the man was saying, she gave no indication. Maddy turned back to the gentleman. "Can you tell me how long before we arrive, sir?"

"Very shortly, miss. Can't you smell the salt air?" He tilted his head back and breathed deeply. "Ah, yes. Restorative to those who love the sea." A sidelong glance had his eyes rising from Maddy's Wellington boots to her bruised face. "Do you travel to Biddeford Pool to watch the boats, miss, or are you part of the city charter celebration?"

"Not likely," Maddy replied, shaking her head and casting another glance at Hetty, sitting stiff as a board. Still no change in her expression. "Are you certain my companion was speaking about finding someone?" she asked the man.

"Indeed. The lady said that in order to find the missing one, your mother sends you to a painting . . . something about La Madeleine by the sea, which I didn't quite understand."

Maddy's doe eyes widened. She leaned forward to grip the wooden bench in front of her, as though to steady herself. A voice in her head was relentless. *But this cannot be. That painting was Mom's last. What could it have to do with finding Patrick?*

Harbor sounds reached them on the wind. Gulls screeching and water slapping wharf pilings on a rising tide. Her thoughts were suddenly jolted. Hetty was pointing ahead, clutching Maddy's arm. *"La mer,* Madelaine, *la mer."*

Beyond the large tidal pool that gave Biddeford Pool its name was a small harbor with an endless vista of the sea. To Maddy, it was like viewing an unfinished miniature of Pool Village as she knew it. Fishing boats, dories and sailing sloops dotted the shoreline. Only a few shacks and a bait shop lined the wharf.

"There she is, ladies," the gentleman shouted, "my schooner anchored out there with her bowsprit pointed north. A beauty to behold, isn't she?"

His enthusiastic smile made Maddy forget her turmoil for a second. She nodded and smiled back. "It is a beautiful ship," she said.

"Fortunately it looks to be a grayslick today, a calm sea, so she'll be easy to board from a dory if my buyer still waits." As the conductor reined the horses to a stop, the ship builder stood and gestured to Maddy and Hetty to leave their seats. "*Après vous,* ladies," he said.

Maddy was first to step down from the car. She didn't hear what Hetty said in rapid French to the conductor.

Hetty stood still beside the horses as the gentleman passenger departed the car. She clutched the market basket close to her side and nodded stiffly to him. "*Bonsoir, monsieur.*" The small civility surprised Maddy.

"*Au revoir,* Madam and Mademoiselle." He bent to Maddy's ear as he tapped his pipe on the side of the car. "Good luck with your search, miss, and may future journeys bring you naught but happiness." His eyes sparkled above his smile.

Maddy opened her mouth to reply but Hetty was tugging her arm. "Come," she urged, turning away from the harbor toward a stretch of sand along the rocky shore.

"Where are we going?"

"A house. *C'est dans la grande maison.* Your *maman* says *la peinture* speaks to you."

There she goes with the painting again. My French is spasmodic at best, but certain words are easy to remember. Maison is house and grande is big. Peinture is painting, of course . . . but Mom's painting? This is not making sense.

"*Tante* Margaret *décrit la peinture.* You will know."

The hair rose on the back of Maddy's neck. "*Tante* Margaret! She described the painting?"

"*Oui.*"

"But why? The gentleman on the horse car said you spoke of information for someone who is missing, so what does a painting have to do with that?"

Hetty trudged on silently, carrying the market basket in the crook of her arm. Suddenly, pursing her mouth, she stopped shuffling her laced-up boots through the soft sand. She cocked her head and pointed away from the shore. "*La grande maison,* Madelaine."

A large house loomed up, ghostly gray against a darkening sky. It stood on high ground beyond the rocks and dunes. Maddy blinked and brought one hand to her mouth. *A vision shrouded in mist from the sea? It was as big as Francois's Fancy, but . . .*

Hetty gave her no time to reconcile whether it was a vision, or real. She lifted her long skirt with one hand and clambered over rocks, balancing the basket in the other. Soon she was taking long steps, pushing through sand and marshy grass, creating a path behind her for Maddy.

"Wait!" Maddy called. "Why are you hurrying so?"

Hetty stopped to catch her breath and pointed toward the harbor. "The horse car," she said, pointing to herself. "I must go."

"You brought me here and you're going back?"

"Oui." She trudged on through the tall grass.

"But you can't just leave me here alone," Maddy called to her. "It's — What will I do?" she shouted.

Clear, unaccented words floated back on

the wind.

"Listen with your heart."

The words were punctuated by Hetty's sudden stop a short distance from the house.

Maddy caught up with her and they both stared at the house that loomed tall on a wide strip of cleared land. Maddy shook her head and shoulders as if to clear her mind. *It is real.* The same gabled roof, but the windows and door were empty spaces, like a child's drawing of a house. Shadowed and skeletal, it looked like a half-built shell of Francois's Fancy. She shivered and reached for Hetty's hand.

Hetty might not have shown her thoughts on the horse car, but she let them show now. She stared at Maddy with mournful eyes. Maddy sensed compassion and struggle in her expression and in her round, dark eyes.

She cupped Maddy's cheek in one cold hand and kissed her forehead. Stepping back she inclined her head toward the house. Speaking slowly and deliberately, her message this time was clear. "I have only power to see." She paused. "To know — not to find. *Allez avec Dieu, ma chérie.* Go with God."

Great dark clouds of a lowering autumn sky suddenly blotted out the sun. Lightning

184

slashed over the rooftop, limning the chimney. A fickle wind sent their skirts clinging to their legs. Thunder rolled and Hetty thrust the market basket into Maddy's hands, the yellow slicker rolled up inside.

Maddy stared at the coat, looked up to the roof, then down at the dark empty space for a door. When she turned, Hetty was halfway down the dunes, tucked up skirt billowing in the wind, legs flying as fast as sandpipers.

CHAPTER SIXTEEN

With the suddenness of storms at sea, sheets of rain blew in, spraying Maddy's cheeks and pelting her head. It felt like needles pricking the sensitive spot behind her ear where Molly had clipped away her hair. She hunched her shoulders, tucking her chin into the collar of her wool jacket. Grabbing the slicker from the basket she put the hood over her head, not bothering with the sleeves.

In one quick look back toward Pool Landing, she could barely see boat masts piercing the gray horizon. Hetty had disappeared into the low-hanging clouds.

A storm was coming with a vengeance. *Like it or not, I've got to get under cover,* she thought.

The house was built on a slope running parallel with the sea. No porch wrapped around it, just three rough steps, the top one level with an opening for a door. She took a deep breath and ran toward it.

Pausing on the top step for a frightful second, Maddy straightened her shoulders and grabbed the wood of the door jamb. It was solid under her hand. Slowly, she stepped through the opening.

A coldness crawled across her skin. Her eyes opened wide, darting left and right. Scant light came through the windowless spaces at the front of the house, but she could see studs, beams and skeleton framing defining arches on either side of where she stood. Nothing but emptiness beyond the left arch. To her right a large stone fireplace dominated the far end of a stark space interrupted only by stacks of framing lumber.

This has to be the center hall. Maddy tried to step forward, but her skirt caught on two-by-fours at her feet, throwing her off balance. With one hand she reached for a beam to hold on to; the other went into her pocket for the flashlight pressing against her hip.

She clicked it on and birds swooped up from the darkness as though flushed out of a nest by gunshot. They screeched overhead, beating their wings furiously toward a weak rectangle of light at the end of the hall. Maddy gasped, heart pounding, the birds' cries echoing in her ears.

A strange sensation coursed across her chilled skin. It felt like warming, soothing fingers across her shoulders, down to the middle of her back, pushing . . . urging her forward. Thunder boomed overhead, echoing in the emptiness. One foot followed the other, cautiously taking timid steps. Maddy moved toward the flashing light.

She stopped stock still at the doorway when a bolt of lightning burst into jagged spheres. A blinding light followed, so bright that Maddy squeezed her eyes shut. A loud whirring sound heralded a whoosh of air, a powerful force ramming into her back, thrusting her over the threshold.

A scream broke the eerie silence. *Was that me?* Her body thrummed, arms and legs feeling like the strings of a fiddle wound too tight. She reeled and wavered. Eyes opening to slits, she peered at windows — double-hung windows over a window seat! Her eyes widened; her face filled with disbelief. Drumming rain made long runnels down the panes. They were real windows . . . squared mullions, old glass. A beam of light wavered to the window seat below, finally coming to rest on her mother's painting stool.

Maddy stared at the stool, then at the shaking flashlight still clutched tightly in her hand. The market basket dropped to the floor. The flashlight followed. Stripping the hood from her head, she let the yellow slicker fall from her fingers. With leaden feet she closed the distance to the painting stool, her trembling fingers reaching to touch the maple wood. She sank to her knees, holding fast to the stool's legs, and laid her cheek against the smooth, hard seat.

Eyes closed and mind whirling, she tried to reconcile the trip to the shadowed and skeletal *Grande Maison.*

Slowly opening her eyes, Maddy's gaze dropped to the oak floor she knelt on, then behind her to the open door. Sandy, wet boot tracks crossed the floor. Looking up at plastered walls she blinked at crown molding over a wall of books. *I'm in my own time. I'm really here at Francois's Fancy. I'm back.*

As she rose shakily to her feet, a strange sensation seized her, propelling her toward the wall behind Jacques's desk. She stared at the bookshelves, rubbing her eyes with her fingers. The paintings that hung beyond the shelves in their familiar symmetrical pattern were pulling her forward as though they were magnets.

Hetty was sending me to a painting.

Her feet moved, tight-jointed like a puppet, toward the last painting. A watercolor of a long, low, white building with a garden at one side, the ocean in front. Carved granite stations on a shell path, each marked with a wild rose bush, marched around the garden in a semicircle enclosing the garden and ending at the door of the house.

She tried to resurrect the memory of that terrible summer when she came home from college to learn that her mother had gone to La Madeleine sur la Mer, a hostel for young women. Unmarried young women. La Madeleine was a place of refuge run by an order of nuns. It was a place dedicated to Mary Magdalene.

Julie Fontaine had volunteered there, teaching therapeutic art to unwed mothers while Maddy was away at school. The nuns urged Julie to come for a retreat and pray with them. She was dying with pancreatic cancer.

Maddy shuddered, rubbed a finger over the picture's frame, trying to rid herself of thoughts remembered, to concentrate on the painting. Her fingers flexed and stopped at the JF at the lower corner of the painting. Julie Fontaine. Stations of the Cross. That's what Mom called the painting. Each stone figure was a station in a garden, graced with roses, sea and sky. It was her last painting . . . from memory when she came home from the retreat.

Predestined? *Oh, Lord. Help me here.* Maddy lowered her shoulders, head down, staring at her shell necklace. She clasped it in her fingers. By the sea — a refuge by the sea for unwed, pregnant young women. Her mouth worked silently, her mind racing. Suddenly she raised her shoulders with understanding.

The moment was shattered by the sound of a door slamming, voices coming from the rear of the house.

"Whew — I'm drenched just running in from the car. Here, darling, let me take the wet coats into the kitchen. Paul, please take your father into the living room and get a fire going. I'm going to bring us a hot toddy."

"Thanks, Kathleen, I really appreciate your coming to the airport. That was a pretty rough flight, but I was lucky to get someone's cancellation for the noon non-stop."

Paul, Papa and Kathleen. But of course. This is home! Relief battled fear with the realization and the reality. Maddy looked down at her clothes, patting the damp skirt that clung to her jeans over the top of dirty boots. Her hands flew to her hair. Strands were pasted wet against her cheeks, but the ivory comb still held a swirl of her long chestnut hair at the nape of her neck.

Voices from the hall were coming closer.

"Well, of course, I'd have come home, Dad. The storm was all over the news and when I couldn't reach anybody, I got hold of CeCe at the hospital. She told me about the flooding and Mad — and . . . uh, well, here I am. From the way Clare talked I thought to find Francois's Fancy swept out to sea."

A flash of lightning from the studio windows stopped their shuffling feet at the studio doorway. Jacques glanced sideways, opened his mouth, then wordlessly closed it. Clutching Paul's sleeve, he stared at Paul, then shifted his gaze back into the gloom of the studio. "Good Lord. Madelaine," he said in a hushed voice. "Is that you in there?"

Paul dropped his father's arm and bolted into the room. His arms wrapped around Maddy, hugging her close. "Sweet Jesus, where have you been?" he whispered in her ear.

He held her at arm's length, giving her a quick up and down. "Look at you, and it isn't even Halloween yet."

Paul's nervous attempt at humor worked, but Maddy didn't know whether to laugh or cry. She held fast to his hand and pulled him toward her father in the doorway.

"Oh, Papa," was all she could manage before a flood of tears came.

Before Maddy could protest, Paul scooped her up in his arms and started down the hall. "Come on, Pa," he called over his shoulder. "Maddy's wet and shivering and I need to get a fire going."

CHAPTER SEVENTEEN

Paul made it into the living room with Maddy several steps ahead of Jacques. He set her down in the wing chair by the fireplace. Leaning forward, a hand on each arm of the chair, Paul fixed her with cool green eyes and spoke in a hushed voice. "CeCe gave me some cockamamie story about a vision *Tante* had. She said your car was found on Pearl Street and . . . and you had disappeared."

He looked over his shoulder. "Get it together, Mad, for Pa's sake. You gotta be careful what you say in front of him. I don't think he knows what's going on any more than I do."

He pulled off Maddy's boots and set them on the hearth. She watched him, a mist of worry in her eyes, but the tears had stopped.

Jacques entered the room, heading directly to Maddy.

"You gave me quite a start, Madelaine.

No word from you since the storm and suddenly, here you are. Are you all right?"

She rose quickly and lifted her hands to her hair, pretending to adjust the comb, but really covering the gash as Jacques leaned to brush a kiss on her forehead. He peered closely at her cheek, then his eyes dropped from her bruised face to her stained and frayed wet skirt, her stockinged feet. He touched her cheek with one finger, his brow wrinkled with concern. "What's happened, my dear? Your clothes . . . Did you fall?"

"Well in a way, yes," she said, a catch sounding in her throat. She sniffed loudly and accepted the handkerchief he offered. "I'm fine really. It's just that there was nothing here . . . I mean there was no one here —" Maddy looked desperately at Paul. "I guess I was just . . . shocked to see Paul."

"Of course you were. We were surprised, too, when we got his call from the airport," Jacques said as he sat in the armchair facing Maddy.

Paul turned from the fireplace, bellows in hand. "Well, it isn't every day that a hurricane blows in and the Saco River overflows. With all the media hype, how could I not come and see if you guys were high and dry."

Kathleen entered the room with a tray.

"Maddy! Gracious, what a surprise. I didn't see your car, dear. Have you been here long?"

"No. I didn't . . . I mean I couldn't . . . I didn't drive. I, uh —"

"Kathleen, why don't you give Maddy my drink," Paul interrupted. "She's chilled and hot cider might help. I'll help myself to Dad's scotch instead. My nerves are shot from that flight." He went to the sideboard and poured from Jacques's decanter. Downing the scotch neat in one gulp, Paul strode directly to his father and sat on the big ottoman at his feet.

"So tell us, Dad, how did you manage with the Atlantic at your doorstep?"

Jacques had settled himself in the wingback chair opposite Maddy. He sipped from the mug of mulled cider Kathleen had given him.

"It wasn't that bad until dusk. The wind was fierce, blowing salt spray, rain and sand with such tremendous force against the front of the house that we couldn't even see out of the windows. The tide was in, but we didn't realize there was such a surge. Waves had risen almost to the porch steps in just a few hours. It was an eerie feeling, hearing the howling wind and crashing waves while this old house creaked and groaned."

"But we were safe and dry, darling," Kathleen said. "Only small leaks in the kitchen when the shingles started flying off the roof. We had candles and the hurricane lamps and didn't know how bad things were until our visitors came."

"Visitors?" Paul asked.

"Yes, it turned out to be two admirers of yours, Madelaine," Kathleen said.

Maddy straightened and stared first at Kathleen, then at her father.

Jacques's lips quirked in an attempt to hide a smile. "It was the Donovans, Rosemary and Patrick."

Maddy's head jerked and her jaw dropped open.

"What in God's name were they doing out here in a storm?" Paul asked.

"You know them, Paul?" Kathleen asked.

Maddy cleared her throat and opened her mouth, but nothing came out.

Paul raised an eyebrow at Kathleen. "Yes. I've met Patrick, and I know that his little sister is one of Maddy's students."

Maddy flashed Paul a quick look of relief and finally found her voice.

"Before the storm worsened and the power went out, I heard on local TV that there was a fire at the Donovans' house. I thought that Patrick . . . well, anyway, I was trying to find out what happened to him and —" She stopped abruptly, looking from one to the other with frightened eyes.

Paul flashed a sympathetic look her way. "Patrick couldn't have known about the fire, else he wouldn't have been out here."

"None of us knew about a fire," Jacques said.

"Then what *did* bring him out here, Pa?" Paul asked.

"Actually it was his sister who explained their presence. Very admirably too, for a young girl. She said she coaxed her brother to bring her out to the university when school let out early. Somehow she knew that's where I teach."

Jacques smiled, lifting his eyebrows while sending an inquisitive look Maddy's way. "Rosemary said Miss Fontaine taught her all about the Pool during Indian times when this land was called Winter Harbor. I think Rosemary reasoned that it was only a little farther from the university to see what the shore looked like in a storm. I suspect your student thinks highly of you, Madelaine, and my guess is she talked her brother into seeing where you grew up."

There was a softness in Jacques's eyes, a sense of compassion, and it gave Maddy courage.

"I did tell the class about Francois's Fancy, mainly because of its historical location in connection with Indian lore we were studying, but I don't understand why Patrick would stop here. He knows that I've moved in to town with Clare."

Kathleen rose from the sofa to pour more cider in Jacques's cup. Her face was flushed and her tone of voice was reproachful. "It wasn't an *intentional visit,* Maddy. It was our roof. Cedar shakes were blowing off and hit the windshield of your friend's truck as he approached on Mile Stretch Road. Then, that clump of birches at the end of the drive split and fell in his path. I was in the kitchen placing pans around for the leaks. I heard the crash and the screech of brakes."

"Was anyone hurt?" Paul asked.

"No, but the girl was really frightened, and the truck had some damage, so of course your father insisted they come in until we could get help out here."

Maddy rose unsteadily. "I do want to hear about the Donovans, Papa, but I need to go upstairs and get out of these wet clothes. I think there might be some old jeans left in my closet. I'll be down in a bit."

Truth be known, Maddy was overwhelmed by everything that had happened in the last hour. So many unanswered questions. Talking about Francois's Fancy and Patrick brought back the horse-car trip to the Pool with Hetty. Only hours earlier her questions were, "Why is this happening to me?" and "What does Hetty want me to discover?" Maddy couldn't put the pieces together. She didn't know how to begin. Neither did she know how to tell them about her trip in time. There was a niggling thought that maybe it had never happened.

Paul rose quickly and followed her. "Put everything on hold, Pa. I just remembered I have a call to make and my cell phone is in my coat pocket in the kitchen." He put a hand on Maddy's shoulder and walked with her into the hall.

"Let me call Clare while you're upstairs, Mad," he said in a low voice, motioning toward the kitchen as soon as they were out of earshot. "From what she told me this morning, she should be finished her shift by now. If anyone can ease this situation, it'll be CeCe, okay?"

Maddy nodded numbly and started up the stairs.

Clare was already on Mile Stretch Road when Paul reached her by cell phone. Paul waited the few minutes in the kitchen until she arrived.

"Am I ever glad to see you, CeCe. I don't know who is more confused, me, my father or Maddy."

Clare rolled her eyes and gave Paul a big hug. "Likewise. I'm freaked out, and that's an understatement. How and when did she get here?"

"Good questions. She was here when we arrived from the airport and so far she seems afraid to talk. Wait until you see her," Paul said, closing his eyes and shaking his head. "I'll back up whatever you say, CeCe, but I think it's best you get her out of here, and I mean ASAP."

Maddy was descending the stairs as Paul and Clare reached the living room arch. Clare took one long look, then lunged forward and drew Maddy into her arms.

"Don't say anything, babe, or both of us will be basket cases before I can get you home. Just follow my lead and send up a prayer, okay?"

With a quiet "Okay," Maddy let herself be guided into the living room between Paul and Clare. She was wearing a pair of faded jeans and one of Paul's old sweaters.

"You look more comfortable, Maddy," Paul was saying softly as they entered the room, "but remember, the sweater is only on loan."

He paused before they got to the center of the room. "Look who the wind blew in, folks. You have another visitor." He ruffled his fingers playfully through Clare's spiky hair. She laughed and jabbed his shoulder with her fist.

"I suppose that's a little better than 'Look who the cat dragged in.' Hi, Mrs. Fontaine and Papa Jacques. I hear you had a small disaster here during the hurricane."

Jacques sat up straight in his chair, casting a look Paul's way. "No, no, Clare. Nothing that can't be repaired."

"Well, I have to tell you, this place looks pretty good compared to some houses along the river. Patrick said he and Rosie rode into town with the tow truck this morning and he couldn't believe his eyes."

Kathleen shot Clare a puzzled look. "My goodness, word travels fast. Maddy just learned about Patrick's accident, yet you —"

"Well, I just happened to be on duty when Patrick came to the hospital this morning to see his Mom," Clare interrupted.

"What happened to Mrs. Donovan?" Paul asked.

"Smoke inhalation. But she's going to be fine. I came out to the Pool to pick up Maddy and check on you folks. I heard the prediction on television that the houses along the beach would take a beating, but I hope I didn't spread a false alarm, Paul, bringing you here from the big city."

"Nah, I'm glad I came. I'm sure Pa can use my help. Have to get someone to repair the roof and cut up the trees that fell."

"I'm glad you are here, Paul," Jacques said, "and Maddy —" He opened his mouth but was interrupted by Kathleen.

"Would you like some mulled cider, Clare?"

Clare caught Maddy's wary expression. "No, thanks, Mrs. Fontaine. I really can't stay. *Tante* Margaret expects us for a hurricane supper." She jiggled her eyebrows up and down *à la* Groucho Marx and flashed a grin. "My *tante* hasn't got her power back yet, so guess who's bringing supper!" She bent to kiss Jacques's cheek. "I told her I'd check on you first, then come right over." Clare sidled up to Maddy and hooked an arm through hers. "All set, Maddy?"

CHAPTER EIGHTEEN

"I gotta be honest, babe. You haven't said much that's believable since we left your dad's. What's more, I get this *déjà vu* feeling. I heard *Tante*'s side about the vision, and I'm lookin' at you with the bruises and a scalp wound, but it still isn't making sense. I think we better wait till after supper and I'll listen while you two put the whole enchilada together. What d'ya say?"

"Fine," Maddy said with a little edge to her voice. "I didn't expect my father and Kathleen to understand, and truthfully I didn't know how to begin to explain it to them. But you. How can you not believe me when your aunt was the one who started everything? Aren't we all on the same wave length?"

"Whoa. You and me, yes, Mad. We think alike, but *Tante* and me, uh-uh. Besides, I didn't say I didn't believe you. I said the *story's* not believable. I love *Tante* dearly, and if she says she saw your mother and her grandmother in a vision, then I gotta believe her. But this psychic stuff and traveling in time is far out. I deal with blood and guts of broken bodies every day, but this . . ." She shivered and shook her head as she pulled her car up in front of the apartment building. "This has me flipped out."

Taking her iPod out of her purse Clare shoved it in Maddy's lap. "Sit tight and listen to music while I go up and fetch dinner out of the oven. We'll hash this out when we get to *Tante*'s house."

Same huge brown eyes, jet-black hair and high cheekbones. The shadow that was Hetty's face in Maddy's memory vanished into Margaret's smile. Her open arms were warm and comforting.

"Madelaine, *ma chérie.*" Margaret held Maddy's face gently between her palms, then moved her hands to Maddy's shoulders. Her head tilted from side to side as she looked closely at Maddy's face. She winced when she saw the scabbed gash and the shorn hair. "Now I know why your mama was so frightened. You are all right, *ma petite?*"

"Yes," Maddy said, shrugging her shoulders and pushing stray hair behind her ear. "It's okay now, but I remember that my head hurt real bad at first. I kept fading in and out and feeling nauseous —"

"It was a concussion, *Tante*," Clare said. "A piece of metal from a sign carried on the wind and struck her head. From what she tells me, your *grand-mère* knew just what to do about it." Clare placed a covered dish on the table. "We better eat this soon, okay? If it gets much colder in here before your power comes back you may have to come to my place for the night."

"The stew smells wonderful, my Clare. We'll keep it covered for a little bit." She nodded toward a grouping of candles in the center of the table. "I lit all these candles so we could see to eat, but it's kind of nice, no?" Her smile was warm and gracious. "Come, sit down, Madelaine, and tell me what happened."

"It's hard to know where to start," Maddy said, "but I'll go back to before we lost power and before you telephoned about your vision." Clare gave her an almost imperceptible nod and she continued. "I was trying to locate Patrick, because the local news program said three females were taken to the hospital after a fire at the Donovans' house." She looked into Margaret's troubled eyes. "You knew about the fire, didn't you?"

206

"Yes, I heard it on the radio before I called you. *Mon Dieu,* that poor *maman.* I was praying for her, you know."

"Well, next you called us and your phone message became so garbled that when you mentioned the mill, I thought you were talking about Patrick. Then the phone went dead and I . . . I left for the mill complex to find him."

"In the hurricane? *Le Seigneur a lapitié.* Lord have mercy. I didn't mean to send you in harm's way."

"Your intentions were good, *Tante,*" Clare said. "Let Maddy finish."

"My car stalled in the flooded street. When I tried to walk through the water in the mill yard, the wind was so fierce it pushed me right up to the door. Something struck my head, and that's the last I remember."

Margaret looked puzzled. "But Clare said my Henriette helped you, *chérie.*"

"That's true, but I didn't know where I was or who she was. I only knew that I was lying on a floor that vibrated with the hum of machinery. I found out later I was in the old mill, the *truly, real old mill.* I was too hurt to get up, and two women were ordered to help me by a Scot who must have been a mill foreman. I found that out later, too."

Maddy paused and passed her fingers over her forehead, reliving the painful memory of the jolting ride in Mr. MacDill's wooden wagon.

"Tell her the women's names and where they took you," Clare prompted.

"They took me to their rooms in the old row houses on Elm Street. One of them was a young Irish girl named Molly, and the other was a woman called Hetty."

Tante's brow furrowed. "Hetty?" she repeated.

"That's short for your grandma, Henriette, but Maddy didn't know that at first either," Clare said. She started to ladle stew onto their plates. "*Tante,* I think we better stop and eat now, okay? The stew will be cold and the candles will be down to stubs if we keep talking."

Margaret flushed and pursed her lips. "I'm forgetting my manners, Madelaine." She rose and reached for a decanter from a small sideboard next to the table. A picture of steadfast control, she poured them each a glass of red wine. "You must be hungry, and my Clare has brought a tempting meal. *Merci,* Clare. *Bon appétit.*"

Maddy was propped up in bed sipping hot cocoa. "Thank God Margaret's electricity came back right after supper. I was so anxious to get into a nice hot tub and be home . . . *really* home, that I'm afraid I was a little short with some of your aunt's questions before we left."

"Nope. I think you squared things in both of our heads . . . for now. *Tante* is bound to have more questions, and she will want to immerse herself in whatever comes next. Believe me on that."

"Clare, I really need your help with this. I have to find a way to tell Papa and Patrick what happened, but I have to know something first."

Clare shot her a wary look. "I'm listening."

Maddy hugged her elbows. "I need to know if you are as convinced as your *tante* that the power that pushed me back in time really came from beyond the grave. Do you really believe I traveled to 1905?"

Clare chewed her lower lip and heaved a sigh. "I dunno, babe. I figure that you couldn't have known the details about Hetty unless you were really with her, but —"

"But you still doubt it?"

"I want to believe it and I want to help. I saw your head and the weird clothes you came back in. After I had your car towed to the garage I knew you were gone *some-place.*"

Clare put her arms around Maddy's shoulders and gave her a reassuring hug. "Would you feel bad, girlfriend, if I asked you to wait a while? Wait to see how things settle and if the clue you got from your mom's painting really leads to anything?"

CHAPTER NINETEEN

After a good night's sleep, Maddy puttered in the kitchen, making toast with jam, just beginning to feel like her old self, when the phone rang. Hesitantly, she picked up the receiver from the wall phone. It was Patrick.

"Madelaine, is something wrong? Twice I've called you, and Clare told me you were unavailable. Rosemary has been bugging me to talk to you. How about it, Miss Fontaine? Can I stop by to see you on my way to the shop?"

Oh, Lord, it's too soon. "Hold for a minute, Patrick." She held her hand over the receiver, her mind racing. She wasn't ready. Patrick was a big part of all this, but how could she explain something that had no real substance? It was only fair he knew about 1905, but her only evidence was a cut on her head and the bruise on her cheek. *Maybe he just wants to talk about his accident at Papa's house, or about his mom and sisters since the fire.* She took a deep breath.

"Okay, but fair warning. I'm not too presentable. I'm just having coffee. I'll save you a cup."

She raced to the bedroom to pull on a pair of jeans. She grabbed Paul's sweater, tugging it over her sleep-shirt as she hurried to the bathroom. In front of the mirror, she tilted her face, chin up, to the bruised cheek that was fading to a purplish yellow. "Oooh. No hope for covering that."

She finger-combed her hair, trying to pull it together on top of her head to cover the gash. She decided there was no time for that. She rinsed her mouth and made it back to the kitchen as the doorbell rang.

Patrick stood in a wedge of light inside the door, staring at her. His eyes narrowed and darkened to a smoky blue. He frowned, reaching to touch her cheek gently with his fingertips. "Is this how you spend days off from school, Miss Fontaine? Looks like somebody packed a hell of a punch."

Maddy grabbed his hand and closed the door. "Come in, Mr. Donovan," she said with a mock smile, "and I'll tell you about it." She poured coffee with trembling hands and straightened her shoulders before looking him straight in the eye. "It was a blow, but it wasn't somebody who did it. It was the hurricane."

Maddy touched her bruised cheek with a finger, then pointed at her scalp as she bent her head forward for Patrick to see. "This happened when the wind threw a missile at me and knocked me to the floor inside the mill."

His frown deepened. "The mill? Are you telling me you came to my shop in the middle of a hurricane?"

"Well, not exactly. I did come to the mill *complex* during the hurricane, but it was because of *Tante* Margaret's vision. I heard about the fire, and I was looking for you, and my car stalled in the flooded street, and . . . oh, Patrick, this is so hard. I know you're not going to believe me." She stood at the kitchen bar, wrapped both hands around her mug and lowered her eyes.

Patrick picked up his mug and reached for her. "Try me," he said tugging her arm toward the living room sofa.

This was the second time Maddy told her story, and the words sounded more unreal in broad daylight. When she described the whooshing wind that pushed her into the mill, the old 1905 mill, her hand flew to her throat and her pulse throbbed beneath her fingers. *Could he know her heart was pounding?*

She watched his unreadable eyes as she told him about Hetty. When she described dressing in Molly's clothes, her eyes flicked from his long legs in jeans to his open shirt and back to his strong hand as it grasped hers, their fingers laced together. His knee pressed against hers, but she took small comfort from their closeness. Her thumb stroked back and forth across the puckered scar on his hand.

She fastened her eyes on their hands. The horse-car ride to the Pool, the skeletal house — becoming her house, Francois's Fancy — and at last, *the painting.* That was the hardest to explain.

When she finished talking, Maddy raised her head and waited. Patrick's frown deepened.

"I can believe that your head was injured and your face bruised in a fall, Madelaine, but falling into a mill that existed in 1905?"

Patrick shook his head. With gentle fingers he raised her chin to gaze in her eyes. "These people you speak of. Dead people who sound more like characters in the stories my grandfather would tell, or people in a dream you had. A nightmare, maybe?" He squeezed her hand gently, a weak smile on his lips.

Maddy's shoulders slumped and her lips trembled. "It *was* nightmarish, but it was real. They were not fairy-story characters. Molly and Hetty were real. They helped me get back to Francois's Fancy, and Hetty led me to the painting. I told you about the house in the painting, Patrick, and how my mother volunteered there. I think there is a message in that painting for me . . . and for you."

He frowned again and shook his head. "For me? I don't get it, Madelaine. You said that Clare's Aunt Margaret believes the people in her vision were all mothers trying to help *you*. They led *you* to your mother's painting of a retreat house. What does that have to do with me?"

"A retreat house for unwed mothers." Maddy felt the weight of silence. A flush of color crept up her neck. "I believe it's a clue, Patrick."

"A clue? To what?"

"A clue to finding your sister Fiona."

Patrick's eyes widened and he immediately released her hand. He leaned forward, elbows on his knees, and held his head in his hands. Rubbing his hands over his face, he straightened and turned to meet her gaze. A muscle at the side of his jaw twitched.

"Visions and seers and time trips, that's weird enough, but —" He shook his head slowly, closed his eyes for a second and drew a breath. "Fiona was confidential, between you and me, Madelaine. Don't you remember how hard it was for me to tell you about her?"

The intensity of his gaze belied his anger. Clenching his fists as though he was trying to gain control, his words erupted like a hoarse cry.

"Sweet Jaysus! How can you expect me to believe this — or even to trust you now?"

She opened her mouth, but he stood abruptly and put both hands up in front of his face. "No more talk. Not now." He looked down at the coffee cup and attempted a humorless smile. "I have to go to work."

His mom was home from the hospital, supervising neighbor ladies who volunteered to help Rosie and the twins clean up smoke and soot from the fire. The downstairs rooms still held the stench of smoke, but luckily, it was only smoke damage. The air hummed with chatter and rattle as everyone worked with pails, sponges and brushes. Patrick had been happy to leave for work this morning, glad to get away from all the females . . . until he talked to Madelaine.

His patience shattered like glass. *How can I trust her again?* He banged the steering wheel of the rental truck, willing his mind to banish the weird scenes Maddy had planted there. *I don't want to be angry with her, but how could she expect me to believe her when she's broken my confidence?*

He had not permitted himself to think much about the fancy big house on the water in the last twenty-four hours, but Rosemary hadn't helped matters. The minute Mom arrived home from the hospital, Rosie told her about Miss Fontaine. She jabbered on and on about Professor Fontaine; what a nice man he was, and all about Francois's Fancy. Bad enough that Maddy invaded *his* thoughts. Now she was the topic of conversation at home.

When he pulled into the mill parking lot, there she was behind his eyelids, wading through the flooded mill yard. Inside the shop, he couldn't work on the band saw, couldn't concentrate. He picked up a small maple box he was finishing. It was not a work-order piece. It was a special gift. His fingers brushed across the satin finish of the lid. *Soft and glowing like her skin.* The greenish-yellow bruise on Maddy's cheek flashed before his eyes. Her beautiful chestnut hair parted by an ugly scab. His lips creased into a thin line, and he set the box down on the workbench.

Pacing to the back of the shop, he thought to find comfort in the familiar, old sofa his mother had given him. He leaned back and tried deep breathing.

There she was, like a film rolling, sitting beside him, having tea on her first visit to his shop. His refusal to talk about her school project angered and confused her and she tried to make a fast exit. He caught her at the door, brushed his lips across her mouth and rested his cheek against hers. Her doe-shaped green eyes flecked with gold in the twilight . . . haunting him, still.

Maddy paced the apartment rooms, turning conversations over in her mind. *Aunt Margaret believed me. Of course she would; her vision started everything. Patrick doesn't believe me. I've angered him and lost his trust. Clare, of all people, has put me on hold. I haven't had the courage to hear Papa's reaction, but* . . . she slapped a hand to her forehead. Paul! She picked up her cell phone and dialed his number.

"Hey, babe, I've wondered when you would call," Paul said. "I've only got the weekend here, and right now I'm out back of the house, trying to stack wood from the birches the tree man cut up. How 'bout I call you back, or better yet, I'll come over there when I'm done with the woodpile. I don't think Pa will mind if I borrow his car and take a lunch break."

"I'd like that, Paul. I'll wait lunch for you." She clicked the phone shut.

Maddy changed into sweatpants and shirt, carefully folding Paul's borrowed sweater to return to him. The sweater sparked a reminder of Molly's old skirt and shirtwaist, folded and tucked away on her closet shelf at Francois's Fancy. She wished the memories could as easily be put away.

The hot bath last night had soothed her aching, tired body, and Clare had shampooed gently around the gash on her head. She could see the healing cut when she held a hand mirror up to the bathroom wall mirror. Brushing her hair carefully into a loose twist in the back, she wound a wide silk scarf from her forehead back over the scab, catching the twist in a loop tied at the nape of her neck.

Wish there had been time to do this before Patrick arrived. Not that it would have mattered much, she thought. *The minute I mentioned Fiona, he closed down.*

219

Clare's small portable radio still sat on the kitchen bar. Maddy tuned in the oldies station as the last strains of a familiar song played. Opening the refrigerator, she straightened and turned her head to catch the disk jockey's voice.

"Nat Johnson here on WBNE. You've been listening to the sultry sound of Sarah Vaughan with a tune from the sixties, *The Nearness of You.*"

Is this karma, or what? Mom's favorite song that played at the wine bar. Patrick gave a toast. "Let's drink to new beginnings," he said. Some new beginning this has turned out to be.

Maddy grabbed a covered bowl from the refrigerator, stashed it in the microwave and set out cheese and bread to make Paul's favorite grilled cheese sandwiches. Clare had left a note to have the chowder for lunch. Perfect combo, she thought. *What would I do without Clare?*

The DJ was signing off. "One last chance, folks, to name the mystery tune. Go to WBNE/Johnson.com and click on *mystery.* You may be the lucky winner of tickets for the fall festival and overnight accommodations for two at Old Orchard Beach Inn."

The Internet! Why didn't I think of that? Maddy glanced at her watch and hurried to her laptop. She Googled: Biddeford, Maine, 1905.

CHAPTER TWENTY

Paul leaned over her shoulder to read the caption on the screen: "City Charter Golden Anniversary 1855–1905." He squeezed her shoulder and ambled back to the sofa.

"That may have happened a hundred years ago, but how does that prove you were there?"

Maddy looked away from her laptop, stood up and shot him a scowl. "Not you, too?" she said. "When I explained everything over lunch, you didn't raise any doubts. Now I need proof?"

"Whoa, Maddy. Not for me. I was only voicing questions others might ask."

"What others? I've told everyone who needs to know, except Papa. I was searching the Internet to see if the things I observed actually did happen. I'm not Professor Fontaine. I don't have Biddeford's history clocked in my brain like Dad does. And I'm not Clare. She says, 'Wait to see if the clues lead anywhere.' I think she's hedging."

"Chill out. Clare's flip nonchalance is only on the surface. It masks her real sensitivity. I think she's trying to shield you, but she'll come around. Count on it. And Pa . . . well, I intend to help you with *him,* but have you forgotten Kathleen? God knows what she's going to ask about. She wants us there for dinner tonight, by the way."

"Oh, Paul, I don't know if I'm ready for that. Telling Papa is one thing, but Kathleen . . ."

"Don't worry. I'll keep her occupied while you talk to Dad. I've got a little plan up my sleeve, and I've got a feeling Big Jacques is gonna be your staunch supporter."

"Maybe. He *has* seemed more caring since he came home from the hospital. More worried about everything, too. Before I moved out of the house, everything centered on Kathleen. I felt like a fly on the wall, for all the notice he took of me."

"Yeah, well that was *then.* No mystery. She's fifteen years younger than him and built like a brick shithouse. She fawned all over him, and Pa lapped it up like a kitten in cream."

Maddy smiled and nodded. "I know. But he's really vulnerable since the stroke. Lately he seems much more aware of you and me. More considerate, too. I think facing mortality scared him."

"You got that right. That's another reason I got here as fast as I could. Clare had me friggin' scared, too. Her call was so frazzled that I imagined all kinds of stuff happening to you and Pa and Francois's Fancy. I don't remember a nor'easter that came into the Pool with such force. In fact, I should be out there now. Dad's got a roofer coming to replace shingles this afternoon. If your car isn't back from the shop, call me when Clare gets home. I'll come back and pick you up for dinner."

Paul jumped up to help Kathleen clear the dishes from the dining table, making small talk as he picked up plates. Kathleen patted Jacques on the shoulder. "Why don't you two go into the living room and relax. Paul will help me bring coffee and dessert in, won't you, dear?"

"But of course," Paul said, giving Maddy the Groucho Marx eyebrows as he followed Kathleen through the butler's pantry into the kitchen.

Jacques took Maddy's arm and headed toward the chairs in front of the living room fireplace. "I don't remember Paul ever being as talkative as he was during dinner. It

224

was hard to get a word in edgewise with all that talk about his work."

"Well, I'm glad he explained about Kathleen's portrait," Maddy said. "I think it's been weighing on his mind since he took the job in New York. He told me this noon that he wants to bring the painting back to you when he comes home for Thanksgiving."

"For Paul's sake, I'm happy that they chose to exhibit it in the gallery, but I still will feel better about it when I actually see the portrait with my own eyes." He looked at Maddy from under his heavy brows and settled into his wing chair.

"Now as to you, Miss Madelaine, are you sure your car is going to be reliable to get you back to school when Saint David's reopens? Paul said you'd probably have it back from the garage, but you haven't told me what happened when the car stalled in the storm."

Maddy clasped her hands tightly. She could hear the voices and faint laughter coming from the kitchen. *Paul is doing his part. Please, God, let me do mine.*

It was an effort not to let her emotions show, to retell her story one more time and make it as succinct as possible, all the while trying to assess Jacques's reaction.

He listened with solemn New England patience until she spoke of Hetty and the painting in the study. Jacques's eyes widened and he leaned forward in his chair. He tilted his head from side to side, equivocating. "You mean to say Henriette had prescience? She knew you were from our time? She knew about your mother's painting?"

Voices in the hall sounded close. Maddy hastily rose and leaned over the arms of her father's chair. She grasped his hand and spoke softly in a plaintive voice. "Please. Let's talk of this another time, Papa, okay?"

Jacques squeezed her fingers and nodded silently as Paul and Kathleen entered the room.

"Attention," Paul blared. "*Mon père*'s favorite, Cherries Jubilee, *à la* Paul." He set a huge tray on the coffee table. A copper sauté pan filled with cherries in an orange-flavored sauce sat next to four bowls of vanilla-bean ice cream. Kathleen doused the cherries with cognac and Paul flamed the jubilee. *"Voilà! Jubilé de cerises."*

Jacques laughed and clapped his hands.

"It was all Paul's idea," Kathleen said. "He even brought the ingredients and put it together. That's what took us so long."

"Very impressive, son. I'd say New York is having a good influence on you."

"Thanks, Pa. At least I was good for something besides stacking firewood this time around."

Kathleen looked up from serving the dessert and pointed a spoon at Paul. "Don't sell yourself short. You have many talents, Paul."

Paul looked at his hands. "I only know that the best one came from my mother."

He looked up when Maddy coughed. Raising his hands, palms up, he smiled at her. "Um, I have to be in the big city to put these hands back to work by Tuesday, Maddy. Do you know whether Clare works the early shift tomorrow? I'm on standby for a ten a.m. flight."

"I know that she starts the night shift next week, but I can take you to the airport tomorrow, if that's why you're asking."

"Your car is back?" Jacques asked. "I thought Clare brought you here tonight."

"She did. My car is back, but Clare was on her way to the Pool with Aunt Margaret, so she dropped me off with the understanding that Paul would bring me home. Clare really wants to see Paul before he leaves, and tonight seemed like the only chance."

"Will they be long wherever they are?" Kathleen asked.

Maddy glanced at her father, then at Paul,

but they were both finishing their Cherries Jubilee. "Actually, Clare was just bringing Margaret with some 'mopping up' supplies for the Star of the Sea Retreat Center. *Tante* Margaret feels that place is her personal mission because some of the old nuns there were her teachers years ago when it was a private school."

"She went to a private boarding school?" Kathleen asked, rather pointedly.

Jacques cleared his throat. "Actually, I know quite a bit about that school, Kathleen . . . and about Margaret. You see, it was once an old hotel and Margaret's father was one of the contractors who turned the property into a school. Margaret was a day student there. Now it is a retreat center." Jacques raised an eyebrow and cocked his head at Maddy. "I wish I had known they were coming out this way, I would have liked to see Margaret."

"What time are they due back at Clare's?" Paul asked.

Maddy looked at her watch. "Right about now, I guess. Clare thought around eight."

Paul rose and started collecting bowls for the tray. "Sorry to bring things to a close, Pa, but I do want to see Clare. Thank you, Kathleen. Dinner was delicious."

"Thank *you*, Paul, for making it so special.

Hopefully next time you come, you'll be able to stay longer. I know your dad appreciated your help."

Paul took car keys from his pocket, dangling them in Jacques's direction. "I'll be back early with your car, Dad." He put the liquor bottle on the coffee table and picked up the tray. "Maybe we can have a nightcap with the cognac."

Kathleen followed Paul into the hall. Jacques rose to give Maddy a hug, holding her for an extra long moment. "I'm glad you were here, too, Madelaine." He tucked a stray hair behind her ear and brushed his knuckles gently over her cheek. "Can you stop by after you take Paul to the airport tomorrow? I believe what you've told me, but there are things we need to talk about."

Chapter
Twenty-One

Clare managed to turn the knob with her hands full, kicking hard with her foot at the same time. The apartment door banged against the inside wall, startling Maddy and Paul. They hurried from the kitchen toward her as Clare stepped into the lighted entry.

"Sorry, guys. I wasn't sure you two were here yet."

Paul relieved her of two tote bags she was balancing. "Watcha got here, CeCe? Trick or treats?"

"*Comment ça va,* Paul?" she asked, reaching up to plant a kiss on his cheek.

Paul cut her a puzzled look. "I'm doin' okay, but what's with the French?"

"Ugh," Clare said as she draped her coat over a barstool. "I've been helping *Tante* mop up black and white tile floors and listening to French nuns for the past three hours. That's how come the French. Only an inch or so of water flooded their first floor, but, believe me, those tiles are damned hard on the feet after a full shift on the hospital floor."

She kicked off her mules and squiggled her toes into the carpet before walking into the living room, balancing as though she were on a tightrope. "This feels so good."

Maddy followed behind her. "Did they feed you?"

"Ohmigod, yes! And filled those bags too. Pumpkin bread, finger rolls, plus Sister Agatha's brandy apple cake. We'll be waddling around like fat geese if we eat all that."

Paul was checking out the tote bags as he placed them on the kitchen table. "I'll gladly take some of this stuff off your hands if you want to pack me a goody bag for the flight," he said.

Maddy put her arm around Clare's shoulder, steering her to the sofa. "Put your feet up, CeCe. We were at my dad's for dinner, and Kathleen sent wine with Paul. He'll bring us a glass."

Clare stretched out on the sofa with a sigh of relief. "Did you tell them, Maddy? I'm dying to know what they had to say."

"Don't I count? How 'bout what I had to say?" Paul asked as he walked toward them with a bottle and glasses. "I did fly here because of your call," he said, raising an eyebrow at Clare.

"Sorry, Paul. I already guessed how *you* would react, but I felt kind of funny when Maddy suddenly was back. Guilty, ya know, thinking that because I panicked, you flew home on a wild goose chase."

Paul shrugged. "In for a penny, in for a pound," he said, handing her a glass of wine. "I'm glad I came, and you're right, I believe her. I might have doubted my sister's judgment a time or two in the past, but *never* her word."

He poured Maddy's wine and held up the glass, feigning a toast. "She's a straight shooter, and she never did have Pa's gift for storytelling." He winked at Maddy.

Maddy sat in the rocker, both hands anchored around her wine glass, smiling at Paul with tears in her eyes. She turned her gaze to Clare. "I feel like laughing and crying at the same time, but I'm glad you called him, CeCe. He had our dad thinking it was the hurricane that worried him enough to bring him home. Paul helped out at the house, and tonight he made it possible for me to talk to Papa alone."

Clare sat up straight, eyes sparking at Maddy. "Kathleen doesn't know?"

"No."

"And what did Jacques say?"

"I didn't have time to finish telling him everything, but he did seem to believe me. Even said there was something he needed to tell *me*. I'll find out tomorrow when I come back from the airport."

Clare nodded her head, solemn-faced. "So, Kathleen doesn't know, and now it looks like Patrick is the Doubting Thomas. What do you think, Paul?"

"Me? It's entirely up to Madelaine — about Patrick, I mean. If it was my sister gone missing, I'd damned well be beating the bushes with any clues I got."

Maddy closed her eyes and took a deep breath. "I'm not trying to make excuses for him, but Patrick's family circumstances are different, Paul. You don't know the whole story, and I really shouldn't have told anyone about Fiona."

Clare swung her feet off the sofa and refilled her glass. "And probably *not* my *tante,* but who could predict her vision, for God's sake! Maddy's really between the proverbial rock and a not-so-soft place," Clare said.

"I'll be as close as a phone call, babe, and I'll want to hear what Pa has to say, so call me tomorrow night, okay?"

Maddy called Francois's Fancy from the

airport just to be sure Jacques was alone. Paul had informed her that Kathleen would be at a Women's Club relief meeting to help flood victims, but Maddy wanted to be sure her father was alone. She let herself in the back door, calling as she entered the kitchen, "Hello, hello. It's me, Papa."

Placing a basket containing a big wedge of Sister Agatha's apple cake on the kitchen table, Maddy jumped at Jacques's "Hello."

He entered the kitchen holding Julie's painting in his hands.

Maddy turned and scowled, moving a step back. She was as puzzled as when she first stared at the painting on her return to Francois's Fancy. "I was just coming in to the study to find you. Why do you have Mom's —"

"Let's sit at the table here, Madelaine, and I'll try to explain."

Jacques sat across from Maddy, placing the painting on the table between them. "The night that the storm raged, I had trouble sleeping. Near dawn, I came down to the kitchen, thinking to warm some milk in the microwave and add a touch of brandy to help me sleep. As I stirred the drink I remembered how you brought ingredients to make your mother's toddy for me when I was feeling sick. I've missed you, Madelaine."

She smiled and reached out to squeeze his hand.

"I guess the toddy and your kindness brought your mother to my mind. I closed my eyes and I could see her behind my closed eyelids. I had the strangest feeling of Julie's presence in the room — a very strong presence. It was as though she took my hand and pulled me out of the kitchen. I found myself in the studio, standing in front of this." He placed a hand gently on the painting. "The only light in the room was a halo of radiance surrounding this painting. Of course I know my way around this house in the dark, so I backed up and sat on your mother's painting stool, drinking my hot milk." Jacques propped the painting upright, gazing intently at it.

"Was this the night of the storm? The night of Patrick's accident?"

"Yes. Of course we had lost our power and there was no possibility of getting back into town with his damaged truck, so your friend Patrick was pretty upset. He couldn't reach his mother at home, and there was nothing to do but offer our hospitality. Eventually, I got him talking about his work and his Grandfather Donovan."

"The *seanchai?* He actually told you about his family?"

"Yes he did. That was wrong?"

"Oh, no. I'm just surprised."

Jacques shrugged his shoulders. "I told him about *your* grandfather. His storytelling, and how this house got its name, so I guess that prompted him. Kathleen tried to teach Rosemary to play chess, so the four of us were up quite late, but I finally insisted that they stay the night. Kathleen fixed the beds in your room and Paul's. I don't think any of us got much sleep."

"I didn't know they were here all night! Oh, Lord, Papa. If I'd only realized that before Patrick came to see me yesterday. He didn't say a word. I told him what happened to me and what I think about Mom's painting."

"And?"

Maddy pursed her lips and shook her head. "I don't think he believed me, but there's a *reason* for his doubting, and you don't know about that."

"Seems you are remiss, then. You haven't told me the significance of the painting, either."

Jacques reached across the table for her hand. "Remember when you were little, Madelaine? You would look for hidden images in a picture and see how many you could find in the pages of your *Jack and Jill* magazine? When you told me about Henriette leading you to your mother's painting, the curious child in me tried to find something in Julie's painting. Something hidden."

He tapped his finger on the frame and lifted one shoulder in a small shrug. "You wouldn't think that history and mysticism would be warring in my mind, but they are, apparently. I couldn't find anything remotely mysterious in the painting, and maybe it's because I didn't think I would."

"Do you believe *Tante*'s vision?"

He nodded his head. "Yes, but this business about Margaret's grandmother — Hetty you call her — leading you?"

"Yes, Hetty was Henriette, *Tante*'s grandmother. According to Aunt Margaret, the vision was about *mothers and hurting hearts* — especially my mother."

Jacques made a low sound in his throat and his eyes suddenly filled with tears. He paused, rubbing his hand over his eyes. "I saw her . . . your mother. Doc Halliday was there when I blacked out and fell. I could feel his hands on me and then I was floating, ever so slowly, down a long hall. The light grew dimmer and dimmer and suddenly Julie appeared in brilliant illumination at the end of a long tunnel-like hall."

Maddy swallowed and clutched her hands together under the table. "Maybe you were dreaming, Papa. I still ask myself if my journey in time could have been a dream."

"No. As much as I don't want to say it — frightening as it was — nevertheless, I believe I had a near-death experience."

A soft mewling sound escaped her lips, but Maddy straightened her shoulders and leaned into the table. She looked intently at the painting, touching the low white building with a fingertip as though it were a talisman. "Maybe Mom's presence was here for both of us, then."

Jacques cocked his head and raised an eyebrow. "What do you mean, Madelaine? What do you see that I don't understand?"

"The retreat house where Mom prayed with the nuns. This is it, right?" she asked, pointing to the building.

"Yes, that is where she taught art therapy to young unwed mothers."

"I think she wants me to go there."

"Go to La Madeleine sur la Mer? Why, whatever for?" The minute the words were out of his mouth he drew in his breath and paled.

Maddy fidgeted, struggling with her conscience, her mind racing. *The truth is out, anyway. The damage done. Maybe only good will come from it if Papa knows about Fiona.*

She reached to cover his hand with hers. "Not for me, Papa." Color pinked her cheeks. "I must go there to search for a lost person. A person who has broken her mother's heart and . . . Patrick's. It's his sister Fiona."

CHAPTER
TWENTY-TWO

The phone call to Paul was tense. Telling him about Jacques's near-death experience was one thing, but trying to get some direction from Paul about what to do next was another, Maddy explained to Clare late that night.

"I believe Papa Jacques *did* have a near-death experience," Clare said. "Yep. Lots of people have told similar stories. The thing that's hard to understand is how it all fits together with your time travel and why *you* are the one predestined to find Fiona."

"I'm not so sure it's me alone who's supposed to find her, but I did discover the clue."

"And you're convinced it's something the mothers are involved in — the dead mothers?"

Maddy nodded her head very slowly. "It was the oddest sensation, listening to Papa talk about my mom and how she led him to the studio, just like Hetty led me back to Francois's Fancy. It's kind of scary, you know."

"Did Paul see it that way? I mean, does he get the connection?"

"Paul always clams up when Mom is mentioned. I know he grieves for her still. He didn't come right out and say he understood, but I think he sees how mothers could be involved in this."

"Well, did he offer to help?"

"You heard him before he left, CeCe. He says it's my decision. *I* should take the next step concerning Patrick. I know he's annoyed with him. 'Can't understand why the guy doesn't jump right on this.' Those were his exact words when I told him about Patrick's reaction."

"Not everybody can follow the yellow brick road, babe. I'm not even sure what I should do, given that *Tante* is in this deeper than January's snow. My late shift ends Friday. What do you say we invite her for dinner Saturday? Things can't get much worse."

Tante Margaret sipped her tea. "My vision was clear, *ma chérie.* I heard about the fire and you had already told me about Fiona, so I was thinking about Patrick's poor *ma-*

man. When loved ones are sad, I feel their pain in my heart, eh. As it happens, so often when I think about a person, it summons their presence. Just so, the shadow of Mrs. Donovan appeared to me when I began to pray for her."

"But you have never even seen Mrs. Donovan," Maddy said.

"*Non,* not herself in person, like Clare saw her in the hospital bed. This is true. Patrick's *maman* was like a shadow . . . a spirit, Madelaine. We have faith even though we can't see, *oui?*"

Maddy nodded her head ruefully. "But, still —"

"Faith is the heart of what we hope for, Madelaine, the evidence of what we cannot see. I could feel Mrs. Donovan's sorrow and her suffering, and that is when the vision started."

Clare poured more tea into Margaret's cup. "Let me get this straight, *Tante,*" she said, cocking her head to gaze directly at her aunt. "You think your grandmother knew all about Fiona Donovan because she is a seer. You also think Maddy's mom Julie knows about it too, and she is sending messages through her painting. So, basically you are saying that mothers are forever."

"*Précisément,* Clare. *C'est bon.* Julie knows

about Patrick and she knows about Fiona, so she is trying to help. Madelaine's *maman* wants her to be happy."

"But the opposite has happened," Maddy said. "Because I told about Fiona, now Patrick is angry with me. The family disgrace was supposed to be confidential, so now he doesn't trust me. He doesn't believe me."

"The road we take on our journeys is not always straight, is not easy to follow. Have patience, *ma petite.* There are ways. Your Patrick will come around."

Houses near the river were beginning to dry out and clean up from the muddy water. Sump pumps were a valuable commodity. County trucks were removing downed tree limbs and debris from the streets, and things were slowly getting back to normal in Biddeford. Saint David's School reopened and Maddy scheduled play rehearsal for the eighth graders.

The play would open on "Old and New Night," close to Halloween. *Daylight saving time is ending soon,* she thought. "Fall back, spring forward." The adage repeated in her mind. Fall back. Double entendre? She wished she could fall back to before the hurricane. She wished she had never fallen back in time.

Rehearsal went smoothly for most of the students, except for Rosemary Donovan. She lingered after the other cast members left. "Can I stay to go over my lines, Miss Fontaine? Would you hear them for me? I'm pretty sure Paddy will wait."

Maddy's lips twitched when she heard Patrick's nickname. Rosie had first introduced him as "Paddy," and he had quickly corrected her. *I wonder if she's trying to get us together?*

"Okay, Rosie, but only for about ten minutes. It's getting dark early now and the streets are still pretty littered from the storm. I'll hear your lines at the beginning of scene two. That's where you need prompting."

"I know I shouldn't use it as an excuse, Miss Fontaine, but my mother hasn't had time to help me since the fire."

"I understand. Sorry I haven't asked before. How is your mother? Is she home from the hospital?"

"Oh, yes. Our neighbors have been real good to us. Mum's breathing is okay now, but the doctors are watching her blood pressure. My brother says she has a problem and I shouldn't stress her out."

"That's good advice. Help her as much as you can, Rosie. There's a special closeness with moms that can't be replaced. I know that all too well."

Rosemary pursed her lips and nodded her head, a faint blush creeping up her neck. "But you still have your dad, Miss Fontaine, and he's the kindest, gentlest man I ever met."

Maddy smiled broadly, nodding her head. "That he is," she said, "Now, come on, Rosemary, let's get started. Go ahead with your opening lines from center stage. Try to feel the sadness of the whalers lost at sea."

Rosemary faltered a few times, needing prompting as the minutes flew by. *Why isn't Patrick coming in after her? It's got to be me. He doesn't want to see me.* The playbook swam before her eyes. She snapped it shut. *If I stay here one more minute I'm going to lose it.* She grabbed their coats from the props closet.

"Time to call it quits, Rosemary. Come get your jacket and we'll walk outside to see if your brother's here."

The shadows were growing thick in the twilight, but there was no mistaking the big silver GMC truck idling next to Maddy's car; the only two vehicles left in the school parking lot.

Rosie's face beamed. "Heh, Paddy's got his truck back. Must be all fixed." She ran around to the passenger side, calling out as she jerked the door open, "Thanks, Miss Fontaine. I'll do better next week."

Maddy hesitated beside the truck. She glanced at Patrick's face, the taut lines of his profile. He looked her way and she saw the determined set of his jaw, the icy blue of his eyes.

"I'm sorry Rosemary's a little late," Maddy said. "I guess we thought you would come inside for her, like you did before."

A muscle worked in his jaw. He cocked one eyebrow. "Like before?" Maddy looked away from his riveting eyes.

"Why *didn't* you come inside for me, Paddy?" Rosemary asked as she fastened her seat belt inside the cab.

"Things change," he snarled, putting the truck in gear. The roar of the engine echoed in the gloom of the empty parking lot, sending shivers down Maddy's spine.

Maddy sat at the small kitchen table, trying to edit poems submitted for the student readings. *Only correct the spelling — keep the images they created just as they are.*

Her mind kept drifting, replaying other images . . . the fierce pain in her head as

246

she lay on the mill floor, unable to move. The vibration had to be from real machinery. It still thrummed in her head. She closed her eyes, running her fingers over the tender spot behind her ear. She could feel the jouncing of the wagon ride from the old mill to the boarding house, the lumpy old bed, the cold chamber pot. She could almost feel the fear that gripped her heart when she peered at the shell of Francois's Fancy.

Stepping through time! Oh God. Shivers raced down her spine. She looked upward. Patrick's eyes blazed at her. *What can I do? How can I convince him that what happened to me has to have meaning, has to have a solution?* She held her chin in her hands, staring into space. Giving up was not an option. All thought stopped at the soft clicking of the door opening and closing.

"Jeez, Mad. You're still up?" Clare said. "Here I'm trying to be real quiet, thinking you must be in bed already."

Maddy shuffled papers and picked up her pencil. "Couldn't sleep, so I'm trying to catch up on the kids' poems for the show. Invitations went home with the students yesterday, and there's only ten days to get this program shaped up. When next week ends, everything has to be all set for dress rehearsal."

"Well, I'll be glad when *this* week ends and the night shift is over. Driving home from the hospital this close to midnight didn't used to bother me, but they haven't cleared all the debris and it's a little wild out there." She looked over Maddy's shoulder at the papers. "Any real talent there?"

"Oh, yeah. Unbelievable. Since the play is about last century whaling days off Biddeford Pool, several of the kids were inspired by early American poets and fashioned their poems in that style. Listen to this one. It's called *Dark and Deep.*

" 'My thoughts drift on an ebbing tide
Out to dark and deep,
In and out of mind they go,
Robbing me of sleep.
Wild as spindrift, crashing waves,
Fathoms dark and deep,
Surging ever seaward,
No mooring will they keep.'

"Who does that remind you of?"

"Are you kidding? You're the teach' here, Mad. I don't know one poet from another, but I think maybe this kid's got something here."

"I know. She's the shyest girl in my class,

and she says she was inspired by Emily Dickinson's poem 'Mystic Mooring.' I've got some Thoreaus, Longfellows and Emersons in this class too. We just finished a unit on early-American poets, and the class talent is unbelievable. I finally had to let everyone vote on the best ones to be read at Old and New Night."

"Tell me no more, babe. I'm gonna be there for you on the big night, but this non-poet has got to get some shut-eye. One last thing before I crash — any word from Patrick?"

Maddy shook her head, put her pencil down and started to pick up the paperwork. "I saw him in his truck after play rehearsal, but all I got from him was a steely look."

"Well if you ask me, he's acting like a stubborn jackass. If I had any of my ancestor shaman's genes I'd sure as hell put a curse on him."

CHAPTER
TWENTY-THREE

The broad strokes of a carefully lettered address puzzled Jacques until he turned the envelope over. Rosie Donovan 12 Bradbury Street Biddeford was crammed together on the flap. He smiled as he tore it open and unfolded two sheets of paper. The top page was a short note from Rosemary, thanking him and Mrs. Fontaine for their "hospitalitee" on the night of the storm. It was sincere and sweet. The page ended with an arrow drawn toward page two with the notation, "I hope you will come."

The second page, on Saint David's School letterhead was a printed invitation to parents from Miss Madelaine Fontaine's Eighth Grade Class:

Please come to Old and New Night
"Winter Harbor" — a One Act play
enacted by
Saint David's Eighth Grade Class

Followed by
Original Readings from Class Poets
October 21st at seven p.m.
Refreshments

"Hmm," Jacques murmured, reading the thank-you note again. "This sounds like an evening I can't miss."

"Are you telling me he hasn't made a move in ten days?"

"Yes, Paul. I keep telling myself to deal with it, but I'm not doing so well. It isn't making me feel better to admit it, either. You called to wish me luck tomorrow and I thank you, but I don't want to think or talk about Patrick Donovan right now."

"Chill out, Mad. Sorry I brought the guy up. You're gonna be fine. You know what you have to do, and you *will* do it. Stay cool and focus on the kids. Everything else will fall into place. I'll be thinking of you at this end, and you'll have Clare and Auntie Mame and Dad there pulling for you —"

"Dad? I didn't tell him about the program."

"But your little star Rosie did. When I called Pa he told me about a thank-you note she sent him with an invitation. Ride with it, babe. Remember, I told you Pa is your biggest supporter. Everything's gonna be fine."

Maddy had a good view of the auditorium's first section from the stage curtains. Jacques was leaning across Clare talking to *Tante* Margaret in third row center left. At fourth row center right she could see the Donovan family, Patrick wedged between his mother and twin sisters. His black curly head was bent over a program that his mother was reading. She watched Patrick flash a dimpled smile when his mom pointed to the program. Her stomach did a flip-flop.

She looked at her watch. Time for the cue. Maddy nodded to the student announcer and the gangly teenaged boy parted the curtain and stepped on stage as the lights dimmed.

The thespians performed without a blunder. No one missed a line, and Rosemary's solo rang out sweet and clear at the end of the one-act play. Applause was hearty as the cast took their bows and the curtains closed. When Maddy stepped through the center curtain, a hush came over the audience. She introduced four students selected by their peers to read their original works of poetry. The audience seemed awestruck and clapped loudly as each in turn read his or her poem.

As the last student left the stage, Maddy came forward, her self-admonishment ringing in her ears: "Look to the very last row and project your voice." She didn't want to look at the first four rows, anyway.

"I am so proud of my class tonight, and thankful that all of you are here. Every student took part in some way — actors, readers, props, lighting, and refreshments. From their studies they have brought you a vision of the past and provided a contrast of talent that will take each of them into the future. I hope you will join us in the cafeteria to congratulate them, but before you do I would like to close our program with an appropriate quote from the present.

"A book by Joan Anderson concludes with 'Life Lines' from Joan Erickson's 'Unconventional Wisdom.' " Maddy paused and dared to look for her father's face . . . for courage.

"This Life Line is called *Dance Beyond the Breakers.*

" 'Having direction and going after something — going after something which gives you purpose, is the way — otherwise your life becomes avoiding trouble, and there is no strength in that.' My wish for my students is that they will all *dance beyond the breakers,* and that you, their parents and friends, will do everything to encourage them."

The applause was long and loud as students came from the wings and the auditorium to stand together on stage with Maddy for a final curtain call.

Maddy shored up her pent-up anxiety and moved slowly through the crowd, shaking hands with parents and relatives. They milled around cafeteria tables set with cups and jugs of cider and plates of doughnuts. She could hear *Tante* Margaret's voice somewhere, but couldn't see her father or Clare. Maddy turned at a tap on her shoulder and looked into Rosemary's smiling eyes.

"Miss Fontaine, I'd like you to meet my mum." Mrs. Donovan stepped forward from between her twin daughters and clasped Maddy's hand. "I'm Eileen Donovan, and happy to meet you at last. Rosemary has been praisin' you to the skies. It's small wonder that your class performed so well tonight. You are a fine teacher and a delight to the eye, to be sure."

Maddy felt her cheeks flush. "Thank you, Mrs. Donovan, but the students deserve all the praise. Rosie has a sweet singing voice. She was a natural for the part."

One of the twins poked her head forward. "Rosie gets that from my brother. He's the best tenor you'll ever hear, except for my grandpa, and he's dead."

Mrs. Donovan closed her eyes for a second, lips twitching to hide a smile. "Moira Donovan, Patrick will be after you for bragging on him like that. Best you sit down and pour some cider for us all. Carefully, please, while Rosemary takes me to Miss Fontaine's father." She patted Maddy's shoulder. "I'd like to thank your dad for his kindness to Paddy and Rosemary during the storm. Come along, Rosemary, and help me find him."

"But Mum, I already wrote him a thank you," Rosie said.

"I know, love, but twice thanked is twice blessed." She took Rosie's arm and steered her toward the other side of the cafeteria.

Maddy worked the room for the next ten minutes, trying to give her attention to parents, all the while dreading a face-to-face with Patrick. She was looking for her father when CeCe came barreling toward her.

Clare rolled her eyes, shifted her head in a beckoning gesture and pushed in the door of the restroom. Maddy reluctantly followed her inside.

"Clare, I need to be out there meeting parents. Mrs. Donovan went to find my dad and I really should be there."

"I know, but you're gonna want to hear this before you get to Papa Jacques. Patrick's mother found him *after* the fireworks, thank God."

"What do you mean?"

"*Tante* pulled off another of her zingers."

"What?"

"Your dad found Patrick as soon as we got into the cafeteria. When he started to introduce *Tante* and me, Patrick told him we'd already met. Then your dad told him that he and *Tante* Margaret go way back. He praised her for helping his family in many times of crisis. He brought up your mother as an example."

"My mother?"

"Yes. 'Course, that was all *Tante* needed to light her fire. She reminded Patrick about the dinner at our apartment when she first met him. She repeated her story about her Indian ancestors and then led right into the vision."

"Oh, God. She actually talked about the vision?"

"Not only talked about it, but talked about you and the courageous thing you did. She told Patrick that his reaction was mocking the truth of the situation. 'Pride is a painful thing,' she said. You know *Tante* — blunt but sweet at the same time. She kissed his cheek and said '*Laissé allez*, Patrick.' He just stared at her without a word. I doubt he knows that means 'Let go,' but I think he got the message. Your father tried to smooth things over, but Patrick was so intense. I left, because just then Mrs. Donovan appeared with Rosie."

Maddy shuddered. "Holy Mother. I better get out there."

In the five minutes that Clare had taken to explain things, the room was clearing. Parents and students were leaving. Maddy stopped at tables to thank them for coming. From the corner of her eye she could see Patrick moving toward her. Striding past the table where his sisters sat, he carried himself with a confidence that was compelling.

She squared her shoulders. *I'm not going to let him spoil this night.*

He placed his hand under her elbow and drew her to the empty food station that lined one side of the room. Maddy smiled at him, furtively. He did not smile back. He took her hand and shook it. To all appearances he was congratulating her, but suddenly he turned his back to the room, pulling her around with him. He wrapped his fingers around their clasped hands. She looked down at the scar, then up into his eyes, nearly losing her resolve when he met her gaze so intently, his blue eyes soft with worry.

"Madelaine?" He swallowed and hesitated.

Her knees felt rubbery. She opened her mouth and took a steadying breath. "I'm sorry about *Tante* Margaret. Clare said she —"

"Don't be sorry. Clare's aunt is one hell of a woman. I swear, she could talk a beggar out of his tin cup." His head shook briefly. "But I needed to hear what she said. When I listened to you up on that stage, Madelaine, I knew I was wrong. I was a fool to let pride come between us, and Margaret just convinced me of that. Can you forgive me?"

Thunderstruck at his words, she opened her mouth and closed it, unable to speak for the knot in her throat. Slowly, she nodded, her eyes brimming with tears. For the space of a heartbeat they stood in silence. She pulled her hand slowly away, wanting to throw her arms around him. Instead she dabbed tears away with the knuckle of her closed forefinger, then gestured over her shoulder, pointing toward the room. "Students are clearing the tables. I should be helping now."

He nodded, a smile dimpling his cheeks. "You did yourself proud tonight, Miss Fontaine."

"In a way, I'm glad Kathleen couldn't come for the program tonight," Jacques said. Maddy gave her father a puzzled look. He had lingered to help her pack things for the car after everyone else had left. "It would have been awkward for me to find a moment to tell you what I've been thinking if Kathleen were here."

He took her hands in his. "Your mother would be so pleased with what you did here tonight; would be so proud of you, Maddy, just as I am. The 'Life Line' quote you gave at the end was just the sentiment Julie would have chosen."

She reached up to hug him. "Thanks, Papa. I needed that. I'm sorry I didn't invite you in the first place, but I was afraid things wouldn't turn out right. I'm glad you were here, though, and I'll bet you're as impressed with my students as I am."

"Indeed I am. Your young poets certainly were inspired to write some beautiful lines." Jacques pulled a small book from his coat pocket. "When I saw your invitation, I decided to bring this along. This was your mother's little pocket Bible. I found it amongst Julie's things after she . . . left us. It has a scrap of paper inside with a quote from a poet named Maya Angelou. I memorized those lines that have special meaning." Their eyes met. "I think she would want you to have it."

He pressed the Bible into Maddy's hands, his gaze never wavering from her eyes. " 'They are not dead in the lives they leave behind — in those whom they have blessed, they live again.' We are blessed, my dear, you and I."

CHAPTER
TWENTY-FOUR

"Yes! Yes!" Clare punctuated each word with a fist jabbed into the air, her PJs swaying with her hips.

"Hold on. Patrick only said he's sorry. Not much more than that."

Clare sat on the edge of Maddy's bed. "I swear, that guy must have had a ton of stuff bottled up inside, but at least now you can feel better about the whole idea of finding Fiona, and it sounds like he might come around too. *Tante* thinks Mrs. Donovan welcomes the idea."

"Whatever makes her think that? She's only just met the woman and —"

"I told you. *Tante* immerses herself into situations. According to your dad, she talked to Patrick's mom real serious-like all the while he was congratulating Rosie and meeting one of her classmates. You know, the one who read the poem 'Dark and Deep.' "

"What did she say to her? I mean *Tante.* What did she say to Mrs. Donovan?"

"God knows what she said to her, but she told *me* on the way home that she plans to go to Star of the Sea Center tomorrow to see if Sister Agatha has any connections with the nuns at La Madeleine."

Maddy held her head in her hands, shaking it. "I already have a connection. My mom taught at La Madeleine."

"I know, but these religious congregations sometimes have spiritual links from one order to another. La Madeleine sur la Mer is not that far down the coast, and miles are short when God's fingers do the walking. Besides, no one knows better than you how influential my *tante* can be."

Maddy sank back against the pillows on her bed. An audible moan escaped her lips. "Sorry, CeCe, but it's been a long day. I'll wait till you get back to your room before I turn out the light, but I have to close my eyes."

"Me, too. I'm on seven to three tomorrow." She jumped up and tweaked Maddy's toes. "Ya done good, Miss Fontaine. Sleep tight."

It *was* good, she thought as she snuggled under the covers. She'd been blessed. The play, the poems. Mom's book of poetry from Papa. Even *Tante*'s lecture to Patrick. His softly shining blue eyes were the last image behind her eyelids before sleep came.

Maddy awoke to a bell ringing and reached for the alarm clock before her senses kicked in. She opened her eyes and stopped fumbling with the small clock. No alarm on Saturday. *It has to be the telephone.* She climbed out of bed and headed for the kitchen, but by the time she reached the phone, the answering machine had picked up.

"Patrick, here, Madelaine. If you're up and haven't had breakfast, come to the shop. There's tea brewin'."

She shook her head, hardly believing her ears. Looking upward, she clasped her hands together under her chin. "You're working miracles again, Lord."

The kitchen clock read eight-thirty. She played the message back, smiled and slowed her steps toward the bedroom. *I should take my time,* she thought.

Forty-five minutes later the bell on the shop door jangled as Maddy opened and closed it. The buzz of a band saw whined to a stop at the same time. She walked slowly toward the entrance to the back room, thoughts tumbling in her mind. *This is like stepping back to September. Everything looks the same. The same smell of oil, turpentine and milled wood.*

Patrick appeared in the open doorway. "Aye, and you must have smelled me mother's scones. Cinnamon and raisin." His lips twitched while he gestured with an open palm and nodded his head. "Top of the mornin', Madelaine."

She strode quickly to him and put her hand in his. "Good morning to you . . . *Paddy.*"

"Uh-oh. Rosemary again, is it?"

"Actually, your mother slipped a 'Paddy' in last night when one of the twins bragged about you."

"The twins bragged about me? They're usually bustin' my chops."

"Well, this twin said you had the best tenor voice that ever was, excepting your grandfather."

Patrick hooted loudly and took her arm to walk quickly to the back of the shop. "That had to be Moira. She's tone deaf." They were both laughing when they reached the Hoosier cabinet on the back wall. "If you would pour the tea, Miss Madelaine, I'll be right back."

Patrick retreated to his workbench while Maddy poured tea and brought cups and a plate of scones to a small bench in front of the sofa. As soon as she sat down, Patrick was in front of her, placing a brown paper-wrapped object in her lap.

She stared at it, puzzled. "For me?" she asked.

"I'm not much at wrapping, but I hope you like what's inside." He nudged her arm as he sat beside her. "Open it."

She pulled off the paper and her mouth made a big O as she drew in her breath. She pressed her fingers over the French-polished top of a beautifully grained wooden box and raised a small brass hasp opening its lid on scrolled brass hinges.

"I lined the inside with cedar. I thought you'd like that."

"Like it? I love it. It's beautiful, but why . . . when —"

His face flushed as he reached for his tea. "Have a scone, Maddy, and I'll explain. I started making the box for you before the hurricane. Actually, right after that dinner at your apartment. I planned it to be a kind of letter box for your desk or dresser." He shrugged his shoulders. "I was going to put an invitation inside to come to my shop with your class and send the box to you as a surprise. Not to worry, though, the invitation *will* come."

"Oh," she said, gulping her tea, swallowing her surprise. Uneasy with what she thought might be coming next, she took a big bite of the scone.

"I didn't tell you some of the bad stuff that happened after Fiona left, but now I want you to understand."

Maddy, sensing his seriousness, nodded her head and folded her hands on top of her gift.

"When my father called a halt to the search for Fiona he became a very bitter man. He had that old-world philosophy, 'You make your bed, you sleep in it.' I told you he drank real hard after Fiona disappeared."

Maddy nodded while Patrick drained his tea. He splayed his hands on his jeans, rubbing his fingers up and down from knee to thigh. "I was still checking out leads on the sly, you know, tryin' to find her. Well, one night Pa carried on something fierce. Ranting and raving about Fiona. He pounded the table and pointed a finger at me.

" 'No fornicating female's comin' back to this house, ever! Brat or no,' he said. 'So quit lookin'.' That hurt my mum real bad, and I promised her that same night that I wouldn't look for Fiona, but if she ever did turn up I'd see to it that she was taken care

266

of. I promised her I'd never be like my father. A week later, Pa died."

He rubbed his hands over his face, his fingertips pressing his temples. "When you told me about the clue you discovered, it brought it all back to me. I didn't want to hear about Fiona. I *was* being like him, and I blamed it on you. Call it fear, pride or stupidity. Clare's aunt pegged it right. I wasn't facing the truth. Thank God Margaret set me straight last night."

Maddy reached to put her hands on his shoulders. "Patrick." She said his name softly as a whisper. "You've had far too much on your plate since your father's death. It's no wonder you reacted as you did." She looked furtively into his eyes. "New beginnings, okay? I'd like to think we can work this out for your mother's sake, and for Fiona. Do you think we can do that? Together?"

He drew her close and her arms wrapped around his neck. His warm, soft lips covered hers, kissing her with infinite tenderness. When he pulled back, he looked deeply into her eyes. "We can try, Madelaine, *a gra.*"

She cocked her head, brow furrowed in a puzzled frown.

He smiled and kissed the tip of her nose. "Gaelic for . . . my love."

CHAPTER
TWENTY-FIVE

Maddy's desk was piled with papers. They were student letters written by imaginary Biddeford residents to relatives abroad. The assignment was to write about their lives working in early nineteenth-century Biddeford mills.

The class had spent a week researching the cotton mills. Their letters described their jobs working at mill looms taller than some of the children who worked alongside them. They told about eleven-hour days working in the picker house, cloth and cotton house, and the counting house of the tall brick factories.

Maddy stuffed them into her briefcase and opened her letter box, releasing a clean cedar fragrance into the stuffy classroom. She lifted a folded letter from the box, held it to her nose and breathed in. Patrick had sent the invitation to school with Rosemary at the beginning of the week.

Patrick Donovan, Cabinetmaker, invites your class to tour his shop as well as two other artisans' micro-enterprises at Biddeford Complex.

Maddy smiled at the word *micro-enterprises*. Perfect choice to emphasize possibilities to her students.

Patrick had arranged with a potter and a candle maker's shop, all set for tours at twelve-thirty tomorrow afternoon. She put the invitation back into the box and glided her fingertips across the satiny smooth lid.

Patrick stood before the group of twenty-six students. "Carding, spinning, weaving — spindles and looms. That's what occupied the huge space of these buildings, guys. These shops produced cloth for one of the most successful companies in the textile industry." He swept his arm in an arc. "As you can see, partitions and new walls have provided craftsmen like me and the owners of two other shops you will tour the space we need to carry on new business for a new century."

Patrick's presence commanded the rapt attention of the students as he guided them through his back room. *He sounds so professional,* she thought. She followed the group around the back room, hearing scraps of words he'd said at her first shop visit: "Skilled fingers and sensitive eyes are the tools . . . an intimate relationship with the wood." She pressed her fingers to her lips, thinking of a different relationship. She thought of his tender kisses, the way he said her name, *Madelaine, a gra.* She *wanted* to be his love.

Patrick demonstrated the band saw, expressing the reason for caution, eliciting oohs and aahs when he showed the students his left hand, injured when he was about their age. He identified all the finishing tools and explained the cabinetmaker's process from drafting design to finished order, illustrating with his current work in progress. A surprise came at the end of the tour when he asked Rosemary to distribute a balsawood bookmark he'd created for each student.

Maddy came forward, smiling. "I think everyone has a better understanding of creative enterprise, Mr. Donovan," she said. "We thank you for your time and talent. Your shop is a great reuse of the city's historic mill buildings, and a fascinating look at an age-old craft. Wait outside at the dooryard please, class, but before you leave, put your hands together for Mr. Donovan."

He caught her arm as the students started filing out the door. "What do you really think, Miss Fontaine?" he asked in a low voice.

"I think they were very impressed." She turned her back on the door and whispered, "Almost as much as I was." An impish look crossed her face. "May I return the favor, somehow?"

Patrick's lips curled in a grin. "Most certainly, Miss Fontaine. I'll pick you up at seven."

Two messages were on the answering machine at the apartment when Maddy came home from school. One was from Paul, wanting to know all about Old and New Night. The other was Clare. True to her word, *Tante* Margaret had visited the nuns at Star of the Sea Center. The good sisters had offered little hope, but did promise to call ahead to La Madeleine sur la Mer, explaining the bare bones of the situation, should Madelaine come there to make an inquiry.

"I won't be home till later," Clare said. "I'm taking *Tante* to a church supper after work. You can make do with a frozen TV dinner for supper, babe, see ya."

Maddy dropped the briefcase of school

papers she had brought home, and pushed aside a stack of magazines and books left on the sofa. No way could she think of eating a TV dinner, or correcting papers, or phoning Paul. Her mind was awhirl with thoughts about La Madeleine and Patrick. She leaned back against the pillows and closed her eyes.

She pictured him at his shop, carrying himself with easy confidence, saying all the right things as he led the kids around. *He's comfortable there; it's his bailiwick. He can be direct and authoritative, even smooth in that setting. It's like he has two sides. Will it always be that way? Today was definitely his macho side.*

She recalled standing in his arms the morning after Old and New Night. That was Patrick's tender side. A soft, vulnerable side. Which side would he show if he came with her to talk to the nuns? Would he even come?

He was everything she wanted, but there was so much in the way. She thought about other men, guys she'd dated in college . . . then, Claude. The longest relationship she had ever had, Claude was steady and convenient, but there was no spark, no desire, no longing for what could be. She was close to dozing off when the phone rang.

No mistaking his deep baritone. He never

said hello — just ran down the bones of his message. "Just had a thought, Miss Madelaine. I'm begging off from my mom's supper tonight. Don't really like liver and onions, so if you haven't eaten, maybe you'd like to come out for a fish fry at Eddie's Drive-In?"

"Er, uh, no, I haven't eaten and yes, I love fish fry."

"I'll be there in twenty minutes."

Maddy checked her watch. Five o'clock. She flew to her room, made a quick change into comfortable jeans and pawed through her sweater drawer. The butter-soft yellow turtleneck sweater. Good, she thought, as she tied her hair back with a bright orange scarf. She looked in the mirror. The scarf's folds touched her glossy hair like tongues of flame settling across her shoulders.

True to his word, Patrick rang the bell at five-twenty. She grabbed a jacket and answered the door.

He looked her up and down, obviously surprised. "Holy God," he said. "I left some students with their teacher this afternoon and here I see a beautiful woman. Have I got the right address?" he asked, cocking his head with an expression of mock confusion.

Maddy jabbed his shoulder with her fist.

"Stop with the blarney, Paddy Donovan. Let's go. I'm starved."

The silver truck eased in and out of Eddy's Drive-In. Maddy juggled a cardboard tray of cold drinks, and two bags containing fish and chips. Patrick drove to Riverside Park and pulled into the empty end of the riverside lot.

A waning moon was rising low in the sky, giving scant silver light to ripples on the river. "It's peaceful here," he said, opening the bags and spreading paper napkins across their laps, "but fog's blowing in. Can you see to eat okay, or should I put the cab light on?"

"No, I can see okay," Maddy said, widening her eyes at Patrick with a smile. "I have cat's eyes, so they say. I do have something I want to ask you about, but it can wait. I'm really hungry." She took a big bite of the fish. They ate in silence, devouring everything in short time.

Patrick stuffed the trash into one bag, stashing it on the floor by his feet. "Later," he said. He grasped her right shoulder, turning her to face him. He brushed a thumb along the orange silk scarf, tracing slowly down to her earlobe and the neck of her sweater, finally closing his fingers on her other shoulder. "Nice colors. You look like a beautiful butterfly, Madelaine."

Pulling her toward him, he pressed a kiss tenderly on each eyelid, the tip of her nose and point of her chin. He angled his mouth to fit and covered her lips with his.

As the kiss deepened, a distinct thudding in her temples and a heated surge took over Maddy's body. She felt that resistance rise that was always present before, but she pushed it back and, for seconds, let desire take over.

Patrick's fingers caressed the curve of her ear, trailed down over the soft turtleneck sweater and gently covered her breast.

Trembling, Maddy suddenly broke away. "Patrick, I can't —"

A thread of moonlight through the windshield revealed her flushed face. Patrick looked closely at her. "Are you okay?"

"Well, not really, I uh, feel, uh . . ." She looked up at him, then quickly down at her lap.

Patrick turned the key in the ignition and pushed a button to roll down the window. "Maybe some air?"

She shivered with the dampness of the river fog and he put his arm protectively around her, gently pressing her head in the hollow of his shoulder.

It was easier to speak if she wasn't looking

into eyes. "When you kiss me like that, my mind gets all crazy. I can't think straight. I can only think of how you make me feel."

He tilted her chin up with one finger, forcing her to look at him. "How *do* I make you feel?"

Maddy swallowed a lump in her throat. "It's hard to talk about, Patrick, and maybe too soon?"

He was silent, all the while watching her eyes. "I hear you, Madelaine, but your feelings can't be unique with me." He brushed a tendril of hair away from her face with the back of his hand. "You've had them before, right?" His voice was husky. "What about this guy, Claude, you told me about? Didn't you —"

She shuddered in his arms, stared at the cleft in his chin. "No, no. I've always thought that when it happened it would have to be with the one I love. I've never . . . wanted . . . anyone to make love to me until you —"

It hit him like a thunderbolt. "Sweet Jesus. I didn't . . . I mean I wouldn't — Oh, Madelaine." Pulling her close, he pressed his cheek to hers, his voice rasping in her ear. "God knows I do want you, Madelaine."

Breathless seconds passed. He reached for

her hand. "But I made a promise to you and I'll keep it. We *will* take it slow from now on."

She could feel his heart thudding, his breath warm on her neck, but it was okay now. She felt safe now, in his arms.

Time seemed to stand still for several glorious moments. It was too soon to tell him she loved him, but she was glad she'd told him her feelings. She was glad he remembered his promise. His arms holding her quietly gave her reassurance. He wouldn't push.

Suddenly, Patrick held her at arm's length, his back ramrod straight. He fixed her with a cobalt-blue stare. His shoulders heaved when he drew in a breath, and his lips twitched with the hint of a smile.

"Now, what was it you wanted to ask me, Madelaine, *a gra?*"

Startled, her eyes went wide. Her lips curved into a smile that wavered around the edges. "I wanted to ask if you would go with me to Madeleine sur la Mer."

CHAPTER
TWENTY-SIX

Maddy was surprised and excited when Patrick agreed to go after only a little hesitancy. He balked at not taking his truck, but since she planned to go on Veteran's Day and he wasn't going to be working, he agreed to go in Maddy's car. As long as he could drive.

Maddy was determined to leave on the morning of November eleventh, the first school holiday since the storm. Her father had written a letter to Mother Superior at La Madeleine. Maddy didn't ask what the note said, but she was grateful that it was one more link, counting the call Sister Agatha made on her behalf.

These were all good signs, she thought, as they drove down the shore road. She closed her fingers around her locket as they approached the tree-lined driveway to the seaside hospice.

It was just as her mother had painted it,

situated on a spit of land jutting into the sea. La Madeleine sur la Mer. They drove into a parking area at the broad end of the property. An iron gate enclosed a small garden beside a shell path. The long, low building, shaped like a cross, faced the sea. Much like Francois's Fancy, a vast expanse of dunes and rocks fronted it. Maddy couldn't see the stone Stations of the Cross, but she felt sure they were there, at the other end of the building.

Getting out of Maddy's two-door Honda, Patrick stretched his long legs and eased his shoulders. "This isn't exactly my style car, Madelaine. I don't mind driving, but I still don't understand why we couldn't use the truck."

"Well, I couldn't resist when my dad offered this car to me last fall. It was my mom's car. Bringing it here is like . . . like she's with me in spirit."

He took her hand and they walked slowly along the shell path circling the small garden. Burlap shrouded the rosebushes against the winter winds, but as they got closer to the entrance of the house, she could see the Stations of the Cross marching like stark gray sentinels across the brown grass bordering the house.

She glanced at Patrick. His face was a

study in concentration, eyes darting from the house to the sea. *Dear God, let this be the right place.*

Seconds after they rang the bell, a nun opened the door. She was as broad as she was tall and if it weren't for the big rosary beads corded around the waist of her long brown jumper, she could have been mistaken for one of the girls sheltered in this place. She wore sandals, no veil, and her short brown hair framed a wide-eyed, unlined, plain face.

"Bonjour," she said, nodding and gesturing for them to enter. They stepped into a small vestibule with doors on three sides. Statues of Jesus and Saint Mary Magdalene looked down from niches on either side of a center door. The sister paused silently in front of the center door, hands folded, staring momentarily at Patrick.

"I am Sister Clare Etienne, Portress here at La Madeleine," she said, her French accent sounding very familiar.

"Bonjour, Sister. This is Patrick Donovan, and I am Madelaine Fontaine. I think we are expected."

"Oui, Miss Fontaine. Mother expects you, but she knows not about the gentleman. *Pardonnez-moi, un moment."* She opened the

door and ducked inside, closing it behind her.

Patrick rolled his eyes. "Shades of *Tante* Margaret. She may be named Clare, but *your* Clare, she definitely ain't." He shot a weak smile at Maddy, then glanced uneasily at the other doors. "Do they know why we're here?"

"I'm sure they do, but there is no way of knowing what Sister Agatha said when she called here, and I didn't ask Papa what he said in his letter to the Mother Superior. He didn't know you were coming with me. Don't worry. She'll see us."

Sister Clare appeared again as if on cue and nodded to them, extending her hand toward a narrow hall. There was an open door at the end of the hall and closed doors right and left. *"Après vous,"* she said, pointing ahead. "Reverend Mother will see you now." She followed until they reached the open door. *"Entrez-vous, s'il vous plaît,"* she said, but when Maddy turned to thank her, the Portress was already retreating down the hall, sandals flapping on the tile floor.

They entered a small, stark room. The only furnishings were a file cabinet, two chairs and a desk. A large crucifix hung on one wall, a *prie-dieu* beneath it. The Prioress sitting behind the desk was a much smaller version of the nun who had ushered them in, with one exception. She wore a brown veil covering her head, pulled taut around an unlined, beautiful face partially hidden behind old-fashioned reading glasses.

"Welcome to La Madeleine sur la Mer. I am Sister Mary Francis." She nodded to them, removed her glasses and laid them on her desk. Her deep-set dark eyes seemed to light up when she peered at Maddy. "You look very much like your mother, my dear," she said.

Maddy was not surprised at the nun's almost perfect English. Jacques had told her that the Prioress had studied in Paris and taught Latin and Greek at McGill University for many years before coming to La Madeleine.

Determined to speak up with words she had rehearsed in her mind, Maddy cleared her throat. "Thank you for seeing us, Reverend Mother. This is my friend Patrick. Perhaps my father explained in his letter that we are here to inquire about Patrick's sister."

"I did receive your father's letter, yes," the nun said. Her gaze flicked from Maddy to Patrick.

Maddy cleared her throat and shuffled her feet, mentally willing Patrick to speak, but he stood like a statue, a muscle twitching in his cheek. He was watching the nun's fingers moving absently back and forth over a folder lying on her desk.

Sister Mary Francis extended her hand, nodding to the chairs. "Please sit down."

They sat as one and Patrick spoke, at last, in a tight voice. "I'm inquiring if my sister came here . . . about a year ago? Fiona Donovan?"

The nun's mouth pursed, briefly. "Why have you waited this long to inquire, my son?"

Color crept up his neck. "My sister didn't wish to be found, and my father wouldn't allow us to search for her," he said.

"That is why our hospice records are generally sealed, you see," Sister said. "We respect our residents' requests for anonymity here."

Agonizing silence lay heavy in the stark room. Patrick glanced at Maddy, then lowered his eyes. No way would he try to explain what prompted this search.

"You do understand our purpose at La Madeleine?" the nun asked. She inclined her head at Patrick, but did not wait for an answer. "Our order is dedicated to honor Saint Mary Magdalene. I'm sure I need not remind you of Christ's forgiveness of our patron saint. We welcome unmarried pregnant women here to a forgiven life."

Patrick shifted on the chair. His eyes had gone the color of storm clouds and the muscle in his cheek was twitching again. Maddy started to place a reassuring hand on his arm, but withdrew it quickly when he straightened his shoulders, and thrust his determined chin forward.

"And did my sister have a child here, then?" he asked abruptly.

Reverend Mother replied with a hint of scold in her voice. "There are extraordinary circumstances in this case, and because of them I have sought God's will. Our sisters have prayed for Saint Magdalene's intercession."

Maddy chewed her lip. Clasping her hands tightly in her lap, she glanced at Patrick. He sat rigidly, staring straight at the nun. *Dear God,* she thought, *help him.*

"Because of certain circumstances, I am prepared to give you some information today."

Maddy closed her eyes with an audible sigh. *Papa must have really pleaded, or there is something that we don't know.*

The nun opened the folder on her desk and put her reading glasses on.

"Fiona came to us November 3, 2004. She

revealed very little of why or how she came to La Madeleine, only that she had worked as a waitress on the shore prior to her arrival. She did give her parents' names for our record, but requested that her residence here not be made known to them." She looked up from the folder. "You are the son of Daniel and Eileen Donovan?"

"Yes," Patrick replied without hesitation, his eyes focused on the folder. "Eileen is my mother, but Daniel is deceased. Fiona wouldn't be knowin' that when she came here, though."

To Maddy, Patrick's words sounded polite, but she could hear the steel in his voice.

The nun continued without pause. "Fiona's pregnancy was monitored by a doctor from Shore Memorial Hospital who volunteers his time here. Some of our sisters are trained nurses and some of our residents do give birth on the premises, but that was not the case with your sister." She looked up at Patrick momentarily, then her eyes went back to the folder. "In her eighth month, Fiona was taken to Shore Hospital with complications." Sister Mary Francis looked up again.

Patrick's face had gone white. "Can you tell us what was wrong?" Maddy asked.

"Simply put, bleeding of the placenta.

Sometimes it stops, but unfortunately, in Fiona's case it did not. Pre-term labor contractions began. The hospital informed us that a premature infant was delivered, but did not survive."

Maddy's fingers flew to her mouth. "Oh," she said at the same time that Patrick spoke.

"Fiona . . . is *she* all right? When did this happen?" His voice sounded cracked and hollow.

The Prioress looked at the folder and traced a line with her finger. "The hospital registered an infant male birth and death as April first of 2005." She paused and looked directly at Patrick as she closed the folder. For the first time, Maddy noticed sadness in the nun's eyes.

"Records forwarded to us show that Fiona was stable after birth, but she left the hospital the day *before* she was to be discharged. Your sister did not return to us at La Madeleine. I'm sorry to say that we have no further information concerning her whereabouts."

Patrick stood woodenly. It was obvious that he was shaken.

Reverend Mother came from behind her desk to stand between Patrick and Maddy. She stood less than five feet tall, but her presence seemed to fill the room. She nodded to Maddy. "We continue to pray for Fiona, as we do for all mothers."

She looked up at Patrick and raised a hand that didn't quite reach Patrick's shoulder. "Our Lord is merciful, my son. I ask his blessings and guidance for you both in your search for your sister. May the good Lord steady your heart and fill the empty spaces with patience and love. *Dieu vous bénisse.*"

Then the Prioress surprised Maddy with a hug. "Your mother would be proud of you, my dear. You have the same redeeming qualities as she. Will you come into the refectory for a cup of tea before you leave?"

Patrick's unease was clear. Maddy could see the hollow look on his face, and his expression troubled her. She started to explain their need to leave, but her words were suddenly drowned out by the sound of bells. The noon Angelus was ringing, calling the nuns to prayer.

The nun nodded and took Maddy's hands in hers. "I understand, my dear. *Allez avec Dieu.*"

Seizing the moment, Patrick bowed his head. "Thank you, Sister," he said. Taking Maddy's hand he turned away quickly, propelling her down the hall. His restless stride and tight grip gave Maddy little doubt how stressed he was. They passed through the vestibule and out the main door in less than a minute.

Outside, the sound of the bells was dimmed by screeching gulls and huge breakers crashing against the rocks. The tide was rolling in and the air was pungent with the smell of the sea.

Patrick stopped on the shell path and stared at the shore. Maddy edged closer to him, barely able to hear his strained voice.

"A few lines on paper. It's like the tide came in and erased all signs that she was ever here." She heard the catch in his voice. "I don't know what I thought we'd find, but, God Almighty, Madelaine. I didn't expect this."

She wrapped her arms around his waist and laid her head on his chest.

CHAPTER
TWENTY-SEVEN

Patrick drove the car like a robot, his face a stony mask. He had hardly spoken since they left Route 1 for the turnpike. There would be no leisurely drive on the scenic shore route. As far as he was concerned, there were no words left to convey either sorrow or hope. Sister Mary Francis had said them all.

Maddy went over and over the nun's information and Patrick's responses in her mind. "A few lines on paper . . ." Suddenly, the memory of the Prioress pointing at the infant death record was like someone pulling her by the arm. She drew in her breath and turned to him. "Patrick, I've just thought of something we're missing."

Without taking his eyes from the road, he shook his head. "I don't know what could be missing, except for Fiona," he said in a strained voice.

"The child's name. Aren't babies given a

name when they're born? If the hospital registered his death there has to be a record. And if we found the record —"

His knuckles were white on the steering wheel. "It died, Maddy. Do you think she would give it — him — a name?"

"I would. And I suspect Fiona would, too. She would want the baby to have a name, even if it could only be Donovan."

The brakes squealed as Patrick suddenly swerved and stopped in the parking lot of a rest area. "God, Madelaine, why didn't *I* think of that?" He shifted into park and slammed his fist on the steering wheel. "If it isn't Donovan, it could be the bastard that —"

The truth was sudden and startling. As sure as shifting winds predict a storm, Maddy knew that Patrick was not just looking for Fiona. There was no escaping the anger in the taut line of his jaw and the midnight blue of his eyes when he turned to face her.

"Finding Fiona hinges on that record. We have to get that record."

Maddy could hear the desperation in his voice. There was never a doubt that Patrick meant what he said. Tension jarred her thinking.

"Yes, well . . . Sister mentioned Shore

Hospital, and, umm . . . I guess you have to know the county. Death notices are recorded in the county, right?"

Her eyes sought his. Her gaze, meant to be heartening, was returned with a scowl. "Not today, Madelaine. It's a holiday. Veteran's Day, remember?"

She knew he was frustrated and probably didn't mean to sound flippant, but that *was* the way he sounded. She could hear Sister's words echoing in her brain: "May He fill the empty spaces in your heart with patience and love."

"We need to think about this, Patrick, and I don't think well on an empty stomach. In fact, I'm getting a headache, so could we please go back to my apartment and have some lunch?"

Patrick reached his arm to gather her to him and kissed her forehead. "No headaches allowed, *Macushla.* I'll have you home before one."

Maddy heaved a sigh of relief. *He's so quick to anger, but so tenderly forgiving.*

Maddy's cell phone rang just as they settled at the kitchen table to eat turkey sandwiches. She jumped up to retrieve her purse from the counter, clicking the phone open just in time.

"Hi." She squeezed Patrick's shoulder as she walked past the table, mouthing *It's Clare.* She checked her watch. "How come you're calling me from work. Is something wrong?"

Patrick watched as she sat down, leaned an elbow on the table and shaded her eyes with one hand.

"Well, yes, we did get some information, but we'll tell you about it when you get here, okay?" Maddy flipped the phone shut and slumped into her chair.

"Clare is actually on her way here, calling to see if we were home from La Madeleine. She's anxious to know what happened, but she called to warn me that she's coming home because she's got a sick headache and a queasy stomach."

Patrick had eaten half of his sandwich and pointed at Maddy's plate. "You better eat that so you'll know whether *your* headache is only because you're hungry. The twins were both sick yesterday, and my mum says there's a bug going around."

Maddy nodded her head and managed to eat half the sandwich before Clare shuffled through the doorway.

Patrick stood. "You're looking pale as this stuff," he said, draining a glass of milk. "Want some?"

"Ugh. No dairy products on an upset stomach, thanks, but I'll try some flat ginger ale if Maddy brings it in the living room."

Clare headed for the sofa. "I've got to put my head down on a pillow before it blasts right off my shoulders. You guys better sit on the other side of the room. I don't know how contagious I am."

Maddy brought a glass of soda, setting it down on the coffee table. Patrick followed her into the living room and sat in Maddy's rocking chair. Moving to the end of the sofa, Maddy removed Clare's shoes.

"Not good, huh, CeCe?"

"It was a long morning, babe, and it got worse."

"Sounds like ours," Patrick said.

"Oh, no. What did the good nuns say?"

Maddy looked at Patrick hesitantly. He nodded his head.

"It was only one. The Mother Superior, and she confirmed that Fiona was there," Maddy said.

"*Was* there. So what happened?"

"Fiona was sent to the hospital late in her pregnancy, and the baby was born prematurely." Maddy swallowed hard and shot another glance at Patrick. He was staring at the floor. "A baby boy. He died, and Fiona left the hospital before she could be discharged."

Silence hung there until Patrick abruptly stood. "End of story." He shot Maddy a wary look. "I think I better leave you guys now so CeCe can get some down time."

Clare sat up suddenly, shoving one hand out like a traffic cop. "Wait. That can't be the end. There have to be records. Every hospital must send birth and death records to the county." She clasped her hands on either side of her head. "Man, I'm beginning to sound like *Tante*. What I mean is, you guys really ought to look for records."

"I thought of that, but we can't," Maddy said, walking to Patrick's side. "It's a holiday and everything is closed."

"Geez, what about the computer? It's right here," Clare said, pointing to the laptop on the coffee table. "Go on the Internet and search for records."

It was like a sudden cloudburst. Maddy and Patrick looked at one another and spoke at the same time.

"I didn't know you could . . ."

"I didn't give it a thought . . ."

Maddy reached to take Patrick's hand. "You have an excuse. You don't have a computer, so you've no reason to think of it."

Clare sipped her ginger ale. "Nothing

stopping you, Maddy. Go for it. I'm out," she said, rising and heading for her room.

Patrick lifted Maddy's hand to his lips and kissed her fingers.

"Let's see these fingers do the walking then," he said, tugging her to the sofa. He sat beside her in front of the laptop.

Maddy was online in minutes. First she checked to see what county Shore Hospital was in. Next she Googled for birth and death records and found a listing for a web page called vitalrec.com.

Clare came out in bathrobe and slippers. "Any luck?" she asked.

"Yep, I just found a page for searching vital records."

"Go to it, Maddy. I'm taking a soda into my room and calling it a day. If I'm lucky, the soda will stay down, and if you're lucky, you won't get any of my germs."

By the time Clare had gone in and out of the kitchen and retreated to her room, Maddy had plugged in location, year, day and the last name Donovan.

"What given name shall I try first? How 'bout I start with A's and plug in Adam, or—"

"I would try Thomas. Fiona loved my grandfather, and she just might have used his name."

Thomas came back "none found."

"Any more suggestions?" Maddy asked.

"Try Joseph. That was his middle name, T.J. Donovan. Remember?"

Joseph wasn't found either, and Maddy could see that Patrick was getting uneasy. "Let's go back to the alphabet. Can you think of any names starting with B?"

Patrick closed his eyes, absently rubbing his scarred hand. "The only Irish names I can think of are Brian or Brendan, but knowin' Fiona, she probably wouldn't even choose an Irish name. She'd probably use some movie star name like Brad."

Maddy tried Brian, Brendan, and Brad. They all came back "none found."

Patrick stood. "Enough. I don't have the patience for this, Madelaine. It's probably why I haven't put a computer system into my shop." He pulled her up, away from the computer and into his arms.

He looked into her eyes. "I should go home to tell my mum what we found out today. I know she's anxious, and it's not going to be easy telling her."

"It'll be okay, Patrick. You'll be gentle with the telling, won't you?"

He nodded, pulling her close, brushing her hair with kisses. She rested her head on his chest.

"Call me if you find anything on the computer," he said. "If not, we'll deal with it tomorrow, okay?"

When he saw the worried look on her face, he cocked his head, a corner of his mouth pulling up in a smile. "Madelaine, *a gra*." He took her hand. "Walk me to the door. There's something I need to say."

When they reached the entry Patrick cupped her face in his hands and kissed her with such tender urgency she could hardly catch her breath.

She looked at him wide-eyed, her heart drumming.

His voice took on a raspy fierceness. "I don't know what to do without you, and I don't want to ever be without you. *Je t'aime*, Madelaine."

The backs of his fingers brushed her cheek. He opened the door and closed it softly while she stood in stunned silence.

Maddy pressed her fingers to her lips, staring at the door for long minutes.

CHAPTER
TWENTY-EIGHT

His presence was everywhere. In the rocking chair, on the sofa, at the door. In the kitchen when she tried to fix a light supper. And finally, in her dreams.

Over and over, she felt his tender kiss. She melted in the blue of his eyes and heard his whispered *"Je t'aime."* She could see his sad eyes staring out to sea and heard his words speaking softly. "It's like the tide came in and erased all signs she was ever here."

Names replayed in her dream like the fast track on video. Her fingers were on the keyboard, typing: Connor, Daniel, Sean, Terrance. None found, none found. The hospital — why didn't we go to the hospital? *"Patrick!"*

She sat bolt upright in bed. *Was that me screaming?* She rubbed her eyes and stared into the darkness. A figure stood in the darkened hall.

Clare spoke from the doorway. "Maddy.

It's the middle of the night. I got up to get a glass of water and heard you callin' out names like your bed was on fire. You must be talking in your sleep. Yelling is more like it."

"I was dreaming about Patrick. At the end of the dream I was searching on the computer. The names all failed, but . . ." She grabbed her pillow, hugging it to her breast. "Patrick loves me, Clare. He told me he loves me!"

"Ohmigod, babe. Were you dreamin' or was he in there with you?"

"No, no. Not in here, and not in a dream. It was before he left this afternoon. He really said it. He told me in French. '*Je t'aime*, Madelaine.' Can you believe it?"

"Hey, it's more important *you* believe it, or more importantly still, what you're gonna do about it. I'm happy for you, Mad, but please, go back to sleep now and have sweet dreams. I've got to get back to my bed. I'm finally able to sleep longer intervals without having to trot to the bathroom, so don't call me in the morning. Tomorrow's my day off."

Maddy couldn't sleep. One thought kept returning. They should have gone to the hospital yesterday. They might have found scraps of information about Fiona. She needed to talk to Patrick about that. A glance at the clock on her nightstand told her it was way too early to talk to anyone. Seven-fifteen. Her alarm usually went off at seven-thirty for school, but today was Saturday. Ordinarily, she would sleep in, but this was no ordinary day.

She slipped out of her pajamas and dressed in jogging pants, sweatshirt and socks. *Time I had a good long run,* she thought. *I've been out of my routine since moving in here.* Carrying her sneakers, she headed for the bathroom.

She was brushing her teeth when she thought she heard the ring of a phone. "Damn. I think I left my cell phone in the kitchen. Who could be calling so early?" By the time she rinsed her mouth it had stopped ringing.

In the kitchen, Maddy checked the stove clock. Seven forty-five. She found her phone, clicked on messages, and listened while she put on her sneakers.

"On my way to work, sweet Madelaine. Just checking on my girls. I hope your headache didn't develop into Clare's galloping crud. I'm okay so far. I don't keep *teacher's* hours, so I'll be here at my shop half day if you need me. Got to get that carriage trade piece finished. Call me later."

"No hello or goodbye," she muttered, smiling to herself and shaking her head. "Just 'checking on *his girls*.' " She tied her sneakers, grabbed a windbreaker from the front closet and left the apartment.

Clare looked up from the kitchen table when the door opened and closed. "Where were you?" she asked.

"Running," Maddy answered. She was in the foyer, leaning forward, hands on bent knees, blowing out quick breaths. "Went all the way to Five Points and around the park. Hey, I'm a little breathless 'cause I'm out of shape." Maddy straightened up, kicked off her sneakers and headed for the refrigerator. "You're up early so you must be feeling better?"

"Yeah, almost back to normal. This must have been a twenty-four-hour virus. Thank God you didn't get it, and I hope Patrick doesn't."

"He was already exposed by his sisters, but he's okay, so far. He called earlier and left a message. Inquiring about 'his girls.' I thought you wanted to sleep in."

"Nice of him to include me," Clare said wiggling her eyebrows. "An eight o'clock phone call jinxed my plans, but I couldn't have stayed in bed any longer, anyway. I'm slept out."

"Who called at eight?"

"Your dad. He's anxious to know about what happened at La Madeleine, but I didn't think it was my place to tell him. I told him you'd call him."

"That's two calls I have to make. Patrick's working and wants me to call him later. In the meantime, there's something bugging me about yesterday. Mother Superior told us about Fiona's bleeding and early contractions, but we never spoke to anyone at the hospital about her delivery. I guess the baby's death was such a shock to Patrick that he didn't think about checking on any details, and neither did I, but I'm wondering now if we should go there."

"I thought you said Fiona left the hospital before she was to be discharged."

"She did, but maybe the hospital records would give us some information. Maybe a nurse in OB would remember something."

"If you're thinking about nosing around at the hospital I don't think it'll do much good. Privacy laws, yuh know."

"Well the county offices aren't open on Saturday, and I haven't had any luck on the computer, so I thought it would be worth a try."

"I don't know much about regulations, but I doubt they'd give you records. That is, unless maybe there's some legal investigation or medical reason to pull the records."

"Well, I'll still run it by Patrick and see what he thinks."

"You do that. I'm gonna watch TV in my room. It's best I isolate for a while yet."

She picked up her cell phone and read a text message: "Can't talk now; the bug caught up with me had to leave the shop early. I'm on my way home. Later, Mad."

He must be really sick, she thought. *He never calls me Mad. He usually comes right to the point on the phone, but never like the text messaging CeCe uses.*

She called her father. Jacques wanted to hear what Sister Mary Francis had to say, and Maddy told the whole story, from their arrival at La Madeleine to the failed computer search. When she explained about Clare and Patrick's stomach virus nixing the likelihood of any more searching, there was a long pause and Jacques suggested a solution that made a lot of sense. She promised to call him back about it.

Maddy showered and dressed in corduroy slacks, a bulky knit sweater and matching wool hat. She peeked inside Clare's bedroom.

"Watching daytime soaps? I've never known you to do that, CeCe."

"Well, I'm still feeling shitty, no pun intended. I'm just flipping the remote here. What's up? You going out again?"

"Yeah. Papa gave me an idea and I'm going to see if it's a possibility. He thinks Mrs. Donovan would be the most likely person to gain information about her grandchild's birth and death, and I believe he's right."

"I dunno. Next of kin might work, but I don't know all the regulations at Medical Records. Not my department, Mad."

"If I remember correctly, Patrick's mother works Saturday mornings at the Café. If I leave now, I might just catch her before noon."

"Are you thinking of taking *her* to the hospital today?"

"That depends. Patrick just told her about it yesterday, so I'll have to go softly. I don't really know her, so I don't know how she'll react."

"Just remember what I said about hospitals, okay?"

Driving down Main Street to the restaurant, Maddy thought about the hospital, and about Patrick. *What would Patrick think of my getting his mother involved?* Tante *says Mrs. D. really wants to find Fiona, but maybe I should be letting him make the decisions. Maybe I should wait until next week—*

A car pulled out of a parking space right in front of the Café as Maddy approached, leaving her with a quick decision. She pulled into the space.

It felt like *déjà vu.* She and Paul had asked the same waitress about Mrs. Donovan weeks ago.

"Yeah, hon, Eileen's just finishing up in the kitchen. What's your name again, so's I can tell her you're here?"

"Madelaine Fontaine."

"Okay, Madelaine, go ahead and seat yourself and I'll be right with you."

Maddy sat in the nearest empty booth and looked at the menu. Minutes later the waitress was back, Mrs. Donovan right behind her.

Maddy tried to rise, but Eileen Donovan waved a hand for her to sit back down. She smiled and placed a hand gently on Maddy's shoulder, putting her at ease.

"What can I do for you, my dear?" she asked.

"If you're not too tired, would you care to sit with me for a bit?"

Mrs. Donovan cocked her head and looked at Maddy the same way Patrick often did. "Why, thank you. It's not often I get invited to sit on this side of the Café." As she sat, she winked at the waitress and smiled at Maddy.

"Were you thinking to have some lunch, Madelaine? I can vouch for the vegetable-beef soup."

"I *would* like a bowl of soup," Maddy said. "It smells good in here. Reminds me that I'm hungry."

"Two bowls, coming up," the waitress said, hurrying off to the kitchen.

"I hope you don't think it forward of me coming here today, Mrs. Donovan. I would have asked Patrick first, but he left me a message a little while ago that he was going home earlier than planned. I think he's got the bug that's going around."

Mrs. Donovan drew in a breath. "Oh, dear. And I left Rosemary home in charge. The twins just got over it, you see."

"If you feel you should go right home, then that's okay, Mrs. Donovan."

"Eileen. Please call me Eileen, dear, and no, I'm sure Paddy will be all right with Rosemary. I'd best have some soup, anyway. It's been a while since breakfast at six this morning."

Maddy twisted her hands together on the tabletop. "Yes, well I'm glad you'll have lunch with me." She looked nervously around and lowered her voice. "But you're probably wondering why I came." She stopped abruptly when she saw the waitress approaching. The bowls and crackers were set down and the waitress said *"Bon appétit"* with a smile, and left the booth.

Eileen reached out to pat Maddy's hand. "Not to worry, Madelaine. The staff here knows about Fiona, and I suspect that's why you're here." Her chin trembled a little, but she picked up her spoon. "I hope you like the soup, dear. It's my own recipe."

Maddy tasted the soup. "It's delicious, and my father's favorite. He's partly the reason I came here to see you. But first I want to tell you how sorry I was to learn about the baby."

Eileen stopped eating and placed a hand in front of her mouth for a second. She sat back against the booth and took a deep breath.

"It's a terrible thing to lose a child. I know that, and now Fiona knows it. But it gives us all the more reason to find her and give her the comfort she needs. I want only for Fiona to come home, you see."

Maddy swallowed a lump in her throat. "I

know Patrick wants that to happen, too. He seemed desperate to get the record of birth yesterday, and there's no way we can do that now — the holiday weekend, you know."

"He told me about your search for records. More's the pity it didn't work."

"I told my father about it, too. I hope you don't mind, but he only wants to help. Did you know that he wrote a letter to the sisters at the hospice? My mother did some teaching there before she died, and I suspect her connection and Papa's letter influenced the nuns to give us the information."

Maddy paused, trying to read Eileen's reaction. She could see the sadness in her eyes, but she also sensed the woman's determination to find her daughter.

"My dad says you would be the likeliest person to obtain information from the hospital where the baby was born."

Maddy thought she could see a little spark of hope brighten Eileen's dark blue eyes.

"He suggested we go there — to the hospital."

Eileen dipped her head and stared at her soup.

There was a worrisome pause. Maddy was reminded of Patrick's frustration, looking out to sea at La Madeleine. She said a silent prayer that she had not gone too far, taking this action without Patrick's knowledge.

To Maddy, it was like looking into Patrick's blue eyes when Eileen looked up. Her eyes had softened and her face held a pensive look.

"You're fortunate that your dad is a kind and caring man, Madelaine. When I met him at your school, I sensed how proud he is of you. If he thinks this might work . . . going to the hospital I mean . . . then I'm inclined to give it a try."

She reached out to squeeze Maddy's hand. "Let's finish our soup and be off."

CHAPTER
TWENTY-NINE

Maddy glanced around the lobby as they walked toward the information desk at Shore Community Hospital. They had agreed that Eileen would do the talking, and Maddy was hoping that Patrick's mother wouldn't be nervous. She glanced sideways at her. If she *was* nervous, it didn't show.

"Can you direct us to the medical records department, please?" Eileen asked the volunteer at the desk.

The elderly woman smiled sweetly at them. "Turn left at the elevators and follow the arrows and signs to the Records Office. It will be on the right side of the hall."

"That was easy," Eileen said. Maddy nodded and took her arm.

It was a small hospital, and in no time at all they found the door and opened it to a booth-like anteroom with a counter. A short, bald-headed man with beady eyes stood behind it. Racks of paper-sleeved records were barely visible in a room behind him.

"I'd like to obtain a copy of my daughter's hospital record. Can you help me?" Eileen inquired.

"Was the record ordered?" the clerk asked.

"Well, no. Is it necessary?"

"Unless you have signed authorization by the patient or you are a physician," he said perfunctorily, hardly moving his lips, "we cannot release records."

Eileen's jaw dropped.

Madelaine's eyes flared. "Excuse me, sir. We're looking for the *birth and death* record of the patient's child. The patient is missing, and Mrs. Donovan is the grandmother."

The man looked from Maddy to Mrs. Donovan, scowled and shook his head. "HIPAA. The privacy laws prevent records going out unless authorized by patient, doctor or law enforcement agency."

Eileen sighed, shrugged her shoulders and turned away.

Outside in the hall her eyes filled with tears. "People can be so difficult. But I suppose it's probably the boring job he does that made him be so snippy to us."

"You're too kind. He was on the edge of rude. Given the kind of record you're after, he could have tried to be considerate." She placed a hand on Eileen's arm. "I'm sure we could both use a little breather after him. Let's see if we can get a cup of tea, Eileen."

They followed a sign leading to a small cafeteria in the next wing. The room was almost empty. "Maybe it's quiet in here because of the holiday weekend," Maddy said. "Everyone seemed to be out on the road when we started down the turnpike."

Maddy chose a small table by the counter, and Eileen sat down while Maddy went to the counter to purchase their tea. She brought back two cups of hot water, tea bags and plastic spoons on a small tray.

"I'd forgotten all about this being a holiday weekend," Eileen said. "Yesterday was Veteran's Day." She smiled to herself as she fixed her tea. "When my girls were younger, their Grandpa Donovan used to take them to the Veteran's Day Parade."

"Patrick told me a lot about his grandfather. He must have been a wonderful man."

"That he was. Thomas Donovan was an inspiration to all my children. That's where they get all their Irish expressions like Da and Mum, and *Macushla*. Their Grandpa Tom had quite a brogue. He always called me Eileen, *a gra*. That means my love," she said smiling at Maddy as she stirred sugar into her tea.

Maddy's lips twitched. She could hear Patrick's "Madelaine, *a gra*" in her head. *I'm glad she's changed the subject to the grandfather, not Fiona,* she thought. *At least she seems to enjoy reminiscing about him.*

"My husband favored Thomas Donovan in looks, but not in temperament." Eileen sipped her tea thoughtfully. "Patrick is like his grandpa in many ways, not just his skills with wood. He'll be disappointed about the records, I know." She looked at Maddy pensively. "Some folks say Patrick resembles me. What do you think, Madelaine?"

The question surprised Maddy. She was thinking that Patrick would be angry at her for dragging his mother down here for nothing. She swallowed some tea and made a pretense of studying Eileen's face before she answered.

"There's no question he inherited his grandfather's woodworking skill. I didn't know his grandfather, but, yes, I think Patrick looks like you. Especially the eyes. I sense tenderness and compassion in Patrick, and I think he's very protective and caring like you, too." Her head moved back and forth thoughtfully. "But at times he does feel strongly about things."

"You've described him well, and if you're

meaning that his temper shows sometimes, you're right, Madelaine." Elaine laughed softly and reached to pat Maddy's shoulder. "My Rosie teases Paddy unmercifully about you. I think he cares a lot for you, my dear."

Maddy blushed. "Let's finish our tea, Mrs. Donovan. You've worked all morning and you must be tired. You'd probably like to get home and check on your family."

Maddy's thoughts on the way back to Biddeford kept returning to Fiona's record. She felt guilty about involving Patrick's mother in such a futile attempt and imagined that Patrick wouldn't like it one bit. She dropped Eileen off with a promise to call later in the evening.

As soon as she saw that Mrs. Donovan was inside her house, Maddy dialed Jacques on her cell phone. Explaining to her father would be lots easier than telling Patrick about what happened at the hospital.

Kathleen answered and Maddy felt another twinge of guilt. *Kathleen knows nothing about any of this.*

"Hi, Kathleen. It's Maddy. Clare is not feeling so good, so I'm out of the apartment for a while this afternoon. I thought I'd check to see if Papa is up to a little visit. What do you think?"

"He's just started out to walk the beach, but I'm sure Jack would love to see you, Maddy. Please do come over, dear."

"Good. I'll be there in twenty. Bye."

Short and sweet, Maddy thought. *Calling him Jack. She's still refusing to use the French pronunciation of Papa's name. Sometimes I think last century's ethnic battles in this town never ceased. Seems like the Irish brickbats are still being tossed at the French. Only they're mostly verbal now.* Maddy drove out Pool Street, mulling everything over in her mind.

She pulled around the circular drive to the front of the house to get a view of the ocean. Shielding her eyes against the dropping sun, she saw Jacques heading up the beach toward the house. She ran down the lawn and clambered over the rocks to meet him.

Jacques gave her a bear hug and took off his peaked boating cap to kiss her cheek. He seemed to be breathing heavily. "What a good sight you are, babe, and what a perfect surprise for sunset."

"Kathleen told me you were out here. Your cheeks are so cold, Papa. Are you sure this is good for you?"

"Oh, yes. Next to the sight of you, walking is the best tonic." He smiled at her.

"Doc says so." He took her hand to climb over the rocks. "Something on your mind for this unexpected visit?"

"Well, I thought I'd tell you about my latest effort to find out about Fiona. I took your suggestion literally, and Mrs. Donovan went with me today to the hospital where the baby was born."

Jacques stopped and looked at Maddy before they climbed the steps to the porch.

"Bad news?"

"Kind of. We found that you have to have signed authorization to get hospital records, and I felt badly for having brought Patrick's mother there with no results."

"Uh oh. I should have known better than to suggest that. I didn't think about authorization. I guess I pre-date all these privacy laws they have now. Sorry, Madelaine."

"Don't worry about it, Papa. I've just been so anxious for Patrick's sake that I've jumped at things without thinking them through."

They climbed the steps to the porch and Jacques squeezed Maddy's hand. "Sunsets have been spectacular lately. Let's sit here a few minutes to watch. To me, the sunset furnishes serenity at the end of a busy or trying day . . . helps to smooth out the wrinkles." He kissed her forehead as though he were doing just that.

Maddy sat in her favorite rocking chair. "I'm glad we had a chance to talk before we go in." She inclined her head toward the door with a meaningful look. "I hoped we could be alone."

"Oh, Madelaine. That's something I should have mentioned to you before. I've told Kathleen about Fiona."

Maddy stopped the rocking chair. She closed her eyes, trying to tamp down the anger and frustration that came with the mention of Kathleen.

"I told her nothing about *Tante*'s vision or about the clues you received from Henriette. I simply told her you were trying to help Patrick find his sister. You know, Kathleen felt badly about your break-up with Claude."

Jacques tried to look into her eyes, but Maddy looked away, fixing her eyes on the crimson and gold streaks stretching above the inky water.

He covered her hand with his. "Since Kathleen met Patrick and Rosemary here during the storm, I thought it might help her to understand your feelings for Patrick if I told her about his family and Fiona. You know, what you are trying to do to help him find her."

Helping him find Fiona is paramount, she thought, *but it really doesn't describe how I feel about Patrick, or he about me. I do want Papa to be happy about us, but why does she have to know?*

Just as she turned to speak from her heart, Kathleen opened the door.

"I heard you drive in, Maddy, and guessed you probably went down to the beach to find your father. I have drinks ready, darling. Come on in before you freeze out here."

Maddy stayed through a glass of wine, nibbled on cheese straws, and tried to carry on normal conversation, but she felt anything but normal in Kathleen's presence.

Jacques mentioned how good it was to be back to work at the University and they talked about his classes. Maddy gave a shortened version of the computer search and the hospital visit, but she wasn't comfortable talking about Fiona with Kathleen. Or about Patrick. She told them about the virus that was spreading in town, and Clare became a perfect excuse to leave.

"I hope you will come more often, Maddy," Kathleen said as they walked to the door. "I'd like to plan a Thanksgiving dinner gathering. The holiday is less than two weeks away and I'm hoping your father and you will help me. I need to know what's traditional for your family."

Jacques pulled Maddy close to his side. "We can do that, can't we, dear? The Fontaines have lots of traditions, and I certainly have much to be thankful for this year."

Maddy fixed her mouth in a tight smile and nodded.

CHAPTER THIRTY

Tante Margaret had come and gone by the time Maddy got back to the apartment.

"I briefed her on the findings at La Madeleine and convinced her that she shouldn't be in our apartment, exposed to this airborne illness. *Tante* left on condition that she'd make a big pot of soup and you would go over to her place and pick it up after mass tomorrow morning, okay?"

Maddy nodded, not sure she wanted to say anything about her visit to Francois's Fancy. Things were muddled enough without adding Kathleen to the mix.

"So give me the scoop, babe. What happened with Mrs. D.?"

"She did go with me, down to Shore Community, and you were right about the hospital, Clare. No records without authorization. It was a pretty tense scene, and now I'm worried about how sick Patrick is and whether he knows about our wasted trip."

"Chances are his mother has smoothed things over."

"Well, I'm going to ring the house instead of Patrick's cell phone."

"Smart move. Let things simmer down a little."

Rosemary answered the phone and that added another measure of tension. Maddy was already uncomfortable with a relationship between teacher and student that could be tricky to handle at Saint David's. Would Rosie brag around about Miss Fontaine being her brother's girlfriend? She didn't think so, but you could never tell with teenagers.

Rosie sounded enthusiastic when Maddy identified herself. She rattled off the condition of everyone in the household.

"The twins are all better. They helped me get supper ready, but nobody ate much. Paddy hasn't left his room all day, except to go in and out of the bathroom a zillion times. My mum is resting right now, too, but I don't think she's been in my brother's room much. She brought him some things to drink when she first came home, but she says he just wants to be left alone."

Maddy thanked her and told her she would call again soon. She didn't want Rosie to know that she would be dialing Patrick's cell phone next time. That's what she intended to do — tomorrow.

A whistling teakettle woke Maddy on Sunday morning. Shuffling into the kitchen, she found Clare sitting at the table having tea and toast.

"Hey, I think I'm gonna live."

"So I see, and you even made tea in a pot."

"Ayuh. The old fashioned way. *Tante* doesn't approve of nuking a cup of water in the microwave. '*Oui, chérie,* you boil the water and steep the tea,' " Clare mimicked her aunt, sounding incredibly like her. "It really is better this way. Want some?"

"I'm up for that, and I'll have toast with it." Maddy put bread in the toaster and took jam from the refrigerator.

"I think the danger of your catching this bug is past, babe. I guess Patrick didn't have your luck though, huh?"

"According to Rosie, he spent yesterday in his bed and in the bathroom."

"Same darned thing. Yuck. It sure throws you for a loop. I've called in to the hospital already. I'm taking one more day, but I'm not up to going to church this morning. You'll stop at *Tante*'s for the soup, wontcha?"

"Yes, and when I come back I have to tackle paperwork. I have tests and essays to correct from last week."

"You better dress warm. The morning forecast said possible snow or freezing rain and the traffic around St. Mary's is usually bad for ten-thirty mass."

Maddy pulled on brown dress slacks and a tan pullover sweater. Buttoning her long wool coat, she threw a scarf around her neck and put on matching gloves and hat.

A leaden sky confirmed Clare's forecast. Maddy let the car warm up until the defroster cleared her frosted windshield. Fine snow whirled around her as she drove to St. Mary's.

Climbing the church steps, Maddy gave little thought to the stone façade and arched wooden doors of St. Mary's. She headed down the aisle to a favored pew in the right transept where she used to sit with her family when she was a little girl. Since a chapel was built at the Pool, Jacques stopped coming to St. Mary's, but the familiar pew, the hymns and prayers and old statues closed the gap, wrapping her in memories.

Today's homily was based on the scripture of Mark. The priest first reminded the congregation of the foul weather, saying they all were familiar with "Red sky at night, sailors' delight; red sky at morning, sailors take warning." Then he drew an analogy to the Pharisees who sought a miraculous sign from Jesus. "Jesus told the Pharisees that they were good at reading weather signs, but only faithless people would ask for miraculous signs."

Maddy thought about their search for Fiona's record. *We're not looking for a miraculous sign here, just a plain old record. Believe and receive. With faith we'll find it.*

Mass ended with "God's Blessing Sends Us Forth," and Maddy rose and sang with the congregation before leaving her pew. Without warning, the calm she had gained in the past hour was suddenly shattered.

Across the aisle, Claude Duval stood sneering at her. She drew in a breath and shivered. A battle played out in her head. She could be polite or give him a taste of his own medicine. Civility won. She suppressed the urge to give him an equally stony stare. Her head dipped in a stiff nod and her lips formed a mirthless smile. She hurried up the aisle and out of the church, hoping he didn't come near.

A dusting of snow covered everything. Maddy slipped and slid her way to her car. The fact that Clare had phoned *Tante* to tell her Maddy was on a tight schedule helped. She managed to leave *Tante*'s after picking up the soup without spending much

324

time with Margaret.

The soup was still hot when she carried the tureen into the apartment. "Chicken soup — good for the soul and the body. Thank God for small favors, huh?" Maddy said as she shed her coat and shoes. "The forecasters were right about the snow. I'll have to dig out some boots."

Clare ladled soup into two bowls. "Thank God for *Tante*," she said.

"Add Patrick's mother to the prayer. She made the soup I had at the Café yesterday. Vegetable beef. I told her it was Papa's favorite. He and Paul both loved my mother's soup."

"Paul called while you were at church."

"Oh. I hope you filled him in. I don't want to repeat about Fiona one — more — time," she said, emphasizing each word.

"I did tell him, but he still wants you to call him."

"Later. Much later. The call to Patrick is the one I'm worrying about."

Maddy worked all afternoon, correcting papers and making lesson plans for the coming week. She listened with Clare to the six o'clock news and weather on TV.

"The first snow of the season caused a major pile-up on the turnpike south of the Biddeford-Saco exit. With temperatures ris-

325

ing rapidly, snow has turned to freezing rain. Warnings are out for icy roads from here to Kennebunkport. Stay tuned for late openings or school closings tomorrow."

"What next?" Clare said, shaking her head. "Hurricane in September, and snow and ice before Thanksgiving."

"Well, that gives me something else to talk about. I've finally screwed up my courage to call Patrick. I feel like I'm cooking up a pot of stew — not knowing what ingredients to put in."

"Hey, you did what you thought was best, Mad. You could have been opening a can of worms, but if Patrick loves you he's not going to cross off the courage it took for you to go to the hospital with his mom. He's gotta know you're only trying to help."

Maddy smiled weakly and nodded at Clare. She went to her room, stretched out on her bed and dialed Patrick's cell phone.

He answered on the first ring. "Talk to me, Madelaine."

"Hello to you, too, Patrick. I called, hoping to find you're better."

"Mum said she was pretty sure you'd call."

"What else did your mother say?"

"She told me you came to the Café and you took her to the hospital and a lot of other stuff about you — all good."

Maddy sighed her relief. "We talked about you, too, Paddy Donovan." Maddy wished he could see her teasing smile.

"Thank God this bug is giving up on me. I need to get back to work tomorrow but my mum thinks it's too soon."

"She's probably right. It took CeCe two days to get over it."

"A man's got to defend himself in these situations and unfortunately, I've got too many females in my life right now."

"Including me?"

"You, Miss Fontaine, are the exception. Can you come to my shop after school tomorrow? I want you with me when I make a trip down county."

Maddy drew in a deep breath. "I —"

"Remember what I said on Friday?"

How could she forget?

"I want you with me always, Madelaine, *a gra.*"

The words took Maddy's breath away.

CHAPTER
THIRTY-ONE

Patrick covered his surprise with a smile when Maddy stepped into his shop at one in the afternoon.

"Hey. I was just thinking of you. I checked the health department for the office hours in Wells. Good thing I did, because the county records office closes at four, and we would have been out of luck. I didn't think calling Saint David's to tell you was a good idea, so—"

He caught her in his arms with an impish grin, dimples denting his cheeks. "I conjured you up, and here you are." He took her mouth with a gentle kiss.

A sweet sensation spread through her. She splayed her hands on his chest and looked up at him, her green eyes gleaming. "Such blarney," she said, tapping a finger on his lips. "I'm here because of icy roads. Saint David's closed early, and it may have worked to our advantage. We can get started for

Wells sooner than you hoped — that is, if you still think we should go today."

"I do. Just let me get my machinery turned off here and I'm good to go."

Outside, Patrick pulled Maddy close to his side as they walked past her parked car. They took baby steps together across the icy lot to his truck. She felt the warmth and the strength of his arms.

He shot her a sultry gaze and hugged her close before helping her climb up to the cab.

"Sweet Jaysus, Madelaine. Even in this icy cold, you don't know what you do to me."

She closed her eyes and smiled to herself as he closed the passenger door.

Patrick darted around the truck to jump in. He steered away from the buildings, pumping the breaks cautiously to stop at an intersection. "It will be a safer trip on my wheels, but I've got to concentrate on the road. This trip is going to take longer than usual. Don't think I'm ignoring you if I'm not talkin'."

They passed a few fender benders and not a few state police cars cruising near the entrance of the turnpike. Maddy clutched her hands together, staring at the road, trying not to show her fear. The freezing rain wouldn't quit, and Patrick was as cautious and steady at the wheel as he was at his woodworking bench. An hour later they entered the county office buildings.

Standing slightly behind him as Patrick faced the clerk in the vital records office, Maddy tried to shake an uneasy premonition.

His voice was firm. "I'd like a copy of the death record for an infant boy born on April first, '05. Last name is Donovan, but I'm not sure if the record shows a given name."

The female clerk looked him up and down. Her brow furrowed. "You're not sure?" she said pursing her lips.

"No," he said, hoping that honesty was the best policy. "The baby died shortly after birth." Patrick looked away for a heartbeat and spoke in a more plaintive tone when he gazed back at the clerk. "He was my nephew, and my mother wants the record for my sister's sake."

The clerk stared silently at him.

"My sister, Fiona . . ." Patrick cleared his throat and started over. "The mother's name is Fiona, but she may not have named the child. I don't think there would be more than one baby-boy Donovan born on April first in this county. Could you please check?"

The woman hesitated for a second. "Okay. That I can do."

Minutes later, Maddy could hear the clicking and purring of a printer, and she squeezed Patrick's shoulder. The clerk came back with a printed document in her hand. "This is the only Donovan death recorded on April one in this county." She shoved the paper forward. "If you'll sign here for the certificate, it will be ten dollars."

Patrick was reaching for his wallet as he gazed at the paper. He frowned as he studied the document, scanning the details. His eyes traveled down and then back to the top. He paused with the money in his hand.

"Is there a problem?" the clerk asked.

"No, no problem. Thanks for your help," he said, handing her a ten-dollar bill. She gave him an envelope and Patrick folded the paper and slid it in. He turned slowly, placed his hand on the small of Maddy's back and steered her toward the door.

She looked up at him as they exited into an empty foyer. "You did it, Patrick." She smiled up at him. "I was afraid it wouldn't work."

The light in her eyes dimmed and her smile faded when she caught the look on his face.

"Let's get to my truck."

The sleet had stopped but a thin glaze of

331

ice covered everything. Patrick helped her into the cab with a firm hand but no sultry words this time. He sat silently, cracking the knuckles of his hand, waiting for the defroster to do its work.

Maddy stared at his profile. "Patrick? What's wrong?"

He narrowed his gaze at her, then pulled the document out of his parka and handed it to her. "See what this means to you," he said, glints of steel flashing in his dark eyes.

Maddy's eyes skimmed the paper. Time and date of death, the medical terms listed for cause of death . . . her eyes flew to the top. Deceased's name: *Claude Donovan.*

Her hand jerked and the paper slipped from her fingers into her lap. Maddy gulped and sat back against the seat, her eyes blinking rapidly.

Patrick picked up the death certificate. The muscle in his jaw rippled, a sure sign he was trying to suppress anger. He stared at the paper.

"How many Claudes do you think there are in Biddeford, Madelaine?"

The question was as startling as the name on the paper. A knot of anxiety twisted inside her.

"I . . . I don't know." Catching her lower lip in her teeth, she struggled to make sense of his question — the inference. "Biddeford has always had a large population of French people. I guess there could be more Claudes—"

"But you only know one. Right?" He folded the paper into its envelope and stuffed it back inside his parka.

Maddy was floundering, like a ship without a rudder. She clutched Patrick's sleeve and looked into his eyes.

"This doesn't make sense. You can't just jump to conclusions."

He tapped his hand on his breast. "For the record, I believe I already have."

The ride back to Biddeford was tense. Maddy knew Patrick needed to concentrate on the road, and her mind was working overtime. Given the question he raised, seeing the name on the document and hearing the insinuation was overwhelming.

Come on, Madelaine, she told herself. *You're the teacher; put things in order. Met Claude last December at Papa's wedding, dated during breaks and over the summer, ended it in September. Last December — Fiona entered La Madeleine.*

Oh, God, how could this be? She couldn't bear the deception, *if* there was deception. Most of all, she couldn't bear risking Patrick's trust. She could almost feel his anger.

She had to say something.

"I know I pushed the envelope with the search for records, but will you bear with me on this, please? The important thing is finding your sister. Please don't let this name be anything but just a name. At least until I've had a chance to do some checking on my own. Will you promise me that, for now?"

Patrick looked at his scarred hand on the wheel. A vision of his grandfather flashed in his mind. *He held my good hand when they wheeled me into surgery.* "I'll bide with you here, lad," he said, placing his hand over his heart. "You'll do just fine."

"I'll bide a while, Madelaine. I'm not angry with you." He tapped his chest. "This isn't about you. It's about Fiona."

When they arrived at Factory Square, he brought her hand to his lips and kissed her fingers. "I'll drive behind you to Elm Street. Nothing is going to happen to you."

"Oh, God," Maddy said, startled when Clare pulled the door open.

"Hey, babe. I was in the kitchen and I heard you stamping your boots in the hall. I've been sitting here, drinking tea and wondering where in blazes you were."

"I should have called, but believe me,

there was no chance."

"Since I got home from work, Paul has called twice. I'm thinking like, all kinds of bad stuff with you driving in this weather."

"I only drove my car from Factory Square to the apartment. We went in Patrick's truck and it took over an hour to get home. Things couldn't be worse, CeCe. He hardly spoke on the way home."

"Whoa, babe. Start at the beginning. Where have you been and what are you talking about?"

Maddy squeezed her eyes shut to keep the tears from coming. "Patrick and I went to Wells to get the baby's death record."

"You went there on a day like this?" Clare shook her head as she took Maddy's coat to the closet. "So did he get the record?"

"Yes, and that's the problem. Just as you said yesterday, I think we've opened a can of worms. Fiona named her son Claude Donovan."

Clare's jaw dropped open. "Ohmigod!"

The house phone rang, punctuating her words. Clare picked up and after a second said, "She's home."

She handed Maddy the phone.

"Hey, Mad. This is big brother hoping it's not *déjà vu* with you disappearing in another storm."

"Oh, Paul, I should give you my cell phone number. CeCe said you've been trying to reach me."

"Yeah, I have, and I do want your cell number. You were out somewhere in the middle of an ice storm! What's going on?"

"It's been pretty awful. I mean the search for Patrick's sister. Did you hear about our trip to the hospice where Mom taught?"

"Yeah, Pa filled me in on that. He called last night, inviting me up for Thanksgiving. That's kind of why I was calling — that and the ice storm. He mentioned that your search for hospital records didn't work. So what's up now?"

"I went with Patrick to the county office to get the baby's death certificate."

"And?"

Maddy swallowed past the lump in her throat. If Clare's reaction was explosive, she could imagine what Paul's would be.

"Fiona named the baby Claude. Claude Donovan."

"Claude! Holy Christ. Did Patrick think the same thing I'm thinking?"

"I'm afraid so. He did promise to give me some time to check things out, but I don't know how to go about it. I don't know what to do."

"I know what I'd do. If it *is* Claude Duval, I'd be the first one to pound in the nails."

"That's why I asked Patrick for time. There's no telling what *he* will do. Do you think I should ask Papa's advice? Maybe Kathleen—"

"Geez, I don't know about her. Pa said Kathleen has been asking about the portrait. I intended to bring it home next week. I had already decided it had earned me enough glory at the gallery, and I thought I'd give it to them as an early Christmas gift. That's what I was calling to ask your opinion about. Given present circumstances, maybe the painting could be like a talisman — you know, soften Kathleen up a little and bring you some luck."

"It might help, but that's a whole week away, and I don't think Patrick will wait that long."

"Give me his cell phone number, and yours. If he'll wait till this weekend, I can probably get away. They're doing major renovations at the museum right up till Thanksgiving, and they won't miss me if I leave for the holiday a little early. Let me call him, Mad. A little man-to-man won't hurt."

CHAPTER
THIRTY-TWO

Maddy told Clare the plan as soon as she hung up the phone.

"Way to go, Paul," Clare said. "I think he can handle this. He'll be good with Patrick, and he can charm most any woman." Clare hunched her shoulders. "Only Kathleen . . ." Clare tightened her lips and shook her head. "She's a mind-boggler."

"I know from experience. Kathleen's been partial to Claude ever since he took her first husband's place in the law firm. There's no telling where her loyalties will lie now."

"Well, they better lie with you and Papa Jacques. Your dad idolizes you, Mad. And don't forget *Tante*." Clare rolled her eyes. "*Tante*'s been prayin' for a solution. She hinted that she's close — but I'm afraid to ask. You know that old saying, 'Be careful what you pray for.' "

Maddy nodded her head. "I know that all too well. I prayed at mass, Sunday. I asked for the record, and look what happened." She picked up her purse and started for her room.

"You got to relax, babe." Clare grabbed her arm and tugged her to the living room. "Sit here for a minute and let's think this thing through."

They had just settled down on the sofa when Maddy's cell phone rang. She pulled it from her purse and listened, mouthing the word *Paul* for Clare's benefit.

Clare watched intently, not wanting to leave her side. Maddy's eyes brightened at first and she nodded several times.

"Yes, I know, and I feel his pain, but, Paul, do you understand about Patrick and me?" Suddenly, tears that had threatened for the past hour spilled down her cheeks. "Okay, I'll talk to Papa. Luv you. Yeah, I will."

"He always says 'Hang tough,'" Maddy said, wiping away her tears with her fingers.

Clare handed Maddy a tissue. "He called Patrick?"

"Yes, and he said Patrick was actually glad to hear from him. That was good. I guess guys understand each other better than we understand them. Patrick agreed to wait until Saturday, and he'll meet with Paul at his shop."

"Does he know how Patrick feels about you?"

"That's what made me cry. He said, 'The guy loves you.' "

"What about your father? And Kathleen?"

"He only wants me to tell Papa that he's flying up on Friday, then wait until we're all together Friday night for the rest."

By midday Tuesday, air temperature was rising and icy roads were a bad memory. Clare came home at four from the day shift to find Maddy peeling vegetables in the kitchen.

"Hey. What's this? You want my job?" Clare asked.

"No, no. I'm not doing supper. I'm trying to remember how my mom used to make vegetable-beef soup. I stopped at the market for these veggies, but I'm glad you're home. I never learned to cook like you did. This soup, if I ever get it done right, is promised to my Dad. I phoned him and told him I'd make soup for him and Paul and bring it Friday night."

"You're in luck, then, 'cause *Tante*'s on her way over here, and she'll have better answers than me. She also said she has some really good news for you." Clare waggled a shaky hand toward Maddy. "I don't know, babe. She's like the battery that won't quit."

Clare was two steps into the living room when a knock at the door stopped her. Maddy opened it to *Tante,* who was balancing a grocery bag, her purse and a cake box in her arms. She marched into the kitchen, followed by Maddy and Clare.

"Ah, Madelaine, I'm so glad to see you," she said, putting things down on the table to give her a hug.

"How about me. I don't count?" Clare teased as she looked into the bag.

"*Mais oui, ma chérie.* I say Madelaine, because I bring good news for her."

Clare pulled a baguette, cheese and a bottle of wine out of the bag. She peeked at a cheesecake in the box. "Yum. What did we do to deserve all this?"

"This," *Tante* said, pointing to the wine and cheese, "makes a treat, eh? No *tristesse.* Okay, Madelaine?"

Clare grinned at Maddy's puzzled look. "She says, 'No sadness.' "

"The cake is from the good sisters at Star of the Sea Center, and with it comes the good news for Madelaine." *Tante* drew a deep breath and looked from one to the other, her dark eyes snapping.

"Sister Agatha went with me to La Madeleine this morning."

Tante inclined her head, raising an eyebrow at Clare. "You remember Sister Agatha when we went to the Center to help after the hurricane, eh, Clare? The one who does all the baking?"

Clare stood still; put one hand on her hip and scowled. "Yeah, I remember Sister Agatha, but *Tante,* Maddy and Patrick have already been to La Madeleine."

"*Oui,* I know." *Tante* sat down and began rummaging in her purse. "But Mother Superior at La Madeleine knows Agatha from long ago. Mother let us talk with one of the nuns who counseled Fiona. This was in the beginning, when Fiona first arrived at La Madeleine."

Margaret pulled a folded paper from her purse. "The nun remembered the name of a shore restaurant where Fiona worked before she came to the sisters." She waggled the paper in front of her.

"Don't tell me you went there with Sister Agatha," Clare said.

"*Oui.*" The smile on her face and her flashing eyes left no question about how pleased she was with herself and her news.

"This place was very near La Madeleine, right on the bay. It was closed for the season, but the owner, Captain Brian, was working inside and he let us in. I think

Agatha's veil impressed him, you know? Anyway, *Voilà!* The good man gave us the name and address of a waitress who works every year for him. He says she would know Fiona. So this is for you, Madelaine." *Tante* handed her the paper. "Praise God, eh?"

Maddy stared at the words printed on the back of a "specials" menu from Captain Brian's Sea Grill.

She threw her arms around *Tante.* "Thank you, thank you, Aunt Margaret. You're unbelievable."

"Ayuh, that she is," Clare said. "Biddeford's own Angela Lansbury. Only this one does her sleuthing with prayer. Right, *Tante?*"

"*Mais oui,*" Margaret said, rising. She kissed Clare's cheek. "And now, I have to go home. It's been a long day, *mes chéries.*"

After Clare closed the door behind Margaret, she turned to Maddy, throwing her hands in the air. "Now what?"

"Lord, CeCe, I don't know." Maddy looked at the address again. "It's in York. I couldn't bear seeing Patrick going there and being disappointed one more time."

"Well, you can't go there by yourself. No tellin' what you'll find."

Clare was quiet for a minute. She rubbed the back of her neck, pushed her hands up and down the front of her white uniform pants.

"Tell you what. My shift changes tomorrow. I'll be on nights from Wednesday to Wednesday, and then I'm off for three days. It works out perfect, 'cause it gives me the long Thanksgiving weekend. Sooo . . . if you could get out of school a little early, either tomorrow or Thursday, I'll go with you and check out this waitress."

"CeCe, you're awesome. What would I do without you?"

Clare smiled. "For starters, open the wine, Miss Fontaine."

A Wednesday teachers' meeting put the trip off until Thursday afternoon. Clare drove while Maddy scanned the streets for the address in York. 154 Main was easy to find. She pulled in front of the Pizza Parlor right next door. They stepped into the vestibule of an old brick building that had seen better days. Two downstairs apartments, two up. Maddy scanned the names on four brass plates and pressed the button next to Fitzgerald: 2-B. No answer came through the speaker.

The stair well was stuffy and smelled like stale cigarettes. Up one flight, Clare unzipped her down vest, fanning herself.

Maddy knocked on the door of 2-B. They listened and waited, but no sound came from within.

As they turned to leave, the door of 2-A opened a crack and an elderly woman poked her head out. She looked them up and down. Clare was dressed in her ER uniform, ready to go to work when they got back to Biddeford.

"If yer lookin' for Kay, she's workin'," the woman said.

"We are. Could you tell us where that would be?" Clare asked.

The woman gave her the once over again. "Are you from the hospital?"

"Yeah," Clare said, "and it's important we find Kay."

"In that case, ask down to the Pizza Parlor," the woman said, closing her door in their faces.

"Thank God for nosy neighbors, and half truths," Clare mumbled as they hurried down the stairs.

Inside the Pizza Parlor, they were surprised to see a tastefully decorated, cozy Italian restaurant. A lone person sat at the nearest table, eating a slice of pizza. Maddy stepped up to the bar and asked for Kay Fitzgerald. The bartender smiled and pointed at a trim, young waitress filling cheese and pepper shakers at tables on the far side of the restaurant. She didn't look much older than eighteen.

"Sit anywhere, ladies," the waitress said when they approached. "We're open for pizza, but dinner doesn't start till five. I'll bring you a menu."

"Uh, we'd just like a Coke for now, and a minute of your time, okay?" Maddy asked.

The waitress checked her watch. "Sure," she said as they sat down.

"We got your name from Captain Brian. He said you may be able to help us," Maddy said.

The waitress gave them a surprised look. "Well, now, let me get your drinks and we'll see about that."

She brought Cokes to the table and called back to the bartender, "I'm on break for a few minutes, Uncle Joe."

The waitress took a good look at Clare's uniform and Maddy's smart-looking clothes. She sat down, leaned her folded arms on the table, and looked at Maddy. "You spoke of my friend, Cap'n Brian, but you guys wouldn't be lookin' for waitress jobs, now would you?"

"Nah," Clare said, "we're lookin' for information about a person. Someone Cap'n said you'd know." Clare inclined her head toward Maddy.

"This girl worked with you at the Sea Grill a year ago. Do you remember Fiona Donovan?" Maddy asked.

Kay pushed straight back in her chair and looked over her shoulder at the bartender. She lowered her voice. "Who's asking?"

"My name is Madelaine Fontaine, and this is my friend Clare Chamberlain. We're from Biddeford, where Fiona used to live."

"You're the ones looking for her?"

Maddy shifted in her chair, twisting her hands under the table. "No. Her mother and her brother are trying to find her. Her brother, Patrick, is my boyfriend and we . . . we just found out about Fiona's baby."

Maddy looked earnestly at the waitress. She was running nervous fingers over the checked tablecloth, listening with her eyes downcast, obviously uncomfortable with the conversation.

"Fiona's mother . . . well, there are things Fiona really should know," Maddy said, trying to see Kay's eyes.

Kay Fitzgerald stood up. "You obviously know who I am, but you really should be talking with my uncle. Just a minute." She walked to the service end of the bar and waited. Her back was to Maddy and Clare, but they could see her talking to the bartender, her hands fluttering as she talked.

"Stay cool, Mad. You're doing fine," Clare whispered. "I think they know something."

The tall, middle-aged bartender came to the table and sat down.

"Ladies, I'm Joe Cerone. Kay thinks I may be able to help you, but what I need to know is *why* you are looking for someone."

Maddy raised her chin and met the man's gaze. She drew in her breath and blew it out slowly. "Fiona Donovan's father died soon after she disappeared from Biddeford, but Fiona wouldn't know that. Her mother lived with the hope that Fiona would return, but she never did. Her brother Patrick and I have only just found out about the hospice that took Fiona in, and . . . about the death of her child."

Maddy looked at Clare and at the waitress behind the bar. Clare gave her a slight nod, but it didn't stop the lump in her throat.

"Clare's aunt found the restaurant where Fiona once worked and her name—" Maddy pointed at Kay, then raised a hand to her forehead and rubbed at her temple. Her head was beginning to ache, and panic was slowly rising. She didn't think that her words were making a difference.

She felt a hand on her shoulder, and she looked up into piercing eyes.

348

"You're sure it's her *family* that wants her back in Biddeford? Nobody sent you here?" Joe Cerone asked.

Maddy looked puzzled. "Yes, of course I'm sure. Her brother and sisters miss her. Her mother is brokenhearted."

Joe Cerone paused, then pulled a card out of his pocket and tapped it against his palm while he studied Maddy's face. "I believe you, miss, but I need more than your word." He handed Maddy the card and stood. "Have someone contact me and we'll take it from there. Have a pleasant evening, ladies. The Coke's on me."

Outside the Pizza Parlor Clare and Maddy stared at the business card.

"Geez, Joseph Cerone owns this place and his home phone's on here, too," Clare said. She put her arm around Maddy's shoulder as they walked to the car. "Getting close, babe. You done good."

"Yeah, but I certainly didn't do it alone. I choked up in there, you know."

"I know, but he believed you. They were cautious and cagey. Did you notice they never really acknowledged Fiona by name?"

"Protective. I think they are protecting her from something or somebody. Now I don't know what to do next. What do you think, CeCe?"

"If it was me, babe, I'd turn that card right over to Patrick and his mother."

"Before we find out about Claude?"

"Well, if they find Fiona first, the question could be answered for you."

CHAPTER
THIRTY-THREE

Maddy looked around the kitchen. The covered pot sat on the stove, the smell of beef and onions still lingering. True to her word, Clare had started the soup for her before they left for York. She looked at the directions that Clare left. *All I need to do is add the vegetables and let it simmer for an hour or so. It'll be ready to bring to Papa's tomorrow, but will I be ready for Kathleen? Ugh. I don't want to think about it. Paul said he'd handle it, so let him.*

Her mind strayed to Patrick and the call she'd made as soon as she and Clare returned. She couldn't tell him the whole truth over the phone. Especially after he said he missed her and guessed he'd have to settle for her in his dreams. She told him that she and Clare had been on an important errand, that she had something to give him, but he'd have to wait till after school tomorrow.

He sets my heart thumping even on the phone. Lord, I need your help here. Everything is jumbling together all at once. Paul will be home tomorrow . . . and Kathleen . . .

Paul came through the back door of Francois's Fancy, suitcase in one hand, big portfolio case in the other. "Hey, something smells good in here." He dropped his gear and pulled Maddy into a hug. "Where is everybody?"

"They're in the living room having a cocktail. I didn't think soup and sandwich on a Friday night called for the usual, so I'm out here to set the table. We're sitting in the kitchen tonight. How was your flight?"

"Flight was good, and I got me a shiny Thunderbird for a rental."

"I wish you had let me pick you up."

"Thanks, but I really needed my own wheels. I'm here for the week, remember? From what you told me last night about your little trip with Clare, I'll probably be needing my own transportation. Tell me now, while we have the chance. How did Patrick react to the business card?"

"Fantastic. I took it over before I came here. He swept me right off my feet. I thought he'd be mad that Clare and I went there without him. I explained about *Tante*

352

going to La Madeleine, and how Clare really wanted to help. Patrick was actually impressed. He said he was anxious to tell his mother about it before he did anything, but he was proud of me, and real happy about *Tante* and Clare. It blew my mind."

"Hey, the guy loves you."

"I thought I heard voices out here. Who loves who?" Kathleen asked, as she walked into the kitchen. "Welcome home, Paul."

Maddy placed napkins on the table and kept her eyes downcast as Paul responded.

"Thank you, Kathleen. I guess there's no sneakin' in on you." He laughed as he picked up his portfolio case and took Kathleen's arm. "Let's go see the big guy. Come join us when you're done, Maddy."

Maddy finished setting the table and hefted Paul's bag. Not a bad reason to stall for time, she thought. She carried it quietly through the hall and upstairs into Paul's room.

A flood of memories assaulted her when she saw the family picture on Paul's dresser. Her mother at her easel, paintbrush in hand, pretending to paint Paul and Maddy, posing on either side of Jacques.

Clare got us all in. Maddy shook her head and sighed, deep in thought. She took the snapshot with her new camera and Paul had it enlarged and framed. Everything was perfect. Then.

She left Paul's bag at the foot of the bed and left the room to go downstairs. *I hope this painting of Kathleen works its wonders.*

"Come see what Paul has brought," Jacques said when Maddy entered the living room. "It's a wonderful surprise."

Kathleen's portrait was propped against the ottoman. Jacques held it up for Maddy to see. Kathleen's red hair and creamy complexion were outstanding in profile against a soft gray background. Voluptuous curves were toned down, but definitely enhanced by the filmy white dress she wore. Maddy looked from the portrait to Kathleen. She could see that the lips tilted up in a smile on the portrait, just as they did presently.

"He's captured her beauty, don't you think, Madelaine?"

"Yes, it's a really good likeness, Kathleen."

"Thank you. It is lovely, and Paul deserves the kudos," Kathleen said, as she strode to Jacques's side. "Remarkable talent your son has, darling."

"I hope this makes up for the anxiety I caused at the beginning, Pa. I'll help you hang it, if you like."

"Well, before we do that, let's have some

of the soup your sister made. It smells so good, it's made me hungry."

"I had a little help with the soup, Papa, and Clare sent a bottle of Pinot Noir, so I'd say we're all set."

Maddy glanced nervously at Paul as she sat down at the kitchen table. His confident smile eased her jitters. She wondered how to get to the subject at hand.

She didn't wonder long. Jacques ladled soup from the tureen and sampled it while Kathleen passed the toasted cheese sandwiches. "Delicious, Maddy," he said. "How did you find time to make it? I tried reaching you after school yesterday and you weren't home."

She shot a look at Paul. He was nodding and smiling, eating his soup.

"Clare and I didn't get back in town until late yesterday."

"Out and about on the first sunny day since the ice storm?" Jacques asked.

"Actually, we were doing a little detective work, Papa. Following a lead we got about Patrick's sister."

"Heavens, Maddy, I would think Patrick should be the one to do that," Kathleen said.

Paul put his spoon down. "As a matter of fact, Maddy's trying hard to help Patrick and his mother through a difficult time.

Does Kathleen know about Fiona's baby, Pa?"

"Baby!" Kathleen said, sending a questioning look from Paul to Jacques.

Jacques nodded his head. "I've only told you that Fiona's been missing, but I did learn that she had a child. A child who died after a premature birth. I felt that if Madelaine wanted to confide that information to you, Kathleen, she would do so in time."

"Well, Pa, there may be no better time than now, while we're all together," Paul said. "We're just family here, and Maddy's already confided in me. What do you think, Mad? Want to tell them the rest?"

Maddy looked down at her plate, then back at Jacques. "Yes. It's okay, Papa." She steepled her hands in front of her face and paused, looking over her fingers at Kathleen. When she rested her hands on the table she spoke in a strong voice that belied the turmoil she felt. "We found out that Fiona had a son out of wedlock and she named him Claude."

It was as though a thunderbolt had struck Jacques. He stared at Maddy, speechless, his eyes seeking understanding.

Kathleen fumbled with her napkin, obviously startled, but not enough to silence her.

"Good heavens. The name Claude? Why, that must be a silly coincidence, wouldn't you say, Paul?"

"No, I couldn't say that, Kathleen, but I damned well would like to find out. Wouldn't you?"

Jacques shook his shoulders and pushed back his chair. "That's a pretty strong statement, son, and the inference in the question puts Kathleen in an awkward position."

"Sorry, Pa. It was an honest question." A flush crept up Paul's neck. "Maddy is involved here, not just Fiona."

"It's all right, Paul. I understand your concern," Kathleen said, rising from her chair. "I'd be very willing to find out about that name, and I'm not in the least afraid of the answer." She squeezed Maddy's shoulder as she passed her. Kathleen ladled more soup into Jacques's bowl. "Family comes first, darling. Right?"

Supper finished quietly; each person deep in his own thoughts. Paul tried to perk things up by talking about historical portraits that had been donated to the museum. Maddy realized that this was his way to draw Jacques into the living room and talk more about the portrait.

Kathleen and Maddy cleared the table and loaded the dishwasher. Kathleen remained unusually quiet, which didn't bode well, Maddy thought. *Either she knows something or she's afraid of what she'll find. Maybe she's as upset as I am about all this.*

Truth was, Maddy was feeling worse by the moment. Tension beat a steady tattoo over her eyes, thudding like the felt hammer of a dead piano key. Her mouth was dry and her eyes felt heavy. She knew she needed to go home. Kathleen was very understanding when she pleaded a headache and made her apologies.

Maddy went to the living room to tell Paul and Jacques. "Sorry to eat and run, guys," she said from the doorway, "but I'm not feeling so good. My head feels like I might be getting a sinus infection. I hate to leave so soon after you arrived, Paul, but I think it's best I go home and doctor up. I hope you don't mind, Papa."

Jacques stood. "I'm sorry you're leaving so early. I wanted to thank you for all that you are doing, Madelaine. You know I'm here for you, always."

"I know, and I'll probably be in and out later, while Paul's home. For certain I'll be here to help with Thanksgiving next week." She blew Jacques a kiss. "Paul, would you carry the soup pot out to my car?"

Paul walked her out and put the kettle on

the front seat of her car. He leaned in for a minute while Maddy turned the key in the ignition. "Is it really a sinus headache?" he asked.

"I don't know. My head really hurts. It could be my sinuses. They act up periodically, but it could be everything building up and spilling over tonight."

"That's more likely. Whatever happens, though, I think Kathleen's gonna be on your side, and of course, Pa is. Get a good night's sleep, Mad, and I'll call you as soon as I get to Patrick's in the morning."

CHAPTER
THIRTY-FOUR

The soft ring tone of Maddy's cell phone woke her at nine-thirty Saturday morning. She made sure the phone was under her pillow the night before so that nothing would disturb Clare's sleep. Clare needed her eight hours after working seven to three in the morning.

Maddy sighed with relief to hear her brother's voice.

"Paul here. Can you meet me at the Café on Main Street ASAP?"

"Hey, I'm hardly awake. What's going on? Why do I need to meet you there?"

"Because I'm already downtown, and because good things may be happening. If you're up to it, I'll be taking you to breakfast. The Café was Patrick's suggestion. He and his mother are in York as we speak, and Kathleen is at Duval's law firm. Does that wake you up?"

Maddy sat bolt upright and shot out of

bed. "You bet. I'm on my way." She was in and out of the bathroom in ten minutes, scribbled a note to Clare and was driving her Honda down Elm Street by ten o'clock.

Paul sat in his rental car in front of the Café. Maddy parked behind him and he motioned with his hand to come inside the car.

She opened the door and stuck her head inside. "Why are we sitting out here?"

"I'm not sure how much we should say in there." Paul pointed at the restaurant. "Patrick's mother said she called in that she wouldn't be going to work this morning, and —"

"Paul. The Café owners are her friends. If anybody learns the good news about Fiona, it will be them. Now come on in. I need good strong coffee while you tell me what's going on."

The same middle-aged waitress whom Maddy remembered from her last visit shot a big smile Paul's way and patted Maddy's shoulder. She brought them to a booth. "Nice to see you again, luv. What can I get you?"

"Two coffees and French toast for me," Paul said. "What else for you, Mad?"

"Just buttered toast, thanks. Now tell me everything, Paul," Maddy said, as soon as the waitress wrote their order.

"Patrick called York last night. He used the home phone number the guy named Joe gave to you. Joe wasn't too helpful at first — not until after Mrs. Donovan talked to him. He asked a lot of questions, like he was making sure they were who they said they were. Patrick thought it seemed like Joe didn't want trouble from a guy he didn't name. Mrs. Donovan wouldn't be put off, though. She volunteered her own information and then asked point blank if he knew where Fiona was."

"Yeah, Eileen!" Maddy said punching her fist in the air, startling Paul. The waitress had just put their coffee down. She chuckled and winked at Maddy.

Paul gave the waitress a quizzical look.

"I'm not Eileen," she said laughing out loud. "She's talking about Patrick's mom. I'll be right back with your order."

"I'm on a first-name basis with Patrick's mom," Maddy said. "It's been Eileen ever since we went to the hospital together."

"Gotcha. Hey, that's good. Anyway, the end of the story is this guy named Joe Cerone said he knew where Fiona was. He agreed for them to come to the Pizza Parlor this morning and he'd see if he could arrange for them to talk with her."

"Hallelujah!" said the waitress as she put their plates down. "Sorry for eavesdropping, folks, but I knew where Eileen was going. When I heard what you said, I thought, praise God. Eileen is a woman deserving of a miracle." She wiped a tear from her eye and left them.

Paul shook his head. "There must be powerful karma around here. Better eat up, Maddy. You're going to need your strength for the last part of this scenario, *the Claude scene.*" Paul poured syrup over his French toast, and cut it with his fork. "Mmm, this is good. Haven't had French toast in a long while."

Maddy sipped her coffee and took a bite of toast. "What did Kathleen have to say before she went to Claude's office?"

"Well, last night she made it clear she didn't want Pa to go with her. Too much stress for him, she said. I told her that I had arranged to meet with Patrick early this morning, so she called Claude. She arranged to meet him there about ten, I guess."

"But didn't she say anything this morning?"

Paul pushed his bottom lip up and shook his head. "Nope, she took my cell number and said she'd call me. Now Patrick, on the other hand, gave me specific instructions. I'm to bring you to his shop between eleven and twelve and wait for him there."

"We'd better get started, then." Maddy finished her coffee. "I'll bring my Honda back to the apartment and you'll follow me, right?"

Paul nodded as he ate the last bite of his breakfast. "Good thing I rented the car. I seldom use one in New York, but having no car in Biddeford is like having a fiddle without a bow."

Maddy had her coat on and keys in hand when the waitress brought the check. "Se ya there in ten, Mad." He counted money out, left a big tip and hurried out.

The Thunderbird was already parked in front of Maddy's apartment by the time she pulled in. Paul sat with his ear to the phone.

"You've got one heavy foot," she whispered as she got into his car.

He raised one finger signaling her to wait and rolled his eyes. She sat and waited. Paul listened for what seemed like forever to Maddy. He groaned and made throaty sounds from time to time and finally he spoke. "Please wait till I get home. Yes, much later, Kathleen." He clicked the phone shut.

"Son of a bitch," he said, pounding the

steering wheel to emphasize each word. Maddy's jaw dropped open. Paul turned to her with blazing eyes, grabbed her hand and squeezed it tight. "It *was* Claude."

"Oh, my God. No. Fiona and Claude? How could that be? She was still in high school a year ago. I . . . I can't believe it."

"Well, I can." Paul shook his head. "I never trusted the bastard in the first place."

"What did Kathleen say?"

"He denied knowing Fiona at first. Kathleen said she laid out the facts, brought up the baby's death certificate and threatened to reveal the whole story to Claude's father. She told him she'd have the firm investigate if he didn't tell her the truth. The truth came out. Duval admitted leaving Fiona at La Madeleine in December, but he refused to talk about the birth. I told Kathleen I'd talk with Pa and her later. She'll have more details, I'm sure."

"Oh, Lord." Maddy held her face in her hands. Part of her felt deceived and angry. Part of her felt broken and wanted to cry.

"How terrible it must have been for Fiona. What do you think Patrick will do?"

"We'll soon see. If they've met with Fiona and this guy Joe, then Patrick may have more answers than we do. Right now I'm taking you over to his shop."

■ ■ ■ ■

Thirty minutes dragged by. Maddy sat on the sofa in the back room of the shop, trying to stay composed. At first she strode around with Paul, pointing out the space, the tools and the machinery. Paul was fascinated by a drawing on Patrick's drafting table, so he was in the front of the shop, examining the exquisite little showroom table when Patrick arrived.

Paul clamped a hand on Patrick's shoulder. "You look a little calmer than you did early this morning. Hope that's a good sign."

Patrick heaved a sigh. "Yeah, well I just brought my mother home and that was a relief. She cried most of the way to Biddeford."

Paul swallowed hard. "That bad, huh?"

"Tears of sadness and joy, I guess you'd say." His own eyes were glistening and he swiped a hand across them. "The Irish, you know."

Maddy appeared in the back room doorway. "I thought I heard voices," she said. She looked closely at Patrick and strode quickly to him. He swept her into his arms and clung to her.

Paul looked aside and cleared his throat. "Uh, I'll wait in the back, okay, guys?"

"No, no," Patrick said, reaching out to grab Paul's arm. "We'll all go to the back room. You both need to hear what I have to say. Today wouldn't have happened without Maddy and Clare."

"And *Tante* Margaret," Maddy said.

"Amen," Paul said, laughing to himself as he perched on a stool near the sofa. "Auntie Mame is a pistol."

Patrick smiled and nodded his agreement. "She did get the ball rolling in the beginning, although I didn't want to believe it." He glanced at Maddy as he sat on the sofa, stretching his long legs out. He patted the cushion beside him, for Maddy to sit. "I'm only going to tell this once, then I want to shut it out of my mind, okay?"

"I want to hear it, Patrick, but first, tell us about Fiona. Is she all right?"

"She is. She wants to come home, maybe even next week. That's the good news that my mum cried about all the way home."

Maddy pressed her fingers to her mouth. "Oh, thank God."

"That little waitress you saw at the Pizza Parlor?"

"Kay Fitzgerald?"

"Yes. She worked with Fiona at the shore

restaurant for about a month, until it closed for the season. They're the same age and got to be pretty close. Kay played a big part in all this. Fiona roomed with her for a while after she left the hospital. Upstairs in the building next door to the Pizza Parlor."

"That was apartment 2-B. CeCe and I went there first," Maddy said.

"Yep. Turns out Joe owns that building, too. Kay's aunt is Joe's wife. Actually Joe Cerone and his wife are the guardian angels in this. They didn't have kids of their own, so they practically raised Kay after her mom died. Gave her the apartment, are sending her to night school, and help her any way they can."

"You said your sister roomed with Kay for a while. Where did she go after that?" Paul asked.

"The Cerones took her in. Fiona went through a bad time after the baby died. Depression, they said. She was filled with shame and regret. It was too much for Kay to handle, so Mrs. Cerone took care of Fiona. She's lived with them ever since. They protected her. Or tried to, but that's the sad part about today."

Patrick got up and began to pace. "It was hard to do, Madelaine, but I brought up the death certificate." He stopped and faced

Maddy. "She admitted that Claude Duval was the father." He watched her eyes, waiting for her reaction.

Compassion for Patrick flooded Maddy. She stared back at him, her thoughts all muddled. *How calmly he said that. This is not the Patrick I know, the protective, fiery guy who wanted revenge for his sister.*

She stood and clutched his arm. "Paul and I found out about Claude too. Just this morning. Actually, Kathleen did. I never had a clue of anything like this. I could hardly believe it." She closed her eyes for a second. "His deceit is staggering to me, but I don't know what to do about it. What can I do to make things better for you, or for Fiona?"

"Nothing. That will be the hard part ahead." Patrick shifted his feet and rubbed at his scarred hand. "Fiona says she really loved him." He looked at Paul and shook his head. "Even after the bastard abandoned her, she named the child after him. Fiona is convinced, *now,* that he never really loved her, and she's okay with that, but it took a lot of counseling. Months of counseling. I can't jeopardize that. My sister wants to come home, but only with the agreement that no one will bring up his name or seek any revenge from Claude Duval. Ever."

There was sudden silence. Maddy drew in her breath. She could see by his expression that Paul was having a hard time with that. *Patrick doesn't really know Claude like Paul does. Doesn't know he's always disliked him.*

With a look of fear that didn't escape Paul, she turned to Patrick. Claude's betrayal of Fiona, added to his deception, was overwhelming. She wished for the comfort of Patrick's arms. Tears slid down her cheeks and she laid her head on his chest.

He tilted her chin up and wiped the tears away with his thumb. "I think maybe Paul should bring you home, Madelaine. We're both drained. This needs thinking through to accept, and I need some time with it. I think you do too."

"That makes three of us," Paul said. "I'll wait in the front, Mad."

Patrick held her ever so gently in his arms, pressing his cheek to hers. "You're the best thing in my life, *Macushla*. I need you now, more than ever." He kissed her tenderly. "Can I call you early in the morning?"

"Better I meet you somewhere. Clare's working nights and needs her sleep. How about the Café?"

He smiled and nodded. "Eight o'clock. Best breakfast in town."

CHAPTER
THIRTY-FIVE

Clare was still sleeping when Paul left her at the apartment, so Maddy curled up on the sofa and did something she rarely ever did. She took a midday nap on a weekend.

She was dreaming about her father. Jacques was sitting at his desk in the study, a book open in front of him. She struggled to see what the book was. His finger traveled back and forth over lines on a page, and stopped. He took notepaper and pen and copied something, closed the book and slipped it into the desk drawer.

When she got close enough to see the note all she could make out was *Jeremiah.*

Jacques was fading into darkness. "Wait, wait," she called to him. "Papa, let me see!"

Someone was shaking her shoulder.

"Hey. You're dreaming again. I've been listening to you snore since I got up an hour ago, but now you're sounding pitiful, so you better wake up."

"Oooh. I'm awake, but I wanted to finish the dream."

"If it was about Patrick and Fiona, I'm dying to know what happened this morning. Was that your dream?"

"No. I wish this morning was all a dream. The one good thing that happened this morning is that Patrick and his mother did see Fiona. She's okay now, and she is willing to come home soon."

"Thank God, and thank you, *Tante!*" Clare shouted to the ceiling.

"I'll echo that. Patrick gives you and *Tante* big credits too. The waitress and bartender we met in York were the big factors in Fiona's recovery. She's been through months of hell, but she's had help and counseling, all because of them. I only got sketchy details, so I'll fill you in later on that. You gotta know the rest of the story, CeCe."

"I have a feeling I know it already. You're gonna tell me the baby's father was Claude Duval."

Maddy nodded her head and closed her eyes.

"Holy hell! No wonder I had bad vibes about that snake."

"So did Paul, but the truth is, nothing will be done about it."

"Why? Because he's a lawyer means he gets away with it? He can ruin someone's life and just say *mea culpa?*"

"No. Because Fiona wants nothing from him and wants that nothing be done. She's lost a love she thought she had, lost her child, and after months of counseling she wants the chapter closed. She wants to get on with her life and Patrick's promised to respect her wishes."

"What about Paul and Kathleen?"

"Paul I've got to talk to, but Kathleen, she's the surprise ending. Kathleen went to Duval's office and threatened him to tell her the truth, and he did. We're going to get those details tomorrow. Paul wants me to come over to the house, so I'll leave for the Pool when you go to work."

Maddy walked into the Café at ten after eight the next morning. Patrick waved to her from the back booth. "You're late, Miss Fontaine, but you look beautiful."

Maddy smiled her pleasure at his compliment. She was wearing her burgundy leather jacket over a green wool dress. "I'm not usually up this early on Sunday mornings. I generally go to ten-thirty mass, so I sleep until nine. How about you?"

"I had other things on my mind this

morning. Five females — no, six to be exact."

"Your mother and four sisters make five females."

"You are the sixth, Madelaine. My mother and sisters haven't stopped talking and planning since I got home yesterday. My mum, and Rosie in particular, are carrying on about Fiona. God help me, they'll continue to do it until it really happens and she's home. They're off to Saint Mary's this morning to light candles and say their rosary. And that's okay for them."

"But not for you?"

Patrick reached across the table to clasp Maddy's hand, lowered his voice to a whisper. "I do believe in God, Madelaine, and I feel his presence in you."

She gulped. "Patrick, you're going to make me cry. No one has ever said such a thing to me." She clutched the shell locket hanging around her neck.

"Well, what I mean is, I think God worked through you to find Fiona for us. However *you* think it happened — Margaret's vision, Clare's help, your trip in time — and I'm still shaky on that one." He smiled and squeezed her hand. "None of it could have happened without you."

Maddy opened her mouth, and her words

came in a whisper. "I love you, Patrick Donovan."

Zing. His heart skipped a beat. He was speechless. He couldn't take his eyes off her. He wasn't aware that the waitress suddenly appeared at their booth.

Maggie's eyes sparkled. "Well, your lordship, your mum called us last night with the news. I'm happy for you, luv." Her smile was broad. "I brought coffee for your lady. I suppose you want the usual order, now."

He shook his head as though to clear his mind. "Yep, and be sure they're over easy."

"Miss Madelaine, what will you have this morning?"

"I'd just like a croissant, please, and a glass of orange juice."

"Comin' up."

Patrick grinned and shook his head as she left the booth.

"My lady. Hmm. Maggie is always teasing me about being the lord of the castle."

Maddy was stirring sugar into her coffee. He reached for her left hand and held her gaze. His eyes were as clear as a cloudless blue sky. "Seeing as you have a title now, and you've spoken your feelings at last, I think I'll make my lordship official. Will you marry me, Madelaine, *a gra?*"

The spoon dropped to the table. Her eyes

widened. He wrapped his fingers around her hand and clasped their hands together.

"Patrick! I —"

"Just say yes, *Macushla*."

Her heart was thumping and her lips trembled, but the answer was certain.

"Yes."

He leaned across the table to kiss her fingers.

"Sorry to interrupt, luv, but your plate is hot," Maggie said, standing at the booth, juggling breakfast dishes in both hands.

"Well, then," Patrick said, "serve away."

The waitress blushed, served their breakfast and left without a word.

Patrick and Maddy looked at each other and giggled. "My mum will know about this before the day is over," Patrick said.

"Do you think she'll be happy about it?"

"No question about it," he said between mouthfuls of egg. "She'll be wanting me to speak to your father, you know, old-fashioned like."

Maddy's mind was whirling. *Mom said, follow your heart. He's what I've dreamed about, prayed about. This has got to be right.*

"I didn't tell you, but Paul asked me to come out to the house later this morning, and I said I would, but I planned to go out to the little chapel at Biddeford Pool first.

They have a ten-thirty mass and I thought I'd go. Will you come with me?"

"Will Paul be there?"

"I can't say for certain, but I think if my father asks him to go with him, he would. Given all that's happened with Kathleen, I'm guessing all three might be there."

"Eat up, Madelaine, and we'll go."

The structure of the modest white building was cruciform, simple but elegant. Its distinguishing feature in front was not the hand-carved cross above the door, but the beautifully painted sign, Saint Mary, Star of the Sea. Maddy and Patrick slipped into a back pew, minutes before mass started.

No choir, only an organist. One altar server, a lector, and a young missionary priest celebrated the liturgy. Patrick held Maddy's hand and shared a hymnal. Hymn numbers were posted on the wall by the altar. She was not surprised at his rich baritone voice. His little sister had told her Patrick had the best singing voice.

She was surprised at the end of mass when Paul, Jacques and Kathleen were first up the aisle following the priest's recessional.

Paul wiggled his eyebrows at Maddy with a devilish grin. "Hey, Mad. Shorter mass out here?" he teased.

Patrick shook Jacques's hand, nodded to Kathleen and clapped a hand on Paul's shoulder. "Worship's the same," he said, looking down at Maddy. "Only the worshipers are different."

"Right you are," Jacques said. "Good to see you, Patrick. Are you coming out to the house, Madelaine?"

"Yes." Maddy smiled up at Patrick. "I'd like him to see it when there isn't a hurricane."

"Amen to that. I'll ride up with them, Pa," Paul said, handing Jacques his keys. "Take a whirl with the T-Bird and we'll follow you."

Paul jumped into the back seat of Maddy's car. "You guys picked a perfect time. I've got to tell you about Kathleen, Maddy, and this is the best chance. She amazed me yesterday. She really ripped Duval up and down. She told us all about it, and I know you don't need the details, but she had to be pretty impressive. Said she wasn't putting up with a duplicitous lawyer. Her clout is that she still has investments and returns for her first husband's half of the law firm."

"I hear you, Paul, and I can appreciate her efforts," Patrick said, "but the bottom line is still *no* retribution. I don't care if the bum gets tossed out on his ear."

"I'm with you, man. I'm just trying to fill

Maddy in on how Kathleen has redeemed herself. I know Pa won't bring it up. My father convinced both Kathleen and me that only what Fiona wants is what should matter. He used a little quote from his Bible. 'More tortuous than all else is the human heart.' "

Maddy turned around in her seat. "Did he say what part of scripture that was?"

Paul scratched his head. "Yeah, I think he said Jeremiah. Why?"

"Oh, Lord. I dreamed it. That very passage was in my dream about Papa."

Patrick pulled in behind Paul's rental car in back of the house. Jacques and Kathleen were going in the door. He squeezed Maddy's hand and whispered as they got out of the car. "I think I've asked a psychic to be my bride."

The welcome was smooth and Jacques, being the dutiful host, served drinks in the living room while Paul lit a fire in the fireplace. Kathleen brought in a tray of biscuits stuffed with ham.

"What do you think of our little chapel, Patrick?"

"I like it. Whoever designed it did a great job. Its beauty is in its simplicity."

"I agree," Paul said. He held the bulletin in his hand. "Whoever took this photo on the cover captured the beauty in perfect light."

Jacques nodded his head. "This is the chapel's first year, and even though the season has ended, it gets good attendance. We've never had a Catholic church out here at the Pool," Jacques said. "It's a beautiful setting."

Maddy studied Patrick's face. *It's almost like I can read his mind,* she thought. *I know what he wants to say.*

Patrick cleared his throat, met Maddy's gaze and reached for her hand. She nodded, and he turned his attention to Jacques.

"Saint Mary Star of the Sea might be just the right setting for a winter wedding. I've asked Madelaine to marry me. Would we have your blessing, Mr. Fontaine?"

There was a second of silence, broken by Paul murmuring, "Oh, man!" as he threw the church bulletin in the air.

Kathleen was about to pass the tray of biscuits. She put it down and stared in amazement at Patrick.

Jacques crossed the room, smiling, kissed Maddy and clasped Patrick's shoulder. "Nothing would make me happier."

Kathleen raised her glass to Jacques. "Let me propose a toast, darling," she said. "To Maddy and Patrick and new beginnings.

Slainte."

Jacques shot Kathleen a puzzled look. "Do I know what *slainte* means?"

Patrick and Maddy gazed into each other's eyes. "We do."

Maddy smiled in her sleep. It was a sweet dream, a gentle voice with an Irish lilt, proclaiming an ancient vow . . .

> By the power that Christ brought
> from heaven,
> May you love me.
> As the sun follows its course,
> May you follow me,
> As light to the eye,
> As bread to the hungry,
> As joy to the heart,
> May your presence be with me,
> Oh one that I love, till death comes
> to part us.

Epilogue

December 1905

Drifts of snow piled at the entrance of the mill. Two figures bundled in coats and mufflers pushed through the snow, hurrying out of the mill yard.

"It was bloomin' cold in the shop today. 'Twill be glad I am to warm my feet in front of the stove. You too, Hetty?"

"Oui."

"I told MacDill the story you told me last night."

"No story. *Vérité*. Truth, eh?"

Molly laughed. "If ya say so, but more likely, I'm thinkin' it was blarney. Miss Madelaine, bein' a beautiful bride, marryin' a handsome Irishman at a little seaside church. Sounds like a story a *seanchai* would tell."

"No, no. *J'ai vu ma petite-fille,* Margaret, *et sa fille,* Clare, *et* Fiona, *jolie demoiselle d'honneur. Beau marriage.*"

"Mother of God, Hetty. You saw your granddaughter, and her daughter, and somebody named Fiona. Three maids of honor! The Irish must have danced a jig at that weddin'. Sounds like a match made in heaven."

"*Mais oui.* God is good, *non?*"

AUTHOR'S NOTE

The characters and places in *Finding Fiona* are fictitious, but the general setting of Biddeford, Maine, and Biddeford Pool exists. Biddeford is still a mill town populated largely by French Canadians. The City Charter's Golden Anniversary was a big celebration in 1905, and the La Kermesse Franco-Americaine Festival is still celebrated in Biddeford every year, in June.

Biddeford Pool, the largest tidal lagoon in the state, connects two bedrock islands to the mainland. Although *Francois's Fancy* exists only in my imagination, large homes like it line the Atlantic dune ridge of Biddeford Pool today, much as they did at the turn of the twentieth century.

The story ends with a wedding prayer in Maddy's dream. It is an "Ancient Irish Wedding Prayer," anonymously written.

Several Web sites and the following books

were used as background information for writing *Finding Fiona:*

Archambault, Alberic A. *Mill Village: A Novel.* Boston: Bruce Humphries, 1943.

Bickford, Cora. *Biddeford Maine: A Historic Sketch on Its Early History, Progress and Development.* Cambridge: Riverside Press, 1902.

Downs, Jacques M. *The Cities on the Saco.* Norfolk, Va.: Donning Co., 1985.

Fairfield, Roy P. *Sands, Spindles and Steeples: A History of Saco, Maine.* Published under the auspices of the York Institute with the assistance of the Saco Tercentenary Committee. Portland, Me.: House of Falmouth, 1956.

Folsom, George. *History of Saco and Biddeford.* Somersworth: New Hampshire Publishing Co.; Portland: Maine Historical Society, 1975.

Guignard, Michael J. *La Foi, la Langue, la Culture: The Franco-Americans of Bidde-*

ford, Maine. With a foreword by Normand Beaupré. New York: M. J. Guignard, 1982.

Knowlton, Evelyn Hope Puffer. *Pepperell's Progress: History of a Textile Company 1844–1945.* Cambridge: Harvard University Press, 1948.

Stories and Legends of Old Biddeford. Prepared by the McArthur Library for the City of Biddeford. Biddeford, Me.: s.n. 1945–1946.

ABOUT THE AUTHOR

Mary Fremont Schoenecker took early retirement as Associate Professor at SUNY College, Oneonta, New York, to live with her husband, Tom, on the Cape Haze peninsula in southwest Florida. Mother of four children, Mary's debut historical novel, *Four Summers Waiting,* depicted true ancestors of her children in an epic story of the Civil War. Always having a profound interest in American history, Mary put a little bit of history into *Finding Fiona.* She is a member of The Historical Novel Society, The Civil War Round Table, and Romance Writers of America. When not writing, reading, or dancing, she enjoys life on the Gulf of Mexico.